Santa Clara County Free Library

REFERENCE

Santa Clara County Free Library

California

Alum Rock
Campbell
Cupertino
Gilroy
Los Altos {Main / Woodland}

Milpitas {Calaveras / Community Center / Sunnyhills}
Morgan Hill
Saratoga {Quito / Village}
Stanford-Escondido

Research Center-Cupertino

For Bookmobile Service, request schedule

THE CITY AT THE END OF THE RAINBOW

San Francisco and Its Grand Hotels

THE CITY
OF THE

San Francisco

AT THE END RAINBOW

and Its Grand Hotels

by DAVID SIEFKIN

G. P. Putnam's Sons, New York

SBN: 399-11742-3

Library of Congress Cataloging in Publication Data

Siefkin, David.
  The city at the end of the rainbow.

  Includes index.
  1. San Francisco—Hotels, motels, etc. I. Title.
TX909.S53   647'.94794'61   75-45100

Contents

Illustrations will be found following pages 96 and 160.

Acknowledgments

Without the original idea from Pat Christopher, the assistance of Don Blum of the St. Francis and Thea Emerson of the Mark Hopkins, the patience of Gladys Hansen and Gene Moore of the San Francisco Public Library, the tolerance of the artists who live in the Goodman Building, where much of this was written, and the critical eyes of Trisha Gornell and Phyllis Uppman, who suffered through early drafts, this book would not have been written. Thank you.

ONE day there was nothing, and the next day there was a city. It had no history, no traditions, no established ways, no established people. It was all new: fresh, crisp and intoxicatingly new. It was called San Francisco.

San Francisco has always been the city of gamblers and dreamers. They were there because they wanted to be; they left the tired and discouraged people behind. They were looking for the dream that had come to them in Ohio or Ireland or Shanghai, a dream of love, perhaps, or wealth, or adventure. They were sure, somehow, that they would find it beside the Golden Gate. San Francisco is the long-sought mistress every man yearns for. It is the city at the end of the rainbow.

Dreamers and gamblers are notoriously rootless, so theirs was a city of hotels. Most cities are lucky if they can boast one grand old hotel; San Francisco has four: the Palace, the Mark Hopkins, the Fairmont and the St. Francis. More big and modern hotels have been built in the city, of course, just as there are now dreamless and smug people there, but those four are the jewels.

This book is the story of those four hotels and of some of the people who passed through their lobbies.

1

San Francisco, 1876

ROME was 2,385 years old; Paris was 1,929 years old; London was 1,833. The United States was preparing to celebrate its one hundredth birthday.

San Francisco was twenty-nine years old.

"Recklessness is in the air," Rudyard Kipling wrote from that new city. "The roaring winds off the Pacific make you drunk to begin with. The excessive luxury on all sides helps out the intoxication. . . ."

The ferries from Sausalito, Martinez, Berkeley and Oakland bumped against the Ferry Building pier, swirling the blue water stained yellow by mud from the Sierra mines and belching smoke from their stacks. Crowds poured over the ferry ramp, through the great shed and out to Market Street, where they were engulfed by a shouting mob of cab drivers and hotel runners, yelling the names of hotels and seizing baggage away from bewildered tourists, loading them into a long line of waiting coaches and horse-drawn streetcars which pulled away with a jerk and a ringing of bells.

"The stranger riding along," wrote an eastern reporter, "will find it difficult to believe he is in a city only a quarter of a century old. But he will also be struck with the absence of architectural unity . . . he will find Corinthian, Gothic, Doric, Byzantine, huddled together in a chaotic jumble of wood and stone and brick and iron. . . . There is the ubiquitous bay window and the ambitious mansard roof, and the elaborate cornice and the somewhat loud front entrance. . . ."

Crowds pushed and promenaded along the sidewalks, underneath signs heralding a dozen brands of steam beer. Looking up from the carriage, the stranger could believe himself in Paris or Baghdad or Hong Kong or Coney Island all at once, by the giddy wooden spires and gilded cupolas leaning over his head. The thumping and blaring of drums, cornets and steam pianos, mixed with the clinking of glasses, rolled out into the street from the open doors of bars.

In front of the tall mirrors of the Pantheon on California Street, black-coated bankers stood at the bar sipping whiskey and eating roast pig, salmon and antelope steak from the free lunch counter. Down the street at Collin's, six bartenders danced to keep up with the crowds pressing against the rail. Nearby, in a "semi-subterranean bar tended by a German with long blond locks," Kipling found customers drinking Button Punch, "the highest and noblest product of the Age . . . shavings of cherub's wings, the glory of a tropical dawn, the red clouds of sunset, and fragments of epics by dead masters."

Passing Montgomery and Kearny, an Englishman wrote, "The pavement is occupied by a crowd of people of all classes—talking, smoking, spitting, anxiously awaiting telegrams from the mines, or the result of Stock Exchange Board meetings."

The marquee of the Metropolitan Theater at Washington and Montgomery announced the imminent opening of *The Black Rook*. A few blocks away, on Market Street, Wade's Opera House was advertising *The Black Crook*. Clergymen were solemnly picketing both theaters, denouncing the tights of the chorus girls as "indecent."

Farther along Montgomery toward Market, the visitor was suddenly surrounded by a fantasy of elegant awnings, flagstaffs and gingerbread roofs, the elegant shops of milliners, toy dealers, florists, mantua makers and jewelers, displaying silks and paintings of Paris fashions in their windows. Young men with canes and polished hats escorted young women through the glass doors of the Maison Dorée and the Poodle Dog restaurants, into elevators and up to private dining parlors.

Three blocks away, outside the What Cheer House, "Old Orthodox" stood on a crate and shouted out fiery selections from the Gospel. On the opposite corner "Old Crisis" answered back in a louder voice. "The King of Pain" held court up the street from the back of his medicine wagon, dressed in scarlet underwear, a velour robe and a stovepipe hat with ostrich feathers. "Oofty Goofty" paraded down the street with a sign declaring himself "The Wild Man of Borneo," offering to let people hit him for a nickel and kick him for a dime.

The visitor could catch a glimpse of one of Andrew Halli-die's new cable cars rocking and clattering its precarious way up Clay Street.

In Pike Street, squeezed between Dupont and Stockton, and on Pacific and Broadway, young ladies stood topless in the windows, beckoning and calling to passersby, while downstairs, in Barbary Coast dance halls, a small girl called "Little Lost Chicken" sang, cried and picked pockets, and an overweight team of sisters called the Dancing Heifer and the Galloping Cow tromped the boards in time with a tinny pi-ano.

The visitor turned to watch the women parading on Kear-ny Street. "San Francisco is a mad city," Kipling wrote, "in-habited for the most part by perfectly insane people whose women are of a remarkable beauty."

"But if the San Francisco ladies dress well," another En-glishman said, "truth compels me to say they are rather too fond of displaying their jewelry in the street, wearing hand-some and massive necklaces and other adornments."

"In eastern cities the prostitutes try to imitate in manner and dress the fashionable respectable ladies," a local reporter wrote. "But in San Francisco the rule is reversed, the latter carrying after the former."

Everywhere the streets and sidewalks were packed with people hurrying this way and that: Chinese in blue blouses and trousers, carrying baskets of vegetables on poles, beard-ed Germans, bankers in black frock coats, gamblers in bro-cade vests with diamond pins, miners in flannel shirts and broad hats, Irish laborers with picks and shovels, firemen in red tunics and stovepipe hats, shouting and jostling and trading and talking. Beer wagons lurched heavily down the streets, followed by polished coaches with heraldry on the doors, pulled by matched horses and driven by men in scar-let and blue livery.

Newsboys ran up to the carriages stopped by the conges-tion of wagons, coaches, streetcars and produce carts, reaching up to sell the passengers papers. The visitor found the front page occupied by the accounts of the recent demise of the 7th Cavalry in a battle with Indians in the Dakota Territory. Inside were advertisements for *Henry V* at the California Theater, more Shakespeare at Baldwin's new theater, and an announcement: "Laura Kendrick, in the interest of Free Thought, lectures this evening, at 7½ o'clock, in Social Hall, 39 Fourth Street. Continuation of her great subject, San Francisco by Night, or What the Darkness does not Hide. Admission 10 cents. The Chinese question discussed at 11."

When the street had cleared enough for the carriage to turn out of the crowded thread of Montgomery into the wide thoroughfare of Market Street, the visitor must have laid down his newspaper and looked up in awe.

There, directly in front of him and towering over everything around it, was seven stories of bay windows, brick, stone and pediment, over which, snapping in the wind, blazed an American flag and a huge white banner proclaiming, in blue letters, PALACE HOTEL.

"It was at least four times too big for its time and place," Oscar Lewis wrote of the Palace, "but then San Francisco never had a sense of proportion." Big was too modest a word. The Palace was, as San Franciscans loved to tell visitors, the biggest and grandest and most elegant hotel in the entire world, boasting no less than 755 rooms, this in a city with only 250,000 people.

The carriage crossed Market and rode down New Montgomery beneath the looming rows of bay windows, turned into a marble-framed archway and entered the Grand Court of the Palace.

Now the visitor would look up in amazement again, for he found himself in a great courtyard seven stories high, roofed in glass 112 feet over his head, encircled by layer on layer of balconies rising from a garden of lemon, orange and lime trees and busy with guests, brightly uniformed employees and gaping sightseers. A marble fountain splashed in the center of the courtyard, gaslit arcades led off to halls of shops, and two grand staircases, embracing a bandstand and ornamented with statues and vases brimming with flowers, led up to a second-floor promenade.

A bellhop led the way to the lobby, a great gaslit and paneled cavern with a high vaulted ceiling and an immense desk. Crowds of people were expectantly waiting in the lobby; there was a whisper of excitement, and the crowd moved toward the door, when the familiar profile of Lawrence Barrett, the Shakespearean actor, appeared, nodding and smiling as he walked from the elevator alongside Henry Jarrett, his manager.

The Palace had no less than five hydraulic elevators, "securely safe and noiseless," leading to its 755 rooms. Each room had its own fireplace and bathroom, nearly all were an astonishing twenty feet on a side, and each was flooded with light from its own bay window, colored with silk draperies and furnished in rosewood and California laurel. Leaving his bags in the room, the guest could step back into the elevator and ride it to the very top, where it opened into the Crystal Roof Garden, just below the glass skylight, where guests strolled among ornamental shrubs, hanging baskets of flowers and statues of Diana and the Four Seasons. He could lean over the railing and watch the carriages entering the courtyard seven stories below.

Outside the Palace, gaslights were beginning to glitter among the domes and spires, and the silver beam of San Francisco's first electric light, a searchlight brought from the 1871 siege of Paris, played on the bottom of the clouds. In the Grand Court, men in evening dress were walking toward the Palace dining room, where they would feast on California oysters, broiled quail on toast and grizzly bear steaks. Above them, the colored gaslights that circled each balcony like a necklace of jewels were being lit, and the sound of violins from the gypsy orchestra in the courtyard floated up toward the roof.

In this city built by gamblers and dreamers, the Palace was the most golden dream of all, a fantasy of a grand European hotel crossed with a Mississippi steamboat and planted, somehow, by the Golden Gate. While it stood, it was the diamond-and-glass jewel of San Francisco, and when it fell in 1906, a whole city and a whole age fell with it.

2

Gamblers

IN the 1870s a river of silver, tapped from the brown hills of Virginia City, Nevada, began to pour into San Francisco. It was to change San Francisco from a muddy mining town into a noisy metropolis of domed palaces and gingerbread mansions which its residents would proudly boast was "The Paris of the West."

Like the great Mississippi riverboats it seemed to copy architecturally, the city was filled with gamblers. Thousands of dollars were handed daily over saloon bars and hotel parlor tables; anything that could be gambled on, from real estate to railroads, rice crops to mining schemes, was, and on a grand scale. Bank presidents and bartenders, financiers and upstairs maids mingled in the corridors of the Mining Exchange, watching their fortunes shoot up and plummet down with every new quotation. But the biggest games in town were being played in the most unlikely place, the quiet office of William Chapman Ralston, the president of the Bank of California.

A gambler from his youth, Ralston had put his very first earnings in the cargo of a Mississippi flatboat only to see it broken up on the wild river and washed away. Undiscouraged, he was soon on the river again as the clerk of a steamboat. Before long his financial shrewdness caught the eye of a passenger, a New York gold dealer named Cornelius Garrison. Garrison talked to Ralston and hired him, first to run his bullion office in Panama, then to run his new office in the ten-year-old boomtown of San Francisco.

Stepping off the ship into the intoxicating golden city in 1858, the thirty-two-year-old Ralston began hunting for something to invest Garrison's money in. He didn't have to look far. Before long he had bought tobacco fields, vineyards, shares in the proposed transcontinental railroad, a clock factory and San Francisco real estate. With shiploads of new residents docking every week, he watched his investments double and triple in value. Before long he had made enough himself to open his own bank, the Bank of California, which, with Ralston's willingness to back nearly any imaginable scheme, soon was the prime financial engine of San Francisco.

One morning in 1864 a small, pale man came to Ralston and asked him for a job. William Sharon explained that, in the confusion of the mining exchange, several brokers had tricked him into buying his own stock from himself. He had wiped himself out. Ralston, who was willing to believe anything and help anyone, agreed to hire him and assigned him to the new branch of the Bank of California in Virginia City.

When Sharon arrived in Virginia City, he found the dozens of once-wealthy silver mines boarded up and abandoned. The easily reached silver had long since been mined and the little companies lacked the money to buy machinery to dig deeper, where they suspected there was much more.

Sharon told Ralston this, and Ralston was intrigued. He bought the mines, ordered the best machinery from the East and started digging. As the miners had predicted, Ralston's engineers hit veins of silver, more silver, in fact, than anyone had ever seen before. They had found the Bonanza of the Comstock Lode.

Since Ralston owned the mines, the mills next to them that stamped the ore, the water pipes that fed the mills, the mountains that fed the water pipes and the railroad that hauled the silver to the mint, he was soon awash in money. He built a new marble Bank of California downtown, a marble mansion for himself outside town, and a theater, which he stocked with Shakespearean actors, to show his out-of-town visitors that San Francisco had culture.

Now he was besieged by people with new schemes. He was offered unbuilt railroads, unbuilt cities, diamond mines in Wyoming and untested inventions, all of which, their backers claimed, would be bonanzas if only they were watered with a little money.

One such young man, Asbury Harpending, proposed to Ralston that the two of them buy up land south of Market Street, which was then only sand dunes, and extend Montgomery Street, the main financial street, to the Bay. Ralston might have questioned Harpending's business sense; the young man's first investment, Mexican gold mines, had got him run out of that country, and his second, a plan that Harpending and some of his southern friends had concocted during the Civil War, to seize the government of California and secede as the independent Republic of the Pacific, had got him thrown in prison for treason, only to be pardoned because he was so young. But Ralston was always intrigued by a new idea. He inspected the sandy hills and decided to buy.

He had bought a strip of land two blocks deep when the owners of the rest of the land realized what he was doing and refused to sell him any more. The angry Ralston convinced the state legislature, which was agreeable to anything for a price, to condemn the land for him. The equally aroused landowners convinced the governor, who was also agreeable to anything for a price, to veto the condemnation. At this point Harpending politely explained that he was called by other matters and left the problem entirely to Ralston.

Ralston tried auctioning off his two blocks. To make sure that he got a decent price, he planted his agents among the audience to keep the bidding brisk. The other owners suspected Ralston's scheme and were silent, letting Ralston's men bid the price up and buy his own land from himself.

He now seemed to be stuck with two and one-half acres of sand and weeds, but Ralston was both a gambler and a thoughtful man. There must be something useful, he thought, that he could put there. This new city needed something that would command attention, something that would make it more than an overnight gambling town. He wanted something grand and awesome that would make people think of San Francisco and invest money there, something as imposing as a cathedral and as gay as a riverboat. William Ralston decided to use his lot to build for San Francisco the biggest, most opulent hotel the world had ever seen.

"Europe's civilization will be judged by its churches, America's by its hotels," Gene Fowler wrote, and this was especially true in San Francisco. Everyone, from the wealthiest railroad baron to the lowliest gambler, seemed to live in a hotel. The city in 1875 had only 200,000 people, but it already had four first-class hotels: the stately Occidental, with its cement Greek portico, where English visitors and Mark Twain stayed; the quiet Cosmopolitan, where the city's minor aristocrats made their home; Lick House, whose riotous bar was the place to get the latest racing stock tips; and the Grand, a three-story confusion of arcades, spires and gilt domes, which William Ralston already owned.

San Francisco's first hotel had been Vioget's Public House, opened in 1840 when the ciy was still the drowsy Mexican village of Yerba Buena. It was renamed the Portsmouth in 1846, after a U.S. sloop moored in the Bay, and that year it was joined by Brown's Hotel. Brown's was nearly blown away that Fourth of July when the crew of the American merchant ship *Vandalia* accidentally fired their Independence Day cannon salute into the lobby.

The discovery of gold in 1848 led to the mad construction of dozens of wood and canvas hotels, filled with stacks of bunk beds and serving meals under canvas awnings. To house the incoming jam of miners, an abandoned ship, the *Niantic,* was hauled ashore, boarded over and opened as a hotel. The old St. Francis Hotel was the first to offer sheets, and the Oriental became the center of social and political life when it raised a canvas ballroom and became the headquarters of the Vigilance Committee, which reprimanded local troublemakers by hanging them from a nearby building.

Now Ralston wanted to surpass them all. He sent his architect, John Gaynor, on a tour of the great hotels then existing in America—the Sturtevant and New Windsor in New York and the Grand Pacific and Palmer House in Chicago— and then set him drawing.

When Gaynor was finished, even Ralston must have been impressed. The architect had designed a seven-story hotel covering an entire city block, which would make it not only the biggest building in San Francisco, but the biggest hotel in the United States. Ralston examined the plans and made only one change; where Gaynor had used bay windows only on the bottom stories, Ralston, a true American democrat, wanted every room to have one; he covered the entire façade with bay windows from the ground to the flagpoles.

Construction began in 1873. Ralston had convinced Sharon who was now a millionaire himself, to join him in the enterprise, promising that the total cost would be $1,750,000. But Ralston, as Sharon soon discovered, took after the pharaohs when it came to lavishness of construction; he spent the $1,750,000 on the foundations and first floor alone.

As awed San Franciscans watched the building on Market Street rise, the newspapers reeled off the statistics: 300 bricklayers laying 31,000,000 bricks; 1,400 men working on the building at one time; 20 miles of gas pipe; 900 washbasins; 435 cast-iron bathtubs. Ralston, in the meanwhile, saw to it that he made a profit even before the hotel was finished; his foundry made the nails and locks, his furniture factory was making the furniture, his clock factory was making the clocks, his tobacco fields were being harvested for cigars, and vineyards were being squeezed for the hotel's wine cellars.

The bricklayers left and were replaced by carpenters, finishers and carpet layers, installing acres of mahogany, rosewood and teak paneling, huge mirrors and marble floors. Finally, there were silk draperies and bedspreads, dozens of paintings of Yosemite and Lake Tahoe and crates of Irish linen and French eggshell china.

Ralston spent his mornings wandering through the unfinished halls, talking with the contractor. Afterward he went to his office and took care of his bank's business, and then, when he was done, he would go down to North Beach and swim in the Bay. He was so preoccupied with his hotel, in fact, that he missed what was happening in Virginia City.

A new mining engineer named James Fair was exploring the shafts of some of Ralston's exhausted silver mines, and he reached the conclusion Sharon had: A little more machinery, and there would be still more silver. Backed by former bartender James Flood and former cook William O'Brien, who had turned tips from their patrons into a considerable fortune, he bought up Ralston's abandoned mines, and as Ralston had, he found a new bonanza of silver.

Ralston, meanwhile, had spent nearly all the Bank of California's money on the hotel. Realizing that he had better do something to refill the vaults, he began buying stock in a mine next to Fair's bonanza, not knowing, as Fair knew, that it missed the lode altogether. Now Fair, Flood and O'Brien saw their chance to finish off Ralston completely. After they sold him all the worthless mining stock they owned, they informed him that they wanted to withdraw their money from the Bank of California to start their own bank.

The stunned Ralston sent a messenger to Flood. "You tell Flood I'll send him back selling rum," he said. A short while later the messenger returned. "Mr. Flood says that, in a short time, he will be able to sell rum over the counter of the Bank of California."

On August 26, 1875, news that Ralston's mine was worthless reached San Francisco. Shortly afterward, the line of depositors trying to withdraw their money from the Bank of California led out the door and far down the street. By two thirty the police arrived to push back the shouting depositors. Ten minutes later Ralston walked from his office to the counter and ordered them to stop payments; there was no money left. The great iron doors of the bank were swung shut on the crowds still pushing outside.

The next day the directors of the Bank of California met, without Ralston present. A quick audit had shown that Ralston owed his bank $4,500,000. On a motion from William Sharon, Ralston was fired as president of the bank.

While this was going on, Ralston was wandering slowly through the unfinished halls of his hotel. The official opening was less than two months away. After talking with the contractor about some minor details, he returned to his office, where he was told he had been fired. After doing some paperwork, he locked his office and went to North Beach for his daily swim. A short while later his lifeless body was carried up on the beach.

Fair, Flood and O'Brien opened their bank and continued to increase their fortunes, Fair by speculating in mining stocks and San Francisco real estate. He became, before long, one of the least-liked men in San Francisco, repossessing the homes of his friends when they were unable to repay loans, denying pay raises to his employees and even bankrupting his wife by selling her and her friends worthless mining stock. His sixty acres of downtown property were easily recognizable, a local newspaper observed, by their "shameful state of neglect . . . paint peeling . . . and doors sagging on their hinges."

In 1883 his wife, Theresa, sued him for divorce. The newspapers and even Fair's old partner, James Flood, supported her, and the bitter Fair retired to two rooms of the Lick House, which he owned. Mrs. Fair took custody of their two daughters, Tessie and Birdie, while James Fair won custody of the two sons, Charles and James, Jr.

The young James died soon afterward, of either alcoholism or suicide. Charles Fair lost heavily in the horse races and eloped with Maude Nelson, who operated what the newspapers called a "questionable resort" on Stockton Street. Both were killed in the spring of 1902 when their Mercedes special spun off the road near Paris.

Birdie Fair married a Vanderbilt, and Tessie married the wealthy and socially elect New Yorker Herman Oelrichs. Neither invited her father to her wedding. When James Fair died in 1894, most of the money went to Charles. The real estate went to Tessie.

Among the plots of real estate was a vacant lot on the crest of Nob Hill, across the street from James Flood's elegant brownstone mansion. It was said James Fair had intended to build his own mansion there. A foundation was laid, but nothing more was ever done until 1904, when Tessie Oelrichs announced she wanted to build a hotel and call it the Fairmont.

3

Heroes and Poets

ON October 2, 1875, five weeks after Ralston died, Willliam Sharon opened the Palace Hotel. Ironically, it was the largest hotel in the world only for a few weeks, until the enormous United States Hotel in Saratoga, New York, opened, but no one could question that it was unrivaled both in grandeur and in the grandeur of the people who came to stay there.

People were beginning to travel then. With the aid of the new railroad system and faster steamships, royalty was discovering the grand tour, statesmen and politicians the junket, artists and authors the touring circuit and financiers and bankers the business trip. Sooner or later nearly all of them passed through San Francisco, and the place to stay in San Fracisco was the Palace Hotel. An endless procession of princes, presidents, generals and business titans came to sleep in the second-floor Presidential Suite of the Palace, with its two parlors paneled in mahogany and satin, private dining room, ebony and quartz-inlaid furniture, antique Egyptian stands and landscapes painted by Albert Bierstadt and Julian Rix.

Civil War hero Philip Sheridan was the guest of honor at the opening banquet, the first of a small army of Civil War generals who discovered that they would be lionized, feted and marched in parades by an enthusiastic public wherever they went. A month after Sheridan, William Tecumseh Sherman came, standing stoically on the balcony while the Palace band played "Marching Through Georgia" and shaking hands with an endless line of veterans and civic delegations. Then came John Charles Frémont, and George Brinton

McClellan, and Ely S. Parker, Grant's secretary at Appomattox, seemingly a general a week until 1896, when the venerable General Benjamin H. Grierson arrived to recount for the few reporters who showed up to hear the story again how he had led from La Grange to Baton Rouge what he modestly described as "the most thoroughly successful cavalry raid of the war."

The most colossal reception was saved for Grant. When the general's ship, the *City of Tokio*, sailed through the Golden Gate on the last leg of an around-the-world tour, 20,000 people crowded the summit of Telegraph Hill for a glimpse of his tiny figure on the deck. Amid a frenzy of cheering and bands playing "When Johnny Comes Marching Home," Grant landed and was borne, tipping his hat and smiling faintly, under a dozen floral arches constructed over Market Street. At the corner of Fifth and Market he was ushered into the reviewing stand and subjected to the longest parade in San Francisco history, an endless procession of singing citizens, saluting veterans, firemen, turbaned fraternal orders, batteries of artillery, drill teams, bands and horse-drawn steam calliopes, invariably playing "When Johnny Comes Marching Home."

When the parade ended, Grant was conducted to the flag-draped Palace Hotel. Crowds jamming all six balconies burst into furious cheers when his carriage pulled into the Grand Court. He bowed, lifted his hat and went inside to his room. The crowds kept cheering, demanding to see their hero again. He reappeared on the third-floor balcony, bowed again and returned to his room, where his staff was frantically searching for his false teeth. By the time Grant learned his false teeth had been thrown overboard by a careless steward on the *City of Tokio* more people had arrived in the Grand Court, and they were shouting for one more look at their hero. He returned to the balcony, said a few words to the cheering throng and listened as Grant's Invincibles, a huge men's glee club, began a song they had written for their idol, to the tune of "The Battle Hymn of the Republic."

> The hero of our nation is the gallant U.S.G.
> He has been away in foreign lands far far beyond the sea,

But now he's coming back again to the land of the brave and
the free,
Yes, Grant is coming home.

Glory, glory hallelujah, etc.
For Grant is coming home . . .

After eight hearty stanzas of this, the Grand Court was
empty, except for Grant's Invincibles, and the Hero of Appomattox was able to return to his room and go to sleep.

The first king to come was Dom Pedro II, the tall and
scholarly emperor of Brazil, who arrived only a few months
after the Palace opened, completing a cross-country tour
from the one hundredth birthday celebration the United
States was holding in Philadelphia. Dom Pedro dutifully visited the opera, inspected the University of California and
made the remark, quoted by Palace managers long after he
had returned home and was overthrown: "Nothing makes
me so ashamed of Brazil as the Palace Hotel."

In 1891 the flag of the kingdom of Hawaii flying over the
Palace was lowered to half-mast when King David Kalakaua,
the last king of the Islands, died in his suite. His staff waved
palm fronds over his body and then carried him through the
corridors and out to a waiting carriage and a place on the
deck of the cruiser USS *Charleston* for the long journey back
to his home islands.

The register of the Palace had become a roster of the great
men and women of the age: Rockefeller, Morgan, Carnegie,
Pullman, Vanderbilt, Huntington, Studebaker, Swift and
Wanamaker; Presidents Hayes, Harrison, McKinley and
Theodore Roosevelt; the Grand Duke Boris, the nabob of
Ranpur, the prince of Siam, Prince Albert of Belgium,
Prince Napoleon Louis Joseph Jerome Bonaparte, Lord and
Lady Randolph Churchill and James J. Jeffries, the heavy-
weight champion of the world.

Jeffries, wearing an undersize straw hat perched jauntily
on his head and an oversize diamond pinned to his tie, arrived in the Grand Court in a coach preceded by a six-piece
band. "This gorgeous pageant surged into the Grand
Court," a newspaper chronicled, "followed by an ardent con-
stituency, attired mostly in sweat shirts. When the crowd dis-

persed the management fumigated the Grand Court and tried to revive the potted palms."

Some visitors were less than kind to the Palace. Rudyard Kipling, a twenty-four-year-old journalist taking the long way back from India, described the Grand Court, the pride of San Francisco, this way:

> In a vast marble-paved hall under the glare of an electric light sat forty to fifty men, and for their use and amusement were provided spittoons of infinite capacity and generous gape. Most of the men wore frock coats and top hats—but they all spat. They spat on principle. The spittoons were on the staircases, in each bedroom, yea, in chambers even more sacred . . . but they blossomed in chiefest splendor around the bar.

Before he left, Kipling managed to find something wrong with the way San Franciscans dressed, ate, walked, drank and talked, and he observed gleefully that one English gunboat could level all the fortifications and seize the city in half an hour. The city got its revenge, however. Today Chamber of Commerce brochures quote him as saying, "The only thing bad about San Francisco, 'tis hard to leave."

Regardless of what they thought of Rudyard Kipling, San Francisco's many admirers of English culture felt their city had arrived when it was announced in 1882 that Oscar Wilde would come lecture there. The twenty-eight-year-old Wilde's appearance in the lobby of the Palace Hotel was spectacular, even for San Francisco. He wore, the newspapers noted, a long black velvet coat, an enormous broad-brimmed white hat, pointed shoes, sienna pants, yellow gloves, a puce tie, a boutonniere of heliotrope, tuberoses and daisies and an expression of utter and complete boredom. When he arrived in his room, the newspapers reported, he took off his coat and flung it across the room, where it was caught by his valet, waiting with arms outstretched in precisely the right spot. He then sprawled on the divan and talked to the reporters.

His lecture at Platt's Hall was entitled "Beauty in Art." For the occasion he wore his lecturing costume, velvet knee breeches and a lily clutched in one hand. Speaking in a barely audible monotone and broadly suggesting that he might

fall asleep at any moment, Wilde informed the eager audi-
ence, "If Life is noble and beautiful, Art will be Noble and
Beautiful. . . . Effect is the essence of design. . . ." and
"Art is eternal because it is Eternally Beautiful."

Afterward, some sporting members of the Bohemian
Club, seeing their chance to show this absurd Englishman
what life was really about, captured Wilde and escorted him
to their club for a drink. The bottles were set out on the table, Wilde set down his lily, and they began. Several hours
later, when the last member of the Bohemian Club had slid
under the table, Wilde got up, picked up his lily and walked
back to the Palace Hotel.

San Francisco adored performers, any sort of performers.
Beginning in June, 1876, when an express train rushed the
entire cast and settings of *Henry V* from New York to open
just four days later in San Francisco, the city was introduced
to the leading figures of the American stage. Edwin Booth,
Edmund Kean, Dion Boucicault and Augustin Daly. Lillian
Russell brought her $10,000 Japanese terrier, and Sarah
Bernhardt took an eight-room suite at the Palace for herself,
her parrot and her baby tiger. There were men destined for
later fame performing in the theaters, too: William Cody,
shortly to be world-renowned as Buffalo Bill, was acting in a
western melodrama called *Life on the Border,* and one member of the visiting London Lyceum Company, a young actor
named Bram Stoker, would one day win fame by writing
Dracula.

San Francisco loved them all, from Sandow, the strong
man, to Adelina Patti, the opera singer, with, as one awed observer said, "an enthusiasm bordering on lunacy."

Sandow was a protégé of the New York impresario Florenz
Ziegfeld, sent to San Francisco to help the city celebrate its
Midwinter Fair. Billing him as the single most magnificent
human body alive, his press agents offered anyone $10,000
who could equal his weight-lifting feats and announced that
he would, on his arrival, wrestle with a lion.

Nearly every reporter in San Francisco was watching when
Sandow, wrapped in a magnificent cloak, made his appearance. His agents produced a small, worried-looking lion
named Commodore, firmly muzzled and paws laced, which
Sandow tossed back and forth for the benefit of the photog-

raphers. Sandow then announced that he would put his body on display in the Maple Room of the Palace Hotel.

The reporters dutifully followed. At the Palace, Sandow appeared in pink tights, flexing and expanding his muscles for the benefit of the spectators who lined up to see him and inviting them to punch him in the stomach, while he explained to the reporters that "my greatest feat, in all probability, is to turn a somersault, blinded, with fifty-six pounds in each hand."

Despite Ziegfeld's publicity efforts, however, and despite his closing performance of lifting and balancing three horses on his shoulders, Sandow took second place at the Midwinter Fair. The first was captured by Little Egypt, who may or may not have been the same Little Egypt who won the admiration of every man to visit the Great Chicago Exposition.

More than any other single performer, Adelina Patti received the adulation of San Francisco. She had sung and had been honored in all the opera houses of Europe, and when, in 1884, it was announced that she would come to San Francisco, the city went into a frenzy. The line for tickets at the opera house began to form the night before the box office opened and soon stretched for eight blocks. Finally, the tickets were put up for auction, selling for as high as $7, an outrageous price then, for a seat in the orchestra. As tickets got scarcer, the city passed an ordinance requiring anyone reselling tickets to buy a license for $100, intended to stop scalping. Seventy-seven people immediately bought licenses, and more followed.

Meanwhile, Patti's journey across the country was being closely followed. She was traveling in a private railway car named the Adelina Patti, embellished with leather-covered walls, a satin couch, a hand-carved piano and leopard-skin rugs. When she felt the whim, the papers reported, she commanded her train to halt and sent her three cooks out to chase prairie chickens for her table.

Her arrival in San Francisco was greeted with only slightly less enthusiasm than the news of the gold discovery. Her room was nearly buried in flowers, crowds filled the Palm Court to cheer her as she arrived and waved her handkerchief to them from the balcony, and everywhere she went her carriage was pursued by cheering crowds.

The night she sang, carriages were lined up outside the Opera House. The enormous crowd literally crushed the box office, crashing through the glass doors. Said the manager, "People were pushed as if shot from howitzers. Several ladies declared that their feet had never touched the ground from the time they got out of their carriages." More people swarmed onto the roof of the Opera House, sawing a hole which permitted 160 of them to sneak into the balcony. By the time the curtain rose every box and every seat and every inch of space in the theater were filled and the air was tight with anticipation.

That night Patti sang *La Traviata*. People who were there recalled it years later in hushed tones, as if recalling the first person they loved. The thunderstorm of shouts, cheers and flying bouquets when she finished was recorded in the papers the next day: ". . . And there was Patti crying and the audience crying . . . and then Patti, who was excited and shaking, sang 'Home Sweet Home' and the audience applauded and shouted and wound up with three tremendous yells."

While this parade of princes and prima donnas flowed through the Grand Court, the aristocracy of San Francisco watched from the balconies outside their suites. The Palace was not only the obligatory place for the visitor to stay, but also, next to Nob Hill, the most prestigious address in town.

"The hotel is the San Franciscan's home," a foreign observer wrote. "A man of domestic habits is a rarity, and women have come to regard family cares and duties as a sort of drudgery without their province." In this spirit Leland Stanford took a suite at the Palace while his Nob Hill mansion was being completed, and William Ralston's widow lived in another suite, as did the new owner, William Sharon. By the 1890s the entire top floor and a large part of the floor below were occupied by permanent residents. The men would sit out on the balcony and smoke and read their newspapers, the women would knit and gossip, and the children would play among the potted plants and peer through the railing at the carriages rattling in and out far below in the Grand Court.

One of the first regular residents was Lillie Hitchcock Coit. No one ever accused her of living a stale life; coming to the wild San Francisco of 1851 as a girl of eight, she was engaged fifteen times before she was twenty. She was a determined poker player, attended cockfights disguised as a man and would, if she felt like it, wash her hair in champagne.

But her first love was the city's volunteer firemen. There was rarely a fire without Lillie Hitchcock cheering on her favorite engine company. When she was seventeen, she dashed out of a wedding rehearsal and chased the fire engines up the hill in her bridesmaid's costume. Her favorite company was Knickerbocker Engine Company Number 5; she attended all their banquets at the Palace, dressed in the fireman's uniform of red blouse, black shirt and fire helmet, and until she died, she signed her name "Lillie Hitchcock Coit (5)."

She finally married the wealthy Howard Coit, but she was too restless to settle down. After they separated, she traveled, sometimes for three days, sometimes for three years, to every corner of the world; but even in Palestine, on the day of the fireman's banquet in San Francisco, she called a halt to the caravan and drank a toast to Company 5. She finally returned to San Francisco and died there in 1929.

Today both tourists and local residents know her for the tower on Telegraph Hill that was built with money she willed the city for its beautification, but the old employees at the Palace fondly recalled the night she invited some particularly stuffy society people to visit her suite at the hotel; they had opened the door to find a ring set up in the parlor, and two boxers slugging it out in a prizefight, cheered on by Lillie Coit.

When the tower in her husband's name was dedicated in 1932, the old fire engine of Company 5 was exhumed from the old barn, polished and pulled up Telegraph Hill; on top rode the black fire helmet of Lillie Hitchcock Coit.

One strange affair took place in the least likely of places, the elegant suite of the Palace's owner, William Sharon. The whole city was astonished one day when an attractive young lady named Sarah Althea Hill claimed that the quiet, pale Sharon was her secret husband, and she wanted a divorce.

Sharon called it "the damnedest lie that was ever uttered on earth." His lawyers claimed that he had never met Miss Hill (whom the newspapers were now calling Rose of Sharon), claimed that when he had associated with her, it had been on a strictly honorable basis and insisted that even if he had associated with her on a less than strictly honorable basis, he certainly never married her.

Miss Hill told a packed courtroom that Sharon had come to her room at the Grand Hotel after she had sought some advice about stock speculation, and had wooed her by singing the verse from Byron, "Maid of Athens, ere we part, /Give, oh give me back my heart!" He then, she said, proposed marriage, saying it had to be secret for political reasons (he was then senator from Nevada), and dictated a marriage contract. She dramatically produced the contract, which was immediately reproduced in all the papers.

Then the attorneys took up the battle. Miss Hill's handwriting experts swore the contract was absolutely genuine; Sharon's denounced it as a bald forgery. Sharon had bought the jury, Miss Hill's attorney charged; Miss Hill had hired a voodoo sorceress to hex Sharon, his attorneys claimed. Miss Hill was a perjurer, Sharon's lawyers shouted, thumping the table. The elderly Sharon was a "Moral Leper," Miss Hill's attorney offered.

It went on like that for sixty-one days. As the trial meandered along the back roads of California law, a reporter leaned over the shoulder of Sharon's attorney and watched him diagram difficult billiards shots. The newspapers faithfully reported what Miss Hill wore each day and printed evidence before it ever appeared in court.

The jury finally reached a verdict the day before Christmas, 1884, finding Sharon guilty. Miss Hill, now Mrs. Sharon, began buying Christmas presents and charging them to William Sharon. But Sharon's attorneys weren't finished; they appealed, and the federal courts ruled that the contract was indeed a fraud. Mrs. Sharon went back to being Miss Hill.

Exhausted by illness and the seemingly endless trial, Sharon died shortly afterward, on November 13, 1885. His funeral was held in the parlor of the hotel. Before long, a new battle began over who would get his estate, including the Palace Hotel.

The persistent Miss Hill, who by now had married her attorney, David Terry, kept pressing her case. In a restaurant Terry angrily confronted the judge who had rejected her appeal and was promptly shot dead by the judge's bodyguard. All the courts ruled against her, and even the marriage contract was destroyed when her house burned down.

Sarah Hill came to sit on a bench in Union Square, telling passersby that she was waiting for her next court appearance. Later she was seen pacing the sidewalk of Kearny Street and standing forlornly in the rain. And once she was seen wistfully strolling through the lobby of the Palace Hotel. Eventually she was committed to the State Hospital in Stockton, where she died in 1937.

Not all the events in the glittering world of the Palace were so unhappy. There were children born there, engagements, and brilliant weddings, like the May, 1900, wedding of a dashing San Franciscan named Scott McKeown to Dorothy Studebaker, of the family that then manufactured wagons. He presented her with a 10,000-pearl necklace, a string of racehorses, and a handmade carriage. "The breakfast cost a thousand dollars exclusive of wine," the *Examiner* reported, "and sixty-five quarts of champagne were consumed by twenty-four guests. Mr. McKeown made the only speech of his life. 'Well, ladies and gentlemen,' said the groom, bracing himself with his hands on the table, 'I'm damned glad it's over.'"

The first child was born in the hotel in 1876, and only a long second thought by her parents spared her from having to go through life named Palace.

And in the days before the Golden Gate Bridge the Palace was one of the most popular places to commit suicide, usually by poison accompanied by a lengthy and sentimental suicide note.

One day the San Francisco county coroner received such a note on the hotel's stationery concluding, "You will find my remains in a room at the Palace Hotel," signed by an A. L. Humison and thoughtfully enclosing a check for $75 to pay for his cremation. A deputy coroner was dutifully sent to the Palace, where, to his surprise, he discovered Mr. Humison was still alive, having changed his mind at the last moment. Humison was very apologetic and the deputy coroner was pleased he was still alive, but getting his $75 back was another matter. It took hours of argument by Humison to convince the coroner's office, which liked to do things by the book, that he was not in need of their services quite yet.

While these more frivolous affairs were going on upstairs, the serious business of politics was being conducted in the Palace Bar. So many of the potentates who made California move assembled there that it earned the nickname of the Unofficial State Capitol. There would be Collis P. Huntington and Leland Stanford and attorney William Herrin of the Southern Pacific Railroad, of which the state legislature then was more or less a wholly owned subsidiary. The governor or any number of legislators were frequently there, listening closely and nodding at what Huntington and Stanford and Herrin would say. There were some thirty bartenders working in this exclusively men's precinct of the hotel, pouring the drinks and keeping the lunch counter covered with large platters of oysters and roast antelope.

There among the businessmen in their black frock coats on occasion was a bizarre-looking man in hobnailed boots, a blue flannel miner's shirt, a wide-brimmed felt hat and a beard like a grizzly bear. This was, spectators would whisper, Joaquin Miller, the Poet of the Sierras. Miller delighted in arriving at fashionable literary salons in New York and London in this outlandish costume to read his poems, which are largely and deservedly forgotten today. In that time, however, it was the height of chicness to have Miller reading his poems about Columbus, California, gold and the mining camps. Some people suspected that Miller had never really visited any of the mining camps that he wrote about and that he had actually spent most of his time in bars in Oakland. One was so bold as to ask Miller if he had really been on William Walker's daring expedition to Nicaragua, as he had suggested in "Song of the Sierras." Miller turned around, glared at him and snapped, "Was Milton ever in hell?"

4

Oysters and Champagne

DINING at the Palace was one of the special joys San Francisco offered in the last century. For instance, this was the breakfast menu one morning in 1876:

Fruit

English breakfast, black and Japan tea. Chocolate. Coffee with cream.

French rolls. Vienna rolls. Muffins. Graham rolls. Corn bread.

Boston brown bread. Graham bread. Wheaten grits. Oat meal. Fried and boiled hominy. Boston cream toast. Milk, buttered or dry toast. Wheat cakes. Rice cakes. Indian cakes. Waffles. Vermont maple syrup.

Broiled:

Porterhouse steak. Beefsteak, plain, with tomato sauce or onions. Mutton chops, plain, breaded, or with tomato sauce. Veal cutlets, plain or breaded. Lamb chops. Calf's liver and bacon. Pig's feet. Tenderloin of pork. Kidneys. Smoked salmon. Fresh fish. Smoked herring.

Fried:

Ham and eggs. Fresh fish with salt pork. Tripe. Fish balls. Bunker's clubhouse sausages. Apple and pork. Clams. Corned beef hash. Stewed kidneys. Salt codfish, Shaker fashion.

Stewed tripe.

Potatoes:

Baked, fried, Lyonaise, and stewed with cream.

Cucumbers. Tomatoes. Green Peppers.

Eggs:

Fried, scrambled, boiled, poached, shirred. Omelet plain, with tomatoes, onions, kidneys or ham.

Cold Meats:

Roast beef, corned beef, ham, lamb, beef tongue, dried beef.

This was not an exceptional meal, simply the ordinary breakfast included, along with lunch, dinner, tea and supper, in the price of a room.

Along with the hotel dining rooms, San Francisco offered an extraordinary assortment of restaurants, the happy result of the combination of a great deal of money, the short distance to the sea, cattle ranches, farms and orchards and the presence of men and women from all over the world who knew how to cook.

The chefs of two millionaires visiting San Francisco decided to abandon their employers and open restaurants of their own, so San Francisco gained two superbly elegant restaurants, the Maison Dorée and the Maison Riche. Nearby was the celebrated Poodle Dog, the rendezvous of actors and young men in tailored clothes with money to spend and their women friends. As you ascended from floor to floor in the Poodle Dog, the dining rooms became smaller and plusher, until you came, on the top floor, to small private rooms with couches, doors that locked from the inside, private elevators and discreet waiters carrying decanters of the finest claret.

At Poppa Coppa's on Montgomery, local artists had painted the walls into a multicolored hurricane of caricature and social comment. Tourists flocked to see the pictures and look at a young curly-haired man who looked like a college football star and a gray-mustached scowling man who looked ready to bite someone as he ate his chicken stuffed into a coconut, Poppa Coppa's specialty. Guides would identify them for their awed guests as Jack London and Ambrose Bierce.

Campi's Italian restaurant claimed credit for introducing

macaroni to America, but it was Campi himself, not his macaroni, that most people came to see. His gallantry, particularly to women, was legendary, and it was this gallantry which was finally his undoing. Campi was vacationing in the mountains, hiking along a mountain trail in Yosemite one afternoon when he encountered two young women coming along the trail from the opposite direction. Chivalrous as always, Campi swept off his hat, bowed deeply, stepped back to allow them to pass and disappeared over the edge of the cliff.

But the dining rooms of the great hotels took no second place to the restaurants outside. Chef Mergenthaler at the Palace had learned his art in Paris and had served the queen of Holland, the grand duchess of Russia and the king of Prussia. Working with him he had five assistant cooks, a chief confectioner from Milan, a chief baker from Vienna, an elderly black named Muffin Tom who baked the corn bread and egg muffins and a staff of 150 waiters in the three dining rooms.

Their specialties came from the Pacific and the California streams and mountains: mountain and valley quail, duck, venison and, while they lasted, grizzly bear steaks. There was rainbow trout, abalone, bass and a particular specialty of the Palace, tiny and succulent California oysters cooked into omelets.

Unfortunately, as Chef Mergenthaler was to lament, not every diner had a palate sophisticated enough for his cooking. Many of the men who had built San Francisco did so while living in tents and rude hotels in mining and railroad towns, and they still had what the chef called "pork and bean" tastes. Worse, they refused to spend any time waiting for their food to be prepared; the American, Kipling said, "stuffs for ten minutes thrice a day."

This determination of San Francisco diners to have whatever they wanted immediately was noticed by another English observer: "The bills of fare are too large and varied to admit of all the plates being well or freshly cooked . . . the American guests insist on having their dinner put before them the moment it is ordered, and essential to have a great variety of dishes to choose from, and to dine at any irregular hour they please between 5 and 7:30. . . ." As a result, he said, "every dish has the general taste of its neighbor, whether it be beef, mutton, lamb or poultry."

Whatever was lacking in quality was made up for in quantity. The English observer saw twelve dishes in front of each diner: a dish of meat cut from the joint, smaller dishes of other entrées, more dishes of game, vegetables, puddings, tarts and ice cream, accompanied by glasses of sauterne and French champagne.

The Christmas season saw the Palace dining room at its busiest. In the Grand Court the house electrician had draped the Christmas tree with necklaces of electric bulbs. Hour after hour a parade of waiters in white jackets and white ties marched back and forth between the dining room and the food-laden tables, coming at last with the premier creation of Chef Ernest Arbogast, Pudding à la Sultan: yellow corn flour baked in sweetened milk, spiced with cinnamon, mint, sliced bananas and dates and served in a sauce of green tea, sugar and hot rum.

This was dinner at the Palace on Friday, December 1, 1876.

SOUP
Clam chowder   consommé Fleury

HORS D'OEUVRES
Deviled crabs à la creole

FISH
Boiled codfish, oyster sauce

RELEVÉES
Leg of mutton, boiled, caper sauce
Roulade of veal, braisé, à la Bourgeoise

ENTRÉES
Samis of wild ducks, with olives
Ragout of filet beef, à la Bordelaise
Calves head, sauce Vinaigrette
Boned Capon Truffée with Gelée
Punch au Mouscatello

ROAST
Saddle of lamb, mint sauce
Ribs of beef
Ham with champagne sauce

GAME
Broiled quails on toast, au cresson
Salad à la Mayonnaise
Vegetables

DESSERT
Indian pudding. Peach pie. Boston cream puffs. Strawberry
Bavaroise. Cranberry tartelette. Gateaux à la Royale. Gelée
au Rhum

Lemon ice cream   fruit   coffee

5

High Society

IN the 1880s the San Franciscans who had made their fortunes in the 1860s decided that they were better than the people who had made their money in the 1870s. Thus was San Francisco society born.

"It was being impressed on the plutocrats—often by their wives—" Oscar Lewis wrote, "that while the rules for accumulating wealth remained pleasantly lax, those governing its proper expenditure were steadily becoming more complex."

For their model, San Franciscans naturally turned to the place where snobbery had long been an established art: New York. Soon San Francisco society columns were filled with the weekly progressions of Vanderbilts and Morgans from Long Island to Saratoga.

There was certainly room for improvement in San Francisco. One woman, who had risen from the position of cook to a great fortune, had a throne installed in her living room and insisted on sitting on it when she entertained guests. W. H. Crocker, one of the wealthiest men in the city, had gone to the Medici Gallery in Florence to purchase some paintings for his mansion and, not seeing what he wanted, had demanded to see Mr. Medici. And as for the manners of the guests at the reception for General Grant: "The military gentlemen, with others, formed a cordon around the tables that no strategy could circumvent. Out of twelve hundred guests . . . many obtained little or nothing. There was no chance for those who were not willing to put both feet in the trough."

In New York Ward McAllister had neatly divided society

into the ins and the outs by making a celebrated list of the "Four Hundred." A plump champagne salesman from Baltimore decided to do the same for San Francisco. What qualified Ned Greenway, the San Francisco representative of Mumm's champagne, to do this isn't precisely clear, other than that he danced well, had an enormous expense account, and looked rather like Field Marshal Paul von Hindenburg. Nevertheless, when he organized the Friday Night Cotillion Club and issued a list of invitations to attend five *very* exclusive dances, San Francisco held its breath to see who had been and who hadn't been invited. The bitterness, intrigue, jealousy, gossip, inflated pride and broken friendships that immediately followed showed that San Francisco had finally achieved real society.

The cotillions were held at the Odd Fellows Hall and ran from 10 P.M. until 3 A.M. Greenway personally led each dance, calling out commands to the dancers: "Grand right and left! Royal arches! Reversed circles!" as if he actually were Von Hindenburg. At midnight the dancing was interrupted for a supper of scalloped oysters, ham and tongue sandwiches, duck, ice cream and champagne, and then the dancing resumed again. Invitations depended largely on how you made your money. If you or your husband or father made cigars, you were in; if they sold them, you were out.

The Cotillion Club was a tremendous success; Greenway was accepted as the arbiter of society. But then he made the mistake of deciding to write a society column for the San Francisco *Chronicle*.

To the editors of the San Francisco *Examiner* anything which appeared in the *Chronicle* was barbarous, underhanded, foul, dangerous and, if it seemed to be successful, worth copying. Thus, they unveiled their own social arbiter, a former steamship officer named William H. Chambliss.

Chambliss promptly organized a Monday night cotillion society, which he announced was the only real society in the city, and suggested that the "Self-elected leaders and dictators of so-called social clubs who claim that a little money and a few false notices in the third-rate newspapers gave high social rating to all the saloon keepers, gamblers, sports, and prize-fighters who attend their money-making functions [a

subtle allusion to Greenway] should be relegated without unnecessary delay to the ranks of colored society."

Publishing his own social weekly with his picture on the
cover, Chambliss traced his own genealogy back to Mississippi aristocrats, ordained that true society people wore white
gloves at all times and offered his opinion of San Francisco's
cosmopolitan population: "I never did like a Chinaman. Personally, I dislike him very much, but I prefer him to the
anarchist and the African at all times. A Chinese exclusion
act we already have. What we sorely need is a European exclusion act that will shut out foreign immigration of all
classes."

Unfortunately, Chambliss' personal financial ventures
failed to prosper as Greenway's had. His plan, which came to
him while reclining in a barber's chair at the Palace, to sell
advertising space on the ceiling of every barbershop in
America was received with less than fervent enthusiasm. As
his financial fortunes declined, so did his social fortunes; his
Monday night club never overtook Greenway's cotillion.

The *Examiner* abandoned Chambliss and launched a new
assault with a new strategy, generaled by Mrs. Monroe Salisbury, who offered nine dances for $5 compared with Green-
way's $20 for only five dances, holding them on the same
night as Greenway and calling them the Friday Fortnightly.
The *Examiner* exulted; "It is no longer sine qua non to belong to the Greenway Club. You might be in society on a five
dollar basis. . . ." When Mrs. Salisbury died, Ynez Shorb
White picked up the standard, formed the New Cotillion
Club and declared that recent balls had been "altogether too
promiscuous." Mrs. White announced that she was removing
200 people from her list. Greenway countered by announcing that from 1906 on no girl could be a member of his club
whose mother had not been a member. San Francisco society
trembled, fearing that, before it was over, there would be no
one left in society but Mrs. White and Mr. Greenway. Luckily
for them, they were saved from this catastrophe by a slightly
larger one, which destroyed not only the Odd Fellows Hall,
but the entire city around it as well, the 1906 earthquake.

It was just as well, for the world was changing. More and
more young people were slipping away from the cotillions

and recklessly plunging into the mad and spinning world of saxophones and ragtime on the Barbary Coast and in the Eye-Wink Dance Hall, and two women, the offspring of British nobility, were seen openly smoking in the lobby of the Palace, "totally unconscious of the many eyes cast in their direction."

The world was changing, slowly and uncontrollably slipping toward the brink. Lenin was feverishly writing in Helsinki, Conrad Hilton was eleven years old, and the Jack Tar Hotel was a malicious gleam in the eye of a yet-unborn child.

6

The Gray Lady and the Gambler

BY the turn of the century the Palace had left behind the gaiety of its youth and had become solid and respectable.

Financially, the hotel had been a magnificent disaster its first ten years. The hordes of European tourists Ralston and Sharon had expected to entertain on their way to the Orient went by way of the newly opened Suez Canal instead. Rooms were empty everywhere in the hotel.

When Sharon died, his businesslike son-in-law, Frank Newlands, took over and reorganized the entire hotel. A new manager was brought in, thirty cooks were fired, all the dining room waiters were dismissed, the grillroom staff were reduced from eighteen to four, and the remaining staff were told henceforth they would be searched going off duty, would have to pay the full price for any food they ate and would have to shave off their mustaches and beards.

As it happened, the economies were unnecessary. In the 1890s advertisements in magazines and newspapers all over the world began luring travelers to the island paradise called Hawaii, and the route passed right through San Francisco. The rooms began to fill.

The Palace prospered, despite new competition. E. J. "Lucky" Baldwin, heady from a quick killing in real estate, raised an ornate wooden palace capped by a delirium of turrets and a Taj Mahal dome on the corner of Ellis and Powell not long after the Palace was opened. Nicknamed Baldwin's Fire Trap, the hotel boasted two mechanical canaries, a ladies' billiard room and a theater, which, Baldwin suggested, "doubtless has no superiors, even in art-loving Europe."

The Baldwin Hotel enjoyed a colorful, if short, life. Lucky

Baldwin himself enjoyed tending the bar of his hotel, joyously throwing any unruly patron out into the street. Old San Franciscans liked to recall the night a guest brought a beer-drinking goat from North Beach into the lobby, which he insisted on taking upstairs to show his wife. Mr. Baldwin and the staff politely declined, and in the ensuing altercation between the staff and the man, his friends and the goat, the lobby was destroyed.

On November 22, 1898, shortly after William Gillette had acted his play *Secret Service* in the theater, a spark flared and caught in a darkened kitchen, and the wooden hotel was suddenly swarming with fire. In the morning Lucky Baldwin poked through the ashes that were all that was left of his hotel. He had no insurance. Eventually he moved to Southern California and bought hundreds of acres of hills and gardens around a sleepy town called Los Angeles.

At the turn of the century the trustees of the recently deceased Charles Crocker looked enviously at the success of the Palace and decided to build their own hotel in the names of the two young Crocker children, Templeton and Jenny.

Built on a lot facing Union Square, the new hotel was to have been called The Crocker, but when it opened, it carried the name of one of the early canvas and board hotels of the gold rush, the St. Francis.

Designed by Bliss and Faville, the St. Francis followed the style pioneered by architect Louis Sullivan in Chicago; its simple face was bare of the bric-a-brac and ornamental frosting that had made much of San Francisco look like a baroque toy shop.

The novelty of a modern new hotel in San Francisco drew the curious from all over to try it out when it opened in 1904. Among them was the gambler Zeb Kendall.

Kendall had lately been losing astonishing sums of money betting on horse races, and his wife had threatened that he would suffer at her hands unless he stopped. Nevertheless, when he had established her in a room in the hotel, he went down to the café and met an old crony, Wyatt Earp. The aging Earp had long since switched from gunfighting to investing in California real estate. The two of them decided to go to the racetrack for one last fling.

When Kendall returned, four days later, his wife was waiting for him. Before he could say a word she seized his suit-case and hurled it through the window. "Wait!" he screamed. "Wait! There's eighty-five thousand dollars in that thing that I *won!*" She looked at him for a moment, and then they both rushed madly for the stairs. "I beat the elevator getting downstairs," she recalled later. "The case was still bouncing when I got there . . . there really *was* eighty-five thousand dollars in it."

A few blocks up the street, on the crown of Nob Hill, another San Francisco family was planning a hotel. Tessie Fair Oelrichs and her husband inspected the site where her father had planned his mansion. Once nearly inaccessible because of its steepness, the hill was now climbed every few minutes by a rattling yellow and green cable car, and all around them were the ornate castles and palaces of the rail-road and silver barons.

By 1904 construction on the new hotel had begun, and a gray granite first story surmounted by five stories of cream marble and terra-cotta, sculpted into the shape of a Euro-pean palace, stood on the site. But things were not so well with Tessie and Herman Oelrichs; their marriage fell apart, and they separated. Tessie, not willing to finish the building, traded it to Dr. Herbert Law, who had made his fortune sell-ing patent medicine, and his brother Hartland, in exchange for several office buildings in the financial district. The Laws continued the work on the hotel, and by 1906 the crates of furnishings were arriving in the lobby, and it was nearly ready to open.

Frank Newlands, in his office at the Palace, had his own problems. For one thing, the newspapers had begun to de-scribe his hotel as "historic," which then was a far from com-plementary term. The huge old building with its great halls and balconies seemed dated, an enormous museum piece. For another, the fashionable shopping and theater districts seemed to be slipping west, away from the Palace and toward the St. Francis on Union Square.

Newlands did what he could. He cut a new entrance far-ther west on Market Street, and moved the bar closer to it. He redecorated the hotel in the gilt and plush style that fash-ion then dictated, turning the grill into a white and gold François I parlor with French mirrors and an ornate fireplace. The bar became Empire style, complete with vaulted ceiling, red African marble and dark mahogany, bronze fittings and amber skylights. Upstairs wood floors were tiled, bright nickel handles appeared on the faucets, and the old iron bathtubs were replaced with gleaming white porcelain ones.

The final sacrifice to progress was the most painful one. Automobiles had begun to appear in San Francisco, after young Charley Fair had driven a Panhard automobile, imported from Paris, down the street, terrifying every horse within blocks.

Now the noisy iron beasts and their chauffeurs, shouting and waving their caps, were clogging the driveway of the Grand Court. The circular driveway had been designed for graceful horse-drawn carriages; no one had imagined the iron and glass monsters that were clattering there now. There was no room for the automobiles to turn, and the lobby was filled with smoke, noise and the angry arguments of chauffeurs fighting for a parking place. In 1900 the Palace gave up, tore up the pavement of the Grand Court, moved in sofas and potted palms, and reopened it as a sitting room. The young girl was gone; she was a gray old lady now.

7

Teddy

A GREAT electric sign with gold-painted bulbs glowed over the dining room of the Palace Hotel: "The land of sunshine, fruit and flowers greets our President." On the long tables vases overflowed with sweet peas and roses and enormous cakes that had been frosted into replicas of San Juan Hill and the Point Reyes lighthouse. The band suddenly crashed into "There'll Be a Hot Time in the Old Town To-night," and Teddy Roosevelt, President of the United States, began to clap his hands and then joined the other 700 men in singing the chorus of the old Spanish-American War battle song. When they were finished he broke into a broad grin, and the men cheered and applauded.

It was May 14, 1903. Roosevelt was the last of a succession of presidents that had begun with Benjamin Harrison to call at the old Palace Hotel. He was received, as every great man was received then, with overflowing tables, endless champagne toasts and endless speeches. Surrounded by his Cabinet ministers, generals and admirals, Roosevelt beamed and sat back to listen to the speeches. The master of ceremonies first reviewed the number of acres of orchards in California, the amount of bank clearings, eulogized "our ever-dear Golden Gate" and the virtues of the California orange, before concluding that San Francisco was destined to be "the largest city in the Union." Mayor Eugene Schmitz followed with a speech that opened, "Seated high on her crested hill, by the limitless western sea," and ended seemingly hours later, when he introduced the next speaker, Governor George C. Pardee. Governor Pardee rose and eloquently reviewed the progress of mankind from 44 B.C. to the present day, sparing no details, before he turned to introduce General Arthur MacArthur, the commander of the army in the west and the father of twenty-three-year-old Douglas MacArthur. MacArthur rambled on uncertainly about the virtues of militarism: "The American Republic today is a most profound and impressive exemplification of the formula as being the rarest combination the world has yet seen of good morals and vitalizing ideas which have been vitalized, unified, and cemented by human blood."

The guests applauded and tried to figure out what he had just said, while Roosevelt just smiled and clapped. He loved every minute of it.

Seldom have a president and a city been more meant for one another than Teddy Roosevelt and San Francisco. Roosevelt charged around the city, making speeches, meeting old Rough Riders, dedicating buildings, accepting awards, saluting soldiers and everywhere being cheered by San Franciscans.

"Our place is with the expanding nations," he shouted to the audience in the Mechanics Pavilion, "and with the nations that dare to be great. All of our people should take this position, but especially you of California, for much of our expansion must go through the Golden Gate!" The audience cheered and clapped, and outside the hall fireworks—skyrockets, Greek fire and bombs—roared a salute to the President.

The next day he drove from the Palace Hotel to Golden Gate Park, where he lustily shoveled earth from the site of a monument to William McKinley.

"Never hit if you can help it," he told the crowd in his high-pitched voice, "but if you hit, don't hit soft!" The crowd, mainly Spanish-American War veterans interspersed with gray-bearded veterans of the Civil War, cheered, and someone yelled, "You're all right, Teddy!" Roosevelt grinned broadly. "It's getting pretty generally understood that that's our foreign policy."

Next, he was driven to the Presidio, where General MacArthur had lined up troops of cavalry and infantry and batteries of artillery for his inspection. Roosevelt leaped from the car, took off his silk top hat and put on a khaki army cavalry hat. A horse was led over to the President, and he climbed into the saddle. He frowned, pulled on the reins and complained that the animal didn't have any spirit. After a frantic search, another horse, this one a veteran of cavalry charges in the Spanish-American War, was led over to the President. Roosevelt changed horses, and when the new horse reared and plunged, he grinned happily.

General Arthur MacArthur turned around to point out a particular regiment to the President and was startled to find that he was gone. Digging his heels in the flanks of his horse, Roosevelt was galloping at full speed across the Presidio golf course. MacArthur and his aides spurred their horses and set off in pursuit. Roosevelt led them on a frantic chase over the golf course and up and down the bordering hills and ravines before he finally turned around and rode back to the parade site, puffing and grinning at the astonished general.

After another banquet with Republican leaders at the Palace Hotel, President Roosevelt boarded a special ferry at the foot of Mission Street and rode through the night across the Bay. As the ferry passed the cruiser *New York* , the crew of the warship, crowding the railings, began to sing "America." A powerful searchlight on the *New York* swept over the ferry and stopped on the rear upper deck, where it illuminated the figure of President Roosevelt, standing at the railing, raising his hat. The crew of the ship burst into a roar of cheers.

A few days later Roosevelt was riding horseback through the awesome canyons of Yosemite National Park, accompanied only by the bearded naturalist John Muir and two park rangers.

"He wrote me asking that I should see him through that country," Muir told a reporter before the trip, "and of course I said I would go. It is only a very little trip. You can't see much of the Sierras in four days, you know, and that's all the President could spare. I lived there for nine years at a time, and found something new all the time."

Completely out of contact with his Cabinet, his advisers and the rest of the country, Roosevelt and Muir rolled themselves in blankets, camped out in the sequoia forests, and walked along the rim of Glacier Point, overlooking the Yosemite Valley. When the four days were over, the President, wearing a khaki suit, army hat and faded handkerchief, rode down to the Sentinel Hotel in the valley.

"Just think of where I was last night!" he exulted. "Up there!" He pointed up toward Glacier Point. "Amid the pines and silver firs, in the Sierra solitude. In a snowstorm, too," he added. "And without a tent!"

8

Cracks in the Rainbow
April 18, 1906, 5:15 A.M.

POLICE Sergeant Jesse Cook, standing in the chill morning outside the produce market, was the first to see it coming.

"There was a deep rumbling," he said, "deep and terrible, and then I could see it actually coming up Washington Street. It was as if the waves of the ocean were coming toward me, billowing as they came."

In the darkness of his room at the Palace Hotel, Alfred Hertz, the conductor of the San Francisco Symphony, found himself gripping the matress of his rocking bed. "Even in this moment I was conscious of sound effects," he recalled. "In opera such elementary catastrophes are invariably orchestrated FFF, while musically speaking, the earthquake gave me the sensation of an uncanny mezzo forte effect—something comparable to the mezzo forte roll on a cymbal or gong."

Walter Courtney Bennet, the consul general of Britain, was rocked awake in his room across from the St. Francis Hotel. He said, "Everywhere there was the noise, like thousands of violins, all at a discord. The most harrowing sound one could imagine."

John Farish, a mining engineer staying at the St. Francis, said, "I was awakened by a loud rumbling noise which might be compared to the mixed sound of a strong wind rushing through a forest and the breaking of waves against a cliff . . . then began a series of the liveliest motions imaginable, accompanied by a creaking, grinding, rasping sound, followed by tremendous crashes as the cornices of adjoining buildings and chimneys tottered to the ground."

Then, after fifty-five seconds of shaking and rocking, the earth was still, and there was an awesome silence. No one knew it then, but San Francisco had been mortally wounded.

Doors banged open on every floor of the Palace, and guests, many half dressed, hurried down the stairs and outside into the cold air, where they joined the stunned residents of nearby apartments and hotels. James Hopper, a reporter for the San Francisco *Call*, left his office and moved through the crowds. "The streets were full of people, half-clad, dishevelled, but silent, absolutely silent," he said. "All of them had a singular hurt expression . . . not of physical pain, but rather one of injured sensibilities . . . as if some trusted friend had suddenly wronged them."

Hertz dressed hurriedly in the dark and rushed to Suite 580, where he found the tenor who had sung *Carmen* so brilliantly in the Opera House the night before. Enrico Caruso was sitting upright in his bed, weeping. "He embraced me hysterically," Hertz said, "repeatedly insisting that we were doomed." Then he claimed he could no longer sing. Hertz urged him to try. They opened the window, and Caruso leaned out. The people in the street at Market and Montgomery were startled to hear a vibrant voice pealing over their heads:

> *La fanta mi salva ,*
> *L'immondo ritrova* . . . .

Satisfied, Caruso dressed, with the aid of his valet, and they hurried down to the lobby. There they found the rest of the Metropolitan Opera Company in confusion, the grand dames in their nightgowns, the rest of the guests hurrying toward the exits and the carpet covered with broken glass and plaster.

Amid this desperate exodus, Hertz remembered: "I could scarcely believe my eyes when I saw an old Chinese servant quietly and calmly cleaning the easy chairs and carpets of the lobby, as if all this was just a daily occurrence."

At five fifty the telegraph operator in the building across the street from the Palace tapped out:

THERE WAS AN EARTHQUAKE HIT US AT FIVE FIFTEEN O'CLOCK
THIS MORNING WRECKING SEVERAL BUILDINGS AND WRECKING

OUR OFFICES. THEY ARE CARTING DEAD FROM THE FALLEN
BUILDINGS. FIRE ALL OVER TOWN. THERE IS NO WATER AND WE
LOST OUR POWER. I'M GOING TO GET OUT OF THE OFFICE AS WE
HAVE HAD A LITTLE SHAKE EVERY FEW MINUTES AND IT'S ME
FOR THE SIMPLE LIFE.

A young page recalled the confusion at the St. Francis: "I
found the floor crowded with screaming guests running every which way. As the elevators were all out of order the
guests headed for the marble stairs, which were broken and
cracked and falling below." The manager, James Woods,
"was in the lobby with only a bathrobe on, trying to calm the
guests." Ignoring Woods, the guests rushed out into Union
Square, along with thousands of others who had fled there to
be clear of falling masonry if there was another quake.

James Hopper reached the little park and observed, "In
the center of Union Square an old man was, with great delib-
eration, trying to decipher the inscription of the Dewey monument through spectacles from which the lenses had fallen."

Soon Hopper was joined by Hertz and Caruso, who went
into the St. Francis in search of breakfast. Waiter Larry Lewis
served them eggs, bacon and toast, recalling that Caruso
"didn't say much, just kept on eating." The singer finished
three eggs and tipped Lewis and the cook each $2.50.

Hurrying out of the St. Francis lobby as Caruso came in
was the young actor John Barrymore, who had been caught
in his room at the time of the earthquake with several empty
bottles of champagne and the wife of another man. He was
still in his evening clothes.

Inside the Palace, a hurried inspection by the management
showed them that their building, like most of those downtown, had suffered no major structural damage. They had
reason to be confident; their walls were two feet thick, rein-
forced with iron, and there was a reservoir filled with
630,000 gallons of water under the pavement of the Grand
Court, connected through pumps run by steam engines to
nearly three miles of fire hose at stations all over the hotel.

But the messages coming in from other parts of the city
were alarming. At the first shock, the recently filled land
south of Market Street near the Bay had sagged six feet,
breaking up and capsizing the clapboard hotels and rooming
houses jammed on its surface. The stoves cooking early

breakfasts had been pitched over and dropped into piles of broken wood and kindling. Within minutes fifty-seven fires were reported south of Market.

The firemen of Engine Company 38 pulled to a halt in front of a blaze on Steuart Street, screwed a hose onto the hydrant and began pumping. Dirty brown water trickled from the nozzle. The earthquake had snapped the fire mains.

Soldiers in khaki uniforms with rifles on their shoulders began to march into the downtown streets from the Presidio, sent to keep order. They found the residents carrying armloads of baggage, pushing steamer trunks mounted on roller skates, even struggling with upright pianos, trying to stay ahead of the rapidly spreading fires that were now sending up billows of gray smoke over Market Street.

At the Palace Hotel the manager saw the danger and sent men to the roof to spray it with hoses. Caruso and Hertz arrived back at the hotel at 10 A.M. to claim their baggage and found "the place had an air of evacuation . . . whereas before people had often tried to pay their bills before leaving, they were now rushing out, wanting to get clear of the place at all costs, taking what they could with them. . . ."

Caruso's trunks were piled on a wagon by Chinese servants, while the singer wrapped a towel around his neck and seized an autographed portrait of Theodore Roosevelt from one trunk, which he tucked under his arm. Then he fled the hotel for the last time.

As the firemen stood by, helpless without water, the dozens of fires south of Market Street joined together on one creeping blaze and began moving toward the business district and the Palace. Shortly after noon the dull crump of explosions was heard over the crackling of the fire, as soldiers tried to dynamite buildings in its path.

The fire had now consumed a square mile of buildings: It had burned through to the Bay on the west, had leaped north into the business district and had eaten its way through to Market Street and was creeping slowly west toward the Palace. As the last guests left, the bartenders handed out the bottles from the shelves. Crowds on Nob Hill watched with fascination as streams of water from the underground cistern danced on the roof of the hotel, now stark against a dirty gray-brown sky.

A wagon filled with brown-uniformed soldiers and crates of dynamite stopped on Annie Street opposite the Palace, and the soldiers carried the explosive into the seven-story Monadnock Building. A few minutes later they were back outside, and a sharp crack shook the building. It refused to fall. The dynamite, hurriedly and poorly laid, had failed to break its steel skeleton. The fire moved closed and closer.

A few minutes later the dancing jets of water on the Palace roof flickered and disappeared. The 630,000-gallon reservoir was empty. The last employees left the roof and the steam pumps clanked to a halt. The hotel was deserted. At two twenty the telegraph operator across the street, who had decided to stay until the last minute, sent a final message:

THE CITY PRACTICALLY RUINED BY FIRE. IT'S WITHIN HALF A BLOCK OF US IN THE SAME BLOCK. THE CALL BUILDING IS BURNED OUT ENTIRELY. THE EXAMINER BUILDING JUST FELL IN A HEAP. FIRE ALL AROUND US IN EVERY DIRECTION. . . . LOTS OF NEW BUILDINGS JUST FINISHED ARE COMPLETELY DESTROYED. THEY ARE BLOWING STANDING BUILDINGS THAT ARE IN THE PATH OF THE FLAMES WITH DYNAMITE. IT'S AWFUL. . . . I WANT TO GET OUT OF HERE OR BE BLOWN UP.

Ten minutes later the Grand Hotel and the Wells Fargo Building were burning, and the flames had leaped to the top floors of the Palace, entering windows popped out by the heat and setting alight the ornate furnishings of the hotel. Within an hour the building was gutted. The crowds on Nob Hill watched as the flames reached up and at last snapped the American flag from its pole over the hotel.

A few blocks away, the crowds of refugees gathered in Union Square realized they were no longer safe. The fire had leaped Market Street and was moving west through the financial district toward them. They fled to the west, leaving the square littered with furniture, baby buggies, dishes, trunks, suitcases, washtubs and upright pianos. The firemen, exhausted and smoke-blackened, set up their line along Powell Street, in front of the St. Francis, determined to stop the fire there.

Late in the afternoon Nob Hill became the command post of the fire fighters. The fifty members of the Committee of

Safety, headed by Mayor Eugene Schmitz, sat in the unfinished ballroom of the Fairmont Hotel listening as General Frederick Funston, commander of the troops in San Francisco, proposed the complete dynamiting of large areas of the city in path of the fire. They could think of no other way to stop it.

As night settled over the city, the glow of the fire could be seen in Sonoma and Santa Clara, fifty miles away. The young Jack London, who had hurried to the city when he heard of the fire, walked along Market Street, which had been crowded with people a few hours before. It was empty now, except for two mounted cavalrymen.

"That was all," he wrote. "Not another person was in sight. In the intense heat of the city, two troopers sat on their horses and watched. Surrender was complete."

An hour after midnight the fire reached the line of firemen on Powell Street, hesitated and then leaped past them. A three-story wooden store across from the St. Francis exploded with fire, and the intense heat cracked the windows of the hotel, setting the curtains on fire. Soon flames were rushing through the hotel, and the firemen were retreating.

On Nob Hill, art students were carrying armloads of paintings and statues out the Gothic doors of the Mark Hopkins mansion, which, since the death of his widow, had been the Hopkins Institute of Art. The Committee of Safety had long since retreated to the west. The firemen on the hill could see that fire was slowly encircling them. The students, unable to find wagons for the art works, abandoned them on the lawn of the Flood mansion. The firemen fought until their water supplies were exhausted and then fell back.

In the early hours of the morning the Crocker house, the cuckoo clock with the seventy-foot tower, burned, followed by the elegant Huntington mansion and the Stanford house, with its marble stairway and great hall. The fire burned around the stone Flood house and its brass rail and, in a frenzy, captured the wooden spires and battlements of the Hopkins mansion.

The wind blew the heat against the white walls of the Fairmont, shattering the windows and igniting the stores of paint, varnish and furniture in the uncompleted rooms. Gertrude Atherton, on a boat crossing the bay, looked back and "forgot the doomed city as I looked at the Fairmont, a tremendous volume of white smoke pouring upward from where its unfinished roof had been, every window a shimmering sheet of gold." By the time the sun had risen the Fairmont was gutted.

Later that morning there was a new sound, the sharp crack of cannon. Using field artillery and teams of expert dynamiters from the Navy, General Funston was turning mansion-lined Van Ness Avenue into a barren firebreak between the fire and the rest of the city to the west. The fire halted at Van Ness and the next morning, seventy-four hours after it began, it was out.

San Franciscans were not the sort to sit and weep over their fate. They set about rebuilding as if the fire had been only a minor inconvenience.

Tent cities sprang up in every park, and hot food stations were hammered together out of canvas and boards on street corners, ladling out bowls of Irish stew, bread and tea to the refugees. A sign over one station read; "Eat, Drink and Be Merry, for Tomorrow we may have to go to Oakland." Another person asked why San Francisco had been destroyed while Oakland was intact. "There are some things even the earth won't swallow," came the reply.

Eight days after the fire the performers of the Orpheum Theater put on a vaudeville show in a downtown park and sang one act of *Carmen.* By August the cable car was running again along California Street.

The old tenants sifted through the rubble and ashes for their belongings. Adolphus Busch, the Milwaukee beer baron, hired a small army of bellhops to sift the wreckage of his rooms at the St. Francis for jewelry and gold coins. The ruins were alive with the sound of hammering and pounding. As insurance adjusters inspected the shells of burned-out buildings, workmen were already putting up the skeleton of a new city.

The brick walls of the Palace were still standing solidly, but, the "Committee of Five" investigators for the large insurance companies reported, "The entire interior of this building, which consisted of wood flooring and finish, has completely disappeared." It was decided to tear down the walls and start over.

The unfinished Fairmont had been more seriously damaged. There were only a few cracks and splinters off the blackened terra-cotta exterior, but inside many of the iron columns supporting the floors had buckled from the heat, making bulges and sinks in the floors. The inside would have to be largely ripped out and replaced.

The St. Francis had survived remarkably well. The copper cornice had warped, and some of the enameled facing bricks had fallen from the blast of heat, but the structure was sound.

Unwilling to concede their guests to Oakland's hotels while their buildings were being repaired, the Palace and the St. Francis each hurriedly constructed wood-frame baby hotels that were miniatures of their great namesakes. The Baby Palace, a twenty-three-room building a few blocks from the old site, opened its grill with Chef Arbogast presiding and offered the best food in the rising city.

The St. Francis was not to be outdone. The Little St. Francis, built in the middle of Union Square, had 110 rooms, a Greek portico, red carpeting, a ladies' parlor upholstered in green velvet, a printing plant, a grillroom and a barbershop. The ground floor of the old St. Francis across the street was cleared of rubble and reopened as a restaurant to feed the guests.

"The gayest, lightest-headed and most pleasure-loving city of the western continent, and in many ways the most interesting and romantic, is a horde of refugees living among ruins," Will Irwin wrote immediately after the earthquake. They weren't for long. The walls and towers rose with almost magical speed. An illuminated phoenix over the entrance of the St. Francis symbolized the rebirth. San Francisco hadn't died; it had simply moved to newer quarters.

It's difficult to say when San Francisco was its old self again. The Chamber of Commerce pointed to the date, shortly after the earthquake, when bank clearings reached and then exceeded their old levels.

The city fathers staged a Portola Festival in 1910, named after the Spanish explorer who discovered the Bay, to celebrate their new city. A huge mission bell of 25,000 lights was erected on one of the hills, its glow visible fifty miles at sea. The city indulged in fireworks and a nonstop five-day party.

"It was as if everyone in San Francisco had suddenly turned to the next fellow and said 'let's get drunk,'" one person remembered, "and they had." Even the citizen selected to don the costume of Gaspar de Portolá drank merrily with his fellow San Franciscans and fell off his horse during the parade.

But the most memorable date was Christmas Eve, 1910. A mall platform had been set up in front of Lotta's Fountain at the intersection of Market, Geary and Kearny streets. Around that platform, in five directions, San Franciscans had gathered and stood hushed. It was said that 100,000 people were there in the downtown streets, but no one really counted.

Onto the platform climbed little Luisa Tetrazzini, in a white gown, gloves and a broad-brimmed hat. She and San Francisco were in love. The city had encouraged her and cheered the rise of her career, until she was one of the nation's most honored opera singers. She, in return, gave all her heart to the city. That night she sang for them.

"Those who heard her said her silver voice seemed to rise to the stars through the still night," one person said. "The utter silence of the great crowd in the dark streets was curiously thrilling."

"I stood two blocks away," a person there remembered, "and every note was crystal clear, every word distinct. Silence, save for her voice, spread over the city, like the silence of night in the desert. Streetcars were stopped, horses and wagons and the few automobiles stood still. The clanging of the cable car bells was stilled. Not a sound came from that audience. She sang again, and if you had closed your eyes you would have thought yourself alone in the world with that beautiful voice. She sang 'The Last Rose of Summer.' When she finished, there was another tumultuous ovation. She held out her arms to her people, asking for quiet, and commenced to sing once more. This time, all San Francisco sang with her. Up and down the streets and alleys and from the windows of buildings high above the street came the song from the hundreds of thousands, and Luisa Tetrazzini sang with them 'Auld Lang Syne.'"

When she finished, there was a deep silence, and then applause and cheers rolled through the steel canyons. Tetrazzini covered her face and wept.

9

The Long Waltz

THE Fairmont was the first of the great hotels to open, just one year after the earthquake, on April 19, 1907. The St. Francis followed in November, and the new Palace opened on December 16, 1909.

They were the serene flagships of an elegant era, the palaces of the leisurely rich in an age with abundant time for leisure. The style of that era would be knocked over just as abruptly by the First World War as the old city had been by the earthquake, but for the moment it seemed that the slow waltz would go on forever.

There were tea dances; there were cotillions; there were summers spent in rambling great resort hotels and hot springs at Monterey and Napa. The American fleet would sail splendidly into the Bay, pennants flying, like a great white armored yacht club, and fill the hotel ballrooms with its white-jacketed officers. There were endless banquets with menus in French and champagne toasts, and one dressed for everything.

Compared to Ralston's vanished bay window fantasy, the new Palace was gray and dignified. Dressed in sedate Milwaukee brick and granite, it looked like an office building, wearing only a single iron balcony below the cornice for ornament. It no longer towered over its neighbors but was shoulder to shoulder with other gray office buildings.

The circular driveway and the Grand Court were gone, replaced by a great glass-canopied room called the Palm Court, framed by double rows of marble pillars and ornamented with mahogany and gilt balconies and potted palms. Adjoining it on one side was the Rose Room, a ballroom with ivory woodwork and rose-colored draperies, and on the other side, through glass doors, was the main restaurant, in stately French decor. Through more glass doors was the men's grill, under a heavy-timbered Gothic ceiling with red tile and white walls reflecting the copper candelabra. Next to the grill was the bar, warmly wrapped in oak panels, lit by leaded sky-lights and displaying over the bar a stylish $10,000 painting of the Pied Piper of Hamelin by the Art Nouveau painter Maxfield Parrish.

Upstairs there were private reception rooms and dining salons, and above that, 900 rooms, including a dignified Presidential Suite.

On top of Nob Hill, Stanford White, the architect who had designed the Boston Public Library and many other noted public buildings of the period, supervised as workmen tore out and replaced 121 columns warped by the fire and finally finished the Fairmont.

The Fairmont was the most imposing building of the San Francisco skyline, crouching like a great marble lion above the rest of the city. An endless line of automobiles and car-riages drove up under the granite porch on Mason Street to the main entrance. On the lower side of the hotel two low wings, like marble paws, enfolded a terrace and levels of gar-dens.

When the guest climbed out of his automobile and walked in the main doors, he found himself in a cathedrallike lobby, reflected in huge Florentine mirrors and surrounded by gleaming marble pillars. On one side a marble staircase marched majestically upstairs; in the center, doors opened into a screened and chandeliered tearoom with a dome of stained glass, flooded with tinted light and hanging baskets of flowers and shrubs. Through this little room, called the Laurel Court, was the dining room, all gold and white in Louis XV style, with tall windows looking down on the gar-dens, Powell Street, downtown and the Bay.

A wrought-iron staircase descended through the middle of the Laurel Court to Rainbow Lane, a collection of fashion and Oriental curio shops along an arcade that led to the Nor-man Banquet Hall, a huge Hollywood-stage-set room with a timbered ceiling and hanging rings of electric candles. Past this was the ballroom, a white and gold corridor with eighteen chandeliers, blue silk hangings and one long wall of full-length mirrors. Lastly, there was the Crypt Grill and Bar, where little wooden chairs and tables huddled under a low, catacomblike ceiling of thick pillars and low arches.

If the austere and dignified furnishings of the Palace made its guests feel important, the Fairmont, by this opulent collection of marble and plush stage sets, seemed determined to make its guests feel as if they were acting in D. W. Griffith costume-epic versions of *Ivanhoe* and *Marie Antoinette*. America's ideas of taste were still copied from picture books of Florence and Salzburg, or whenever possible, bits of Florence and Salzburg, like the mirrors in the Fairmont lobby, were bought, crated and shipped to America. William Ralston had tried to furnish the Old Palace entirely with California products: Edwardian hoteliers tried to import European culture in bulk.

Travelers came to San Francisco in Wagner palace cars pulled by the big locomotives of the Southern Pacific. No two palace cars were alike; inside they were miniature Louis XV and Louis XVI salons, paneled with rosewood and vermilion, furnished in mahogany and hung with tapestries. The Sunset Limited, traveling between San Francisco and New Orleans by way of Los Angeles, trailed behind it, in addition to the palace cars and pullmans, a bath car, a ladies' parlor car, a barbershop, a car for maids, a club car and a library. Others arrived on one of the great black-hulled steamships of the Pacific Mail Line, the *Manchuria* or the *Korea* or the *Siberia* or the *Mongolia,* coming from Honolulu after long tours of the Orient.

They brought with them piles of trunks, valets and governesses for their children, settling in for two- and three-month vacations. For their benefit, the Fairmont provided "a completely-equipped school, featuring out-of-door work and play, music, dancing, and French in all grades." These long-term guests seldom felt the need to leave the hotel. There were quiet teas in the Laurel Court, bridge games in the salons, reading in the parlors and afternoon concerts in the lobby. For the more adventurous, there was polo in Burlingame or trips to look at the buffalo or the grizzly bears in Golden Gate Park, or for the both wealthy and adventurous there was the grandest Edwardian sport of all, motoring.

The Edwardian automobile, a lush garden of leather, glass, chrome and brightly colored fenders and cowls, was virtually a land yacht. Each machine was lovingly and expensively put together; their names alone summon memories of vanished craftmanship: Winton, Stearns, Stoddard-Dayton and Stevens-Duryea, Thomas Flyer and Pierce Landau and Logan Blue Streak. They were nasty-tempered, smelly, noisy inefficient machines, prone to explode, turn over or belch clouds of steam and oily smoke, but their owners loved them and showed them off as if they were precocious children. Their owners proudly assembled them in great herds and drove them to the beach, to Yosemite or to the Del Monte Hotel in Monterey, where they would park under the trees in long lines, tiny American flags fluttering on their hood ornaments, while their owners ate dinner inside.

Resort hotels like the Del Monte were the center of San Francisco social life during the long and lazy Edwardian summers. In late May, when eastern visitors began to take over the Fairmont and the Palace, San Franciscans would move out to the Del Monte, the Rafael in San Rafael, the Hotel Bon Air in Ross or the Monte Rio on the Russian River near Sonoma, advertised as "The Switzerland of California."

They were modeled after the great resort hotels of Saratoga, great, white, rambling buildings with wide, covered porches and cupolaed towers and gingerbread trim, surrounded by acres of gardens, strolling paths, croquet courts and flower beds. The Del Monte offered tennis, shuffleboard, a racetrack, polo, band concerts, carriage rides along the beach and swimming in the ocean or in one of the four swimming pools, each filled from the ocean daily and heated to a different temperature.

When "taking the waters" caught on as a treatment for nearly any ailment, Northern California's hot springs became nearly as popular as the resort hotels. Most, like the Geysers near Napa, offered a natural mineral stream and hot mineral plunge baths, enclosed in wooden pavilions with cottages and a hotel nearby. Vichy Springs, in Mendocino, advertised that its waters had been "Pronounced by experts a natural skin beautifier." Gilroy Hot Springs informed readers: "The waters contain sulfur, alum, iron, soda, magnesia, iodine and traces of arsenic, and are very efficacious in cases of rheumatism, neuralgia, rheumatic gout and kidney and liver diseases."

Back in San Francisco, the Fairmont was entertaining its guests with afternoon concerts in the lobby and the Laurel Court. One afternoon the Fairmont Orchestra was joined by Margaret McKee, who whistled "The Sunflower Dance," "Invitation" and assorted "Bird Raptures."

Oriental customs, or what Americans imagined to be Oriental customs, were particularly fashionable. In February, 1908, the lobby and dining rooms of the Fairmont were hung with paper lanterns to celebrate a "Blossom Festival." The program featured ice cream, lemonade, Japanese girls in kimonos reading palms and elaborate tableaus:

"Miss Cherry Blossom"
Song: Chinese Lady picking mulberries—by Miss Lillian Niggle
Tableaux of Same
Tableau: "Three Little Maids from School"

Two years later, in December, 1910, the Fairmont played host to the officers of a squadron of the Japanese fleet, lately victorious in the Russo-Japanese War. Two hundred and fifty white-uniformed Japanese naval officers from the cruisers *Asama* and *Kasagi* and their escort ships paraded into the Fairmont Ballroom, decorated for the occasion with a huge American flag hanging from the balcony. They solemnly joined their American hosts in shouting three *banzais* for President Taft. One of the junior officers that evening paying tribute to President Taft was twenty-six-year-old Isoroku Yamamoto, who, thirty-one years later, as the commander of the imperial Japanese combined fleet, would give the order for the attack on Pearl Harbor.

At night, San Francisco came alive with lights and music. New restaurants, brighter and more luxurious than before, occupied the new "Uptown Tenderloin" surrounding Powell and Market. Across the street from the Orpheum, the leading vaudeville theater in the city, was Tait-Zinkand's, where the vaudeville performers, including the young Charlie Chaplin and the Marx Brothers, re-created their acts for each other in the middle of the ocean of tables. All around them swarmed crowds of diners, spectators and waiters, an orchestra played in the gallery, and electric lights played on shimmering cascades and fountains of water. Nearby were the huge and equally crowded Portola-Louvre, the Odeon, Techau's Tavern and the Indoor Yacht Club.

"The Great White Way" began one block away on Mason Street, a gay parade of automobiles, crowds, bars and electric lights. Pacific Avenue featured the great dance halls, the Moulin Rouge with its facade of sculptured plaster nudes, Lew Purcell's So Different Saloon, a black dance hall where the turkey trot was said to have originated, and above all, the Olympia, with its round dance floor surrounded by galleries and booths from which wealthy "slummers" could watch the madness below.

It was to the Olympia that the photographer Arnold Genthe brought the little dark-haired ballerina Anna Pavlova after a performance of the Ballet Russe. The two of them began dancing in the middle of the dense and noisy crowd that jammed the floor. When they finished, they realized they were alone on the floor. The rest of the dancers had formed a circle around them to watch the graceful Pavlova, and when she stopped, they burst into cheers.

The culmination of that grand and stately age came in 1915, when the city celebrated the opening of the Panama Canal by holding the Panama-Pacific Exposition. All that remains today is the crumbling pavilion and lagoon of Bernard Maybeck's Palace of Fine Arts, but in 1915 a mile-long pastel fantasy of sea-green domes, palaces and fountains glittered by the Bay, overlooked by the seven-story Tower of Jewels. At night a powerful battery of searchlights called the Scintillator threw a halo of colored light on the clouds over the exposition.

The exposition opened on February 20, 1915. As the 500-voice chorus finished the last note of "The Star-Spangled Banner," the president of the fair picked up a long-distance telephone and asked President Wilson, in the White House, to push a key on his desk. Wilson did, and the key sent a wireless message to San Francisco. Suddenly water began cascading around the horseback figure of Hercules astride the Panama Canal in the Fountain of Energy, the doors of the Palace of Transportation swung open, and the great wheels in the Palace of Machinery began to turn. As the crowd cheered, a fragile biplane circled the Tower of Jewels, scattering doves behind it.

And those were only the first of the miracles. While the architecture and decoration tended toward the romantic, such as California's stucco Mission and Turkey's replica of the Sultan Ahmed Mosque, the inside of the buildings were gleamingly and noisily twentieth century. The crowds admired the French landscape paintings and the heroic statuary; but they were awed by the functioning model of the Panama Canal, whose workings were explained by a recorded voice crackling over an Edison talking machine, and they gazed in wonder at the Ford assembly line in the Palace of Transportation that turned out an endless procession of shiny new automobiles, each one just alike.

In October, 1915, Thomas Edison and Henry Ford, arm in arm, stepped off the ferry in San Francisco to see the exposition.

"I see you are traveling like a prima donna," Ford told Edison.

"It's my first vacation, I've a right to," Edison said pleasantly. "I hope they will let me see some of the exposition."

Surrounded by reporters, the two men checked into the Inside Inn, a special guest lodge built on the exposition grounds. Edison sat down in an armchair in his room, lit a cigar and listened to the questions of the reporters who gathered around him.

What was his favorite invention? someone asked. "Oh, I like the phonograph best."

Was he really a wizard? "Wizard?" He laughed. "No, no! That's a fake! Why, I have five thousand men working for me, and five hundred are experimenters. We work and watch all the time. I get along with four hours' sleep in twenty-four. You could do it yourself by six months' training. I don't eat much, that's why I'm never tired."

Would we be able to hurl thunderbolts at the enemy in the next war? "No," Edison said. "Not as we know electricity now."

What was he working on? "I am going to reproduce all the symphonies of Beethoven by phonograph," he announced, "so that one can hear them as perfectly as if listening to a big philharmonic orchestra. I am constructing a concrete bowl forty-two feet in diameter, arranged with wires, which will catch all the sound waves. I will place all the musicians underneath and not a single sound wave will escape reproduction."

In the next room Henry Ford was also surrounded by reporters. "The militarists who caused this war and will profit by it are the bankers of Wall Street, London, Berlin, Paris and St. Petersburg and, of course, the ammunition makers," he was telling them. "I can stop the war in Europe in two weeks if I can speak to the people through the press of the afflicted country. I have started a bureau in Detroit to distribute educational material throughout the world on the subject of peace and war. I don't suppose that the countries now at war will permit our articles to be published, but I'll guarantee that if the soldiers read the articles they will stop fighting inside of two weeks; the soldiers would drive the militarists out of their country or set them to work."

"But supposing the United States were unjustly attacked?" a reporter insisted.

"If we are decent and just to other people we will never be attacked. If Standard Oil suffers a setback in some corner of the world, is it necessary for us to go to war over it?"

The next day, arm in arm, Edison and Ford strolled through the exposition. Together they admired Edison's talking machine at the model of the Panama Canal, and then they watched Ford's assembly line making automobiles. Ford threw off his jacket, pulled on coveralls and enthusiastically jumped into the assembly line, bolting fenders on the cars as they slowly moved by. At the General Electric pavilion, they ate a banquet cooked on the stage in electric skillets and finished their meal on miniature Ford automobiles made of nougat. They traveled by car to the Stanford Court apartments in Nob Hill, where they climbed to the roof to view the city.

On a suggestion made in the San Francisco *Examiner* every office building in the city had turned on all its electric lights, which normally were extinguished at dusk. Every building in sight was lit with strings of electric bulbs; across the Bay, Oakland and Berkeley, for the first time, glittered with lights; out on the Bay, the warships of the U.S. fleet turned on the searchlights and shone them into the sky; the Southern Pacific Building and Bank of Italy were covered with lights; the electric wires of the trolleys crackled with blue sparks; and while 10,000 people cheered in the street below the apartment building, a huge electric sign was lit, proclaiming, "Long Live Edison; the Greatest Man on Earth." Edison smiled and shook his head.

Everyone seemed to have come to San Francisco to see the exposition: Camille Saint-Saens came from France to conduct his compositions in the Festival Hall; Flo Ziegfeld sent one hundred of his beauties; Paderewski came to play Chopin; Helen Keller danced after supper at the St. Francis, touching her partner's lips; and evangelist Billy Sunday came to preach the Gospel.

The little ex-baseball player charged into the lobby of the St. Francis, followed by his wife and two sons, scrawled his name in the register and immediately began to map out to the reporters following him his plans to save San Francisco.

"Satan is entrenched much more strongly than he should be in this wonderful city of God," he began. The reporters nodded. He certainly was. "I shall load my guns with dynamite, rough-on-rats and barbed wire and the trenches of Satan will be stormed as I never stormed them before!"

Sunday jumped down on his knees and shook his fist. "I am going to stoop down like this and and defy Satan to get out of his hole. I am going to come and ask him to fight the Christian men and women of San Francisco in the open!"

He jumped back on his feet. "He has been fighting them with evil dances and with whiskey. Now whiskey is all right in its place . . . but its place is in hell!"

The next day Sunday took his crusade to the Court of Abundance at the exposition, where 15,000 people had gathered to hear him. He jumped on a table and began to preach, launching a vivid denunciation of "your old bastard theory of evolution."

"My own views are that between the latest scholarship and the word of God, the latest scholarship can go to hell!" he shouted, using his hands for a megaphone. "I don't read modern authors because I haven't the time. I haven't the time to swim through fifty feet of sewage to get a scintilla of truth." He leaned back, spread his arms and roared, "O-o-o-o-o, you infidels! Don't tell me there's no God! If you're a doubter, it's evidence of a pygmy intellect or a black heart!"

When they had finished listening to Sunday, the crowd rushed next door to the Zone, an amusement extravaganza for those bored by exhibits of machinery or the glories of the Panama Canal. It featured such attractions as Underground Chinatown, the Maori Village, and the '49 Camp, an "authentic gold rush mining town" that was so authentic that the exposition officials and vice squad ordered it closed down and cleaned up. Burlesque was offered as Art with a capital A:

> The Living Venus in the Zone—
> not a picture, but a
> Singing, Dancing & Dramatic Performance
> of Great Beauty!
> Pretty Girls in Barefoot Dances
> Sensational Climax showing the most beautifully
> formed woman in the world!

As one strolled among the crowds in the Court of Abundance, watching the footraces between cash-register girls from the city's department stores or cheering on San Francisco's firemen in a tug-of-war with the sailors of the battleship *Oregon*, it was easy to forget that in Europe great armies were facing one another across the blasted farmland of Flanders and Poland.

Ignace Paderewski in his hotel room at the Palace saw only blank faces on the reporters as he tried to explain to them the sufferings of his native Poland. As he listed churches destroyed and villages burned, he realized they had been hearing the same stories for years about Belgium, France and Italy.

At last the tall, fiercely mustached pianist declared, "No words can describe the suffering of Poland." He sat down at the piano in the room and began to play Chopin's A-flat Polonaise. Few of the reporters recognized it because he played the gay and dancing polonaise as a slow funeral march.

Neither the British nor the Germans had pavilions, but

people gathered regularly outside the French Pavilion to sing the "Marseillaise" and urge American entry into the war. Inside, as a subtle hint, the French were displaying Lafayette's sword and the flags French soldiers had carried at Yorktown in aid of General Washington.

The Savoy Theater was showing five reels of official German war films, which, the advertisements said, "portray, in minute detail, in some four hundred scenes, the actual movements and activities of the German Army . . . it is pointed out by the sponsors of the pictures that they show conclusively that the Emperor's troops are well-fed and invariably cheerful." At a climactic scene in the film showing the charge of the Uhlan cavalry, the German-Americans in the audience leaped to their feet and cheered.

One afternoon the sound of brass bands and tramping boots filled the Court of Abundance; the exposition was honoring German-American Day. Thousands of German-Americans had marched from German House at Turk and Polk Street down to the exposition, after hearing Mayor James Rolph Jr.'s secretary read a message from the mayor: "The German cities are the best governed . . . . Germans have written the sweetest songs . . . the life of no American is complete without the German influence . . . we cannot have too much in San Francisco of the spirit of Germany."

Now the brass bands oompahed, joined by an incongruous bagpipe band representing the Irish Republican Army, and the crowd sang "Deutschland über Alles" as old veterans of the Franco-Prussian War of 1870, wearing their old uniforms, goosestepped proudly through the Court of Abundance.

The newspapers were becoming filled with the debate over whether the United States should join the war. Each day, the papers reported, American merchant ships were torpedoed by German submarines. Finally President Wilson sent a stern ultimatum to the kaiser, and San Franciscans read that Secretary of State William Jennings Bryan, the leading spokesman for staying out of the war, had handed Wilson his resignation.

Two weeks later Bryan stepped off a train on the Oakland mole and was handed a bundle of mail by the assistant manager of the St. Francis. Nodding and smiling at the crowd that had come to meet him, he walked to the ferry that would take him across the Bay to San Francisco.

"The Great Commoner" was now fifty-five years old. When he was thirty-six, as the "Boy Orator of the Platte," he had stampeded the Democratic National Convention with his "Cross of Gold" speech, only to lose the election to McKinley. Twice more his oratory won him the nomination, and twice more he was defeated. His political misfortunes never dimmed his popularity in rural America, however, and he returned their affection by fighting their battles for them with his deep, organlike voice, speaking pacifism, prohibition and the old-time religion. He came to San Francisco to rest and to speak at the exposition, which declared the next day "William Jennings Bryan Day." His mail in hand, he registered at the St. Francis and walked solemnly to the elevator through the awed crowd.

Bryan mounted the steps to the platform in the Court of the Universe the next day under gray and threatening skies. Ironically, his speech followed a long military parade. As Bryan stood, enormous in his long black coat, he was watched by lines of soldiers, leaning on their rifles.

"This nation," he declared, "more than any other nation, is at liberty to put God's Truth to the test. . . . With an ocean rippling on either side, with a mountain range along either coast, we are singularly free from the possibility of invasion. . . ."

He raised his hands. "Thou shalt not kill could not be violated by a nation with impunity any more than by individuals. Enough people cannot be brought together to violate the laws of the Creator. Across the seas our brother's hands are stained in brother's blood—the world has run mad! They need a flag that speaks the sentiment of the human heart, a flag that looks toward better things than war. . . ."

When he finished his hour-long speech, Bryan bowed to the applause, walked off the platform and was driven back to the St. Francis.

On July 20, while Bryan was avoiding the summer heat by relaxing in his hotel room, there was an enormous commotion outside the Ferry Building. A crowd of 10,000 let go a cheer, a troop of cavalry began to clatter down Market Street, and an open car pulled away from the building following the cavalry, carrying, beneath an enormous white sombrero, the unmistakable face of Teddy Roosevelt.

Roosevelt waved the sombrero and grinned at the crowds along Market Street. With a whoop, a veteran Rough Rider leaped from the crowd, jumped onto the running board of the motorcar, pumped Colonel Roosevelt's hand and leaped off back into the crowd. Roosevelt grinned even more.

The cavalrymen halted in front of the St. Francis, and Roosevelt sprang from the car and into the lobby. Crowds surged around Roosevelt as he went to the desk to register. Socialites in evening dress stood on the chairs and sofas to get a glimpse of him.

"How are you feeling, Colonel?" someone yelled from the crowd.

"Bully!" Roosevelt roared. "Just bully!"

"What are you going to speak about at the Exposition tomorrow, Colonel?" a reporter asked.

"I am heartily sick and tired of this bleating, puling, inane cry about having peace at any price," Roosevelt said. "I shall talk about 'War and Peace' at the Exposition tomorrow, but I might just as well have entitled my address 'Damn the Mollycoddles.'"

With that and a grin, he made his way to his hotel room. He was no longer president now, having been beaten in a bitter three-way battle with Wilson and Taft three years before, but he was still by far the most famous Republican and the most energetic politician in America. As the most enthusiastic spokesman in the country for preparedness, he would offer to lead a division when the war finally broke out, a request denied by President Wilson. Instead, Roosevelt sent his four sons to war, and his favorite son, Quentin, was killed. It broke Roosevelt's heart, and he didn't live until the next Republican convention.

July 21 was Theodore Roosevelt Day at the exposition. People began arriving in the Court of the Universe at ten o'clock, carrying sack lunches. By noon the court was impassable with 60,000 people, half of them so far away that they would be unable to hear a word; they simply wanted to see Roosevelt.

Back at the St. Francis Hotel, another crowd had gathered in the lobby. Seated there, asking to see Colonel Roosevelt, were a dozen men and women who said they had peace plans, one man with a model of a perpetual-motion machine, a man with the design of a bicycle that would run backward and forward and a man with an invention that he claimed would convert soapsuds into butter.

Colonel Roosevelt's secretary met each one of them. "I'm sure the colonel will be very interested in this," he told each one. "Just a moment." He walked up the stairs toward Roosevelt's room, waited a few moments and came back down. "The Colonel is delighted you came," he said. "And he wants to meet with you on Sunday." Roosevelt, of course, was leaving on Saturday.

Now, in the Court of the Universe, Roosevelt was mounting the platform, waving his hand to the tremendous cheers of the crowd. The president of the exposition stood up to introduce him. "Who built the Panama Canal?" he asked the crowd.

"Teddy!" the crowd roared back. Roosevelt grinned.

He got up to speak, and the thousands far back in the crowd cupped their hands behind their ears, hoping to hear.

"I have a very strong feeling about the Panama Exposition," Roosevelt's high, strong voice said. "It was my very good fortune to take the action in 1903, failure to take which in exactly the shape I took it, would have meant that no Panama Canal would have been built for half a century!" The crowd roared its approval; they knew what he meant: Teddy had sent gunboats to Panama to help that country break loose from Venezuela and had got the Canal Zone in return.

"I advocate preparedness against war as the best type of peace insurance. We have been culpably, well-nigh criminally remiss as a nation in preparing ourself. If we continue with soft complacency to stand naked and helpless before the world we shall excite only contempt and derision if and when disaster ultimately overwhelms us. . . .

"No nation ever amounted to anything if its population was composed of pacifists and poltroons." Roosevelt slammed his fist into his palm. "Men who are not ready to fight for the right are not fit to live in a free democracy!"

Roosevelt quieted. "To conclude, I would like to quote from the 33rd chapter of Ezekiel: 'If the watchman see the sword come, and blow not the trumpet, and the people be not warned, and if the sword come, and take any person from among them . . . his blood will I require at the watchman's hand."

There was a dead silence over the crowd, and then a roar began, continued as Roosevelt walked off the stage, continued as he walked down to the waiting car and continued while he drove away.

Bryan read the speech in the newspaper in his room the next day. "The trouble is," he told a visitor, "you can't find a soft voice with a big stick. If a man has a soft voice he doesn't want a big stick. If he gets a big stick he loses his soft voice."

Downstairs, Roosevelt's secretary gave the St. Francis house detective a stack of brass plaques with the colonel's name on them and pointed to the man with the perpetual-motion machine and his friends waiting patiently in the lobby. "Tomorrow, give these to each of them," he instructed, "and tell them Colonel Roosevelt regrets he was called away on urgent business."

There was another commotion as Roosevelt appeared, hurrying through the lobby toward his car, pursued by his exhausted party.

"By George, this is a wonderful city," he called to the reporters trying to follow him, "and the air is wonderfully invigorating. By George, it's simply great!" With that, he charged out of the hotel.

10

War—April, 1917

"THE declaration of war issued this week will touch
this nation lightly," the *News-Letter* predicted. San Francisco
went to war as people went to a Fourth of July picnic, with
speeches and the waving of flags and the anticipation that it
would be over by the next morning.

In February San Francisco society had come out, as it did
every year, to the Mardi Gras Ball. In 1917 it was held in an
enormous barnlike annex raised next to the St. Francis Hotel, decorated for the theme, "The Court of the Czar." Ed-
munds Lyman had been the czar, and Mrs. Talbot Walker
the czarina. While balalaikas played, the guests had paraded
in dressed as counts, gypsies and cossacks, as Chinese court
ladies, and as peasants, their embroidered blouses strung
with pearls. The "czarina" arrived in a sleigh borrowed from
the museum in Golden Gate Park, and then prizes were giv-
en to the wearers of the best costumes. Miss Gertrude Hopkins, dressed as Madame DuBarry, won first prize. "I'm so
thrilled I can hardly move," she murmured, and the Crock-
ers, Floods, De Youngs, Camerons, Theriots and Tobins applauded graciously.

Of course, San Francisco had been aware before April,
1917, that a war was going on; the French chefs and
chauffeurs at the hotels had been called back to their country, merchant ships leaving the Bay were searched for con-
traband that might compromise America's neutrality, and
arms buyers from England and France, in their checkered
caps and kepis, has been a familiar sight in the hotel lobbies
since 1914. Mrs. Crocker and some other society women had
dressed as peasants, opened a booth in Union Square and

auctioned off some of their spare jewelry for Belgian War Relief. And San Francisco was visited by both a hero and a spy.

The hero was a pilot named Bert Hall. He had been a chauffeur on the East Coast. When the war broke out, he had packed his bags and sailed to France to enlist in the Lafayette Escadrille, was taught to fly and in short order shot down six German planes. His proud French sponsors granted him a two-week leave to visit the United States for a series of Red Cross benefits.

Hall showed up at the St. Francis, kepi tipped rakishly on his head, six medals pinned on his breast, and was the immediate star of San Francisco society. He was invited to every parlor in Burlingame and to a banquet at the Fairmont, where he modestly recounted, using his hands to trace out the dogfights, how he had nearly destroyed the German Air Force. Seemingly every woman in town adored him.

He took such a liking, in fact, to being a touring war hero, that he never made it back to the war. He continued his tour to Los Angeles, and late in 1917, the French Air Force was still trying to find out where he was.

The spy was Franz von Papen, who one day would be the chancellor of Germany, Hitler's sponsor, and the Nazi foreign minister. In 1915 he checked into the Fairmont Hotel under the name of Pope.

His nemesis was the valet at the Fairmont, a young man named Henry Kalfain, who had come to work at the Fairmont from Turkey the year before.

Henry was an enterprising young man. When he had come to apply for the job, he had found the room full of applicants who had come before him. The telephone had rung, and the interviewer was out of the room; Henry had rushed up and answered the phone. It was Phoebe Apperson Hearst, the mother of William Randolph Hearst. Could someone come upstairs and get some clothes to be pressed? Henry rushed upstairs and claimed the clothes, took them out, had them pressed, returned them and proudly took his seat again in the waiting room. Mrs. Hearst telephoned downstairs to thank him, and the amazed interviewer quickly hired him.

Now Mr. Pope sent down to have his trousers pressed.

Henry claimed them, took them to the valet's room, laid them out and started to press them, but he was obstructed by a bulge in the pocket. Taking a paper out of the pocket, he saw the name "FranzVon Papen, Imperial German Embassy, Washington." Henry, who read the newspaper, took the papers to the manager, who called federal agents.

The lean, mustached Van Papen was surrounded by reporters when he emerged from his room. "I have nothing to say," he said in German.

"How long do you intend to stay with us?" a reporter asked.

"Until I leave," Von Papen said. Since he had broken no laws, the agents let him check out of the hotel. Shortly before April, they arrested him again, this time on charges of trying to organize spy rings around the United States, and sent him back to Germany.

And ever since Teddy Roosevelt had spoken for preparedness at the exposition, San Francisco had been eagerly going to training camp. Fifty members of the Burlingame Polo Club banded together and declared that henceforth they would be known as the San Francisco Cavalry Troop. On weekends they mounted their polo ponies on the parade ground of the Presidio, performed a dizzying series of wheels and counterwheels and a few spirited charges and then dismounted, sat back in lawn chairs and were served gin fizzes by their valets. In Berkeley the University of California students enthusiastically formed a company, but their numbers were seriously depleted when the cook at one of their field exercises inadvertently piled the campfire with poison oak.

The Regular Army was not to be outdone. Borrowing seven cars from the local Studebaker agency, they loaded them with 101 men and several machine guns and drove the thirty-seven miles from the Presidio to Half-Moon Bay in less than an hour, demonstrating that they knew the meaning of "lightning war" and could repel any invader who gave them sufficient notice.

The whole city demonstrated its readiness in a Preparedness Day Parade in 1916, featuring among its units a whole platoon of bellhops from the hotels, led by the chief of bell service at the St. Francis. The parade was marred by an explosion at the corner of Steuart and Mission which killed one person and injured a dozen others; a labor organizer named Tom Mooney was quickly accused and convicted of the crime on what would later prove to have been entirely fabricated evidence.

By March, 1917, events seemed to have got out of human control. The kaiser declared his submarines would torpedo any American ships in the war zone and the czar of Russia, Nicholas II, was overthrown.

The next morning the double eagle and the word "Imperial" on the door of the Russian consulate were covered by a piece of cardboard. The consul general to San Francisco, one Artemy M. de Wywedzeff, told reporters, "Well, we naturally expect to have some changes in view of what has taken place at home, and the paper was fitted over the door merely as an experiment. I am awaiting instructions from the Russian Embassy in Washington, and in the meantime I am continuing to act as Consul General as if nothing has happened."

Count Ilya Tolstoy, the fifty-five-year-old son of Leo Tolstoy, arrived in San Francisco a few days later aboard the *Siberia Maru* to lecture on "Universal Peace" at the Orpheum Theater. He was told the news. "It is impossible to be an optimist with regard to the Russian Revolution," he said sadly. "I am very happy I was on the ocean when it took place."

San Francisco moved closer and closer to war. Army recruiters set up tents and a Gatling gun in front of the Hippodrome Theater; soldiers staged a mock battle, complete with barbed wire and an armadillolike tank, in the sand dunes at Sloat Boulevard and Thirty-seventh Avenue, filmed by Hearst-Pathé newsreel cameramen; the Emporium began selling American flags; and, the most ominous sign of all, the *Examiner* unfurled American flags on its masthead.

It came at last on April 16: CONGRESS VOTES WAR , the huge headline on the *Examiner* declared. It reported that both Theodore Roosevelt and William Jennings Bryan had volunteered to fight, Roosevelt offering to lead a division, Bryan offering to enlist as a private. Motor launches full of American sailors pulled alongside the German merchant ships anchored in the Bay, boarded them and raised the American flag. The mayor of Oakland announced that any home or business not flying an American flag would have its occupants arrested, and the German consul in San Francisco, Franz Bopp, was arrested by federal agents and taken by boat to Alcatraz.

For the first few months following the declaration of war most of the war effort in San Francisco consisted of loud singing of "The Star-Spangled Banner" and the enthusiastic sale of Liberty bonds. Business in the hotels was frantic as military delegations from the Allied countries moved in and businessmen arrived to compete for the new war contracts.

On September 4 San Francisco sent its first men off to war. The 196 men were given a party at the St. Francis, ancient veterans of the Civil War in their Grand Army of the Republic uniforms clapped them on the back, and the mayor presented each of them with a button with the seal of the city. Then, between an honor guard of firemen, high school cadets and boy scouts, they marched to the train depot and took their seats on a train heading east.

At the end of October Artemy de Wywedzeff returned from a trip to Russia, greatly relieved that things had been straightened out and that he could keep his job. He proclaimed himself an enthusiastic supporter of the new provisional government and said that its leader, Alexander Kerensky, "may prove a Russian Lincoln."

A few days later Kerensky was overthrown by Lenin, who, a few weeks earlier, had led a march down the Nevsky Prospect in Petrograd to the American consulate, demanding that Tom Mooney be freed from jail in San Francisco for his alleged role in the Preparedness Day bombing.

Artemy de Wywedzeff was beside himself. "I will resign!" he shouted. "I cannot possibly reconcile myself with the criminal and insane policies of the so-called Bolsheviki." A few days later he changed his mind, withdrew his resignation, and insisted he would remain as consul general until someone with a letter from the provisional government showed up to replace him.

"The present government will last only a few weeks," the visiting Russian commissioner, A. J. Sack, confided.

"My poor country!" lamented Admiral Alexander Kolchak, the commander of the Russian Black Sea fleet, who was also in San Francisco. "Russia seems to have reached the limit of her troubles. Things cannot possibly become worse than they are at the present."

But of course they did. Admiral Kolchak departed from San Francisco to Siberia to lead the armies against Lenin that plunged Russia into civil war.

The first American soldiers arrived in France that November, and the first San Franciscan died on March 14, 1918. He was Private Giuseppe Vanucchi, an Italian citizen who lived with his godparents on Vallejo Street.

The war in France, which San Franciscans had expected to be over in weeks, bogged down. The battlefield, the San Francisco Cavalry Troop found, bore little resemblance to a polo field, and the Germans refused to stand up to be shot. Day after day the *Examiner, Chronicle* and *Call* carried the names of obscure French crossroads and lengthening casualty lists. The city began to feel the effects of shortages; cheese disappeared from the free lunch counters at the hotel bars. "Meatless Tuesday" was joined by "Wheatless Wednesday" and "Ice Creamless Thursday," and the hotels were persuaded to cancel their wheat orders altogether. Promoting the food economy drive, the St. Francis unfurled two huge banners, "Food Will Win the War" and "Every Kernel a Bullet for the Hun." At the Fairmont a man was turned over to federal agents for eating three breakfasts, one after another, despite the food economy appeals on the menu.

In July local draft boards called up all the remaining elevator men and bellhops at the hotels, leaving them run by women and elderly men. San Francisco had become a city at war. The city was soon filled with army trainees from all over the country, gaping at their first sight of a big city. One of them, an officer trainee from a tiny outpost in New Mexico, was particularly awed by the towering buildings and crowded streets around him. His name was Conrad Hilton.

As San Franciscans had once been urged to hate the Chinese, they were now urged to hate the Germans. The *Examiner* ceased using the world "Teutons" in its headlines and replaced it with "Huns." Large signs were posted in all government buildings and in the hotels, proclaiming, under the word " SPIES":

Report at once any suspicious persons and acts.
Don't trust anyone you don't know.
Don't criticize military conduct.
Be continually on the lookout to detect German
   propaganda.
Always look with suspicion on strangers.

In the Palm Court of the Palace, a Monterey judge told the State Council for Defense, "I don't favor violence, but unless Congress comes to our aid with legislation providing for stripping American citizenship from those showing disloyalty, we shall have to return to the practices of the vigilantes and compel respect for the flag."

Evangelist Billy Sunday, staying once more at the St. Francis, was less restrained: "If you turned hell over, you would find 'Made in Germany' stamped on the bottom. It is the Kaiser against the President, Bill against Woodrow, Hohenzollern against Uncle Sam, Germany against America, hell against heaven. Pacifism or indifference at this time is treason."

Many people took them literally. In Berkeley a group of University of California students marched to the canvas tabernacle of the Church of the Living God, accused the Reverend Joshua Sykes of preaching pacifism and commanded him to sing "The Star-Spangled Banner." The organist rose and began to sing the song for him, but the students shoved her down, seized Sykes and his two sons and threw them into the baptismal font. Then they wrecked the furniture and set fire to the tabernacle.

As they marched away from the blazing tent, they were met by the police chief of Berkeley. "Boys, what you did tonight was done in a thorough fashion and you sure went 'over the top,' " he said. "It was bad from a police standpoint, but we are with you."

At the Hofbrau Restaurant in San Francisco, where local residents had long drunk beer and sung along as the band played "Where has My Little Dog Gone?" a group of sailors crashed through the door, stood in front of the band, and ordered them to play "The Star-Spangled Banner." The members of the band either didn't understand or refused, and the sailors pushed them off the stage, trampled their instruments and wrecked the restaurant.

By November, 1918, the lines showing Allied advances on the huge map on the *Examiner* building on Market Street were steadily moving toward Germany. The street below looked like a huge hospital ward, for an influenza epidemic was raging, having already caused more than 1,000 deaths, and everyone on the sidewalk was wearing a gauze surgical mask. The news in the headlines was getting, day by day, better and better. Finally, on November 11, bombs, sirens and bonfires signaled the end of the war. Market Street was flooded with men waving derby hats and men in coveralls, standing on the roofs of the streetcars and fire engines and singing what they knew of the "Marseillaise" and "The Star-Spangled Banner." Mayor Rolph stood in the middle of them and shouted, "This is the world's greatest day in the age-long fight between good and evil!"

But the soldiers knew better. When San Francisco's sons returned from Europe a few weeks later and began marching down Market Street for their triumphal welcome in the Civic Center, they began seeing their old bars and taverns along the way. One by one, and then by entire units, they dropped out of the parade to visit their old haunts. By the time the parade reached city hall there was hardly anyone left in it. It had been that kind of war.

11

Wilson

IN 1919 Woodrow Wilson came to San Francisco in a losing fight to save his dream. His dream was a League of Nations, and he was to fight for it until it divided the nation, broke his party and broke him.

A few months earlier the austere, bespectacled Wilson had landed in Europe and had been hailed as a savior. The streets and rooftops of Paris had been filled with people shouting his name, and children strewed flowers in his path. He had ridden down the Champs-Élysées under banners proclaiming HONOR TO WILSON THE JUST. "I do not think there has been anything like it in the history of the world," Premier Georges Clemenceau said.

In Rome he was met by banners reading HAIL THE CRUSAD-ER FOR HUMANITY, and people kissed his hands. In London the king and queen came to the train station to greet him. In that euphoria before the Paris Peace Conference all things seemed possible for the college professor with his smile and his extended hat.

Then it soured. When he sat down at the table, Wilson wanted principles; the other allies wanted German land and money. Most of Wilson's principles were lost in a wilderness of intrigue. But, after a long and wearying conference, Wilson came home with one precious prize: a peace treaty containing a plan for a League of Nations.

But when Wilson presented the treaty to the Senate, he made another mistake; he presented it the way a professor would an assignment to his class, telling them he wanted it ratified, and quickly. The Senate, wary of being dragged into any more European wars, reacted with bitter hostility. Senator Hiram Johnson of California told a crowd Wilson was "seeking to hand over American destiny to the Secret Councils of Europe." Europeans, he said, were filled with "duplicity unequalled in the history of the world, and when the President seeks to keep up the duplicity by binding our sons to guarantee it, I say it shall not be!"

Next, the patrician Massachusetts Republican Henry Cabot Lodge began to attack the treaty. Wilson quickly called him "contemptible, narrow, and selfish." Lodge told friends he "had never expected to hate anyone as he hated Wilson."

While Wilson had been at Versailles, things had got worse at home. Thousands lost their jobs as war industries shut down, and other thousands were battling police on picket lines. Even Boston policemen went on strike, and Governor Coolidge called in the Army.

RULE BY SOVIET SEEN IN BOSTON POLICE STRIKE, the San Francisco *Chronicle* warned. "Logical Sequence will be Unionizing of Army and Navy—Says Senator. PRESIDENT IS BLAMED—His Tolerance of Radicals Held to Promote Nationalizing Industries." The senator was Warren G. Harding of Ohio.

Faced by an immovable Senate, Wilson chose to take his case for the treaty directly to the people. "I don't care if I die the next minute after the treaty is ratified," he told a reporter.

On September 3, 1919, he boarded the Mayflower, his blue private railway car, and his seven-car special train pulled out of Washington station for the West.

Each day the train made a dozen stops, and Wilson spoke to crowds at fairgrounds or auditoriums or from the rear platform of the Mayflower, pleading for the League. As the train rushed through the night, he wrote the speeches for the next day.

In Columbus, Indianapolis, St. Louis and Kansas City the crowds were curious and quiet. They grew larger and more enthusiastic as the train came to Des Moines, Sioux Falls, Omaha, Bismarck and Billings, Spokane, Seattle and Portland. Veterans saluted their old chief, women held their children up to see him, and the crowds applauded his speeches. Watching the crowds, Wilson sensed he could win.

San Francisco would be a crucial test. On September 17,

when Wilson arrived, the *Chronicle* , which carried the brand "This Newspaper Is One Hundred Percent American" every day on the front page, warned him "he will find while in this city he is in hostile territory."

There was much truth in that. The huge Irish-American community was angry at Wilson for not pressuring England for Irish independence, and the Italians in North Beach were equally angry because he had let Yugoslavia take a chunk of their homeland at the Peace Conference. Further-more, the city was the home of the leading fighter against the League, Senator Hiram Johnson.

Yet when Wilson, gaunt and pale from exhaustion, stand-ing in the back of an open car holding out his silk top hat in one hand, rode down Market Street, the reception was thun-derous. Thousands of San Franciscans jammed forward on the sidewalks to cheer him. At the Civic Center he was greet-ed by city officials, 60,000 schoolchildren waving red, white and blue striped caps and more thousands waving handker-chiefs. Even the *Chronicle* conceded it was a "welcome un-precedented in recent years."

Wilson was driven to the St. Francis, where he entered by the Post Street entrance to avoid the crowds in the lobby, and then went up to his suite for a short rest.

Then Wilson was driven to the Palace, where he was to make his first major speech in the city. One thousand people were waiting to see him come through the lobby, waving and smiling, and inside the Palm Court 1,600 women rose from their tables, waved tiny flags and cheered as he came through the glass doors. Hundreds of men pressed up against the glass of the adjacent men's grill to watch. Wilson waved his hat and took his seat.

By the time Wilson had finished his fried sea bass and roast chicken and was introduced by his wife, "The place was warm enough to suit the most tropical tastes," one reporter wrote. Wilson cleared his throat, rose, waited for the ap-plause to stop, and then began to speak.

"I have come to get the consciousness of your support and of your sympathy," he began, "at a time in the history of the world, I take leave to say, more critical than has ever been known during the history of the United States."

One by one he raised and answered the criticisms of the

Treaty and explained the reason for a League of Nations: "We have shown Germany that upon occasion the great peoples of the world will combine to prevent an iniquity. But we have not shown how that is going to be done in the future with a certainty that will make every other nation know that a similar enterprise must not be attempted.

" . . .The moral compulsion among us, who at the critical stage of the war saved the world . . . the moral compulsion upon us to see it through is overwhelming. We cannot now turn back.

"The weak and oppressed and the wronged peoples of the world have never before had a forum made for them to which they could summon their enemies in the presence of the judgement of mankind." That, Wilson argued, was what the League of Nations could be. As he finished and sat down, smiling at the prolonged applause, reporters noted that he was completely exhausted.

His doctor ordered him to cancel planned visits to Stanford University and Letterman Hospital, but that night he spoke again in the Civic Auditorium at Civic Center, where 20,000 people had waited two hours for a chance at the 11,000 seats. Again he forcefully argued the case for the League and answered his critics, and again he was greeted with almost deafening applause and cheers.

The next day Wilson was back in the Palm Court of the Palace Hotel to deliver the most important speech of his visit, an address to 1,500 members of the Chamber of Commerce, the business leaders of the city. They applauded politely when he rose.

"I was saying to some of your fellow citizens here yesterday," Wilson began, "how touching it has been to me to have women whom I subsequently learned have lost sons or their husbands come and take my hand and say . . . God bless you, Mr. President.

"Why should they say God bless me? I advised the Congress of the United States to take the action which sent their sons to their deaths. As Commander in Chief of the Army and Navy I ordered their sons to their deaths. Why should they take my hand, and with tears on their cheeks, say 'God Bless' you?

"Because they understood, as I understood, they understood as their sons who are dead upon the field of France understood, that they had gone there to see that in subsequent generations women should not have to mourn their dead. . . .

". . . If this great enterprise for which we fought should fail, then women with boys at their breasts ought now to weep because when those lads come to maturity, the great battle will have to be fought over again."

Speaking to the women, Wilson had been the college professor; now, to the businessmen, he became the sales manager: "It is mighty hard to hate a fellow you know, and it is mighty hard to hate a nation you know." The United States had spent thousands of lives and $32 billion on the war, expecting nothing in return. That was the "biggest advertising item I ever heard of."

Those nations are "expecting us to lead the free world . . . because they trust us . . . they really and truly trust us. . . ." Wilson stretched out his arms. The small nations were saying, he declared, "Can't you come help us?" The businessmen jumped to their feet and cheered.

"I do not believe," Wilson finished, "there is any body of men, however they concert their power or their influence, that can defeat this great enterprise, which is the enterprise of democracy, and peace and good will."

Wilson sat down to loud cheers, but his prediction was wrong. A few weeks later the United States Senate, gathered around Hiram Johnson and Henry Cabot Lodge, would defeat the treaty, because its champion was no longer able to defend it.

After his speech at the Palace, Wilson had gone directly on to San Diego, Los Angeles, Reno, Salt Lake, Cheyenne and Denver. It seemed that by the sheer force of his spirit he was succeeding in putting over the League.

In Pueblo, Colorado, his voice stuck in the middle of a sentence, and he turned pale, but he finished the speech.

"I believe that men will see the truth eye to eye and face to face," he told the crowd in Pueblo. "There is one thing that the American people always arise to and extend their hand to, and that is the truth of justice and of liberty and of peace. We have accepted that truth and we are going to be led by it, and it is going to lead us, and through us the world, out into the pastures of quietness and peace such as the world has never known before." When he finished, there were tears in his eyes.

That night Wilson collapsed on the train. The rest of the tour was canceled, and the train rushed back to Washington, where doctors found the President had suffered a thrombosis and was now completely paralyzed on his left side. He would be too weak to fight for the treaty, too weak even to leave the White House for the rest of his term. He never fully regained his health, and he died, broken, in 1924.

Had he lived until 1939, he would have seen his warning of the children of 1919 fighting another war grimly fulfilled. But had he lived until 1945, he would have found, in the same San Francisco civic plaza where he had spoken, men putting together the first tentative pieces of a United Nations, and heard President Truman say, "By this Charter you have given reality to the ideal of that great statesman of a generation ago, Woodrow Wilson," followed by the applause of the delegates of twenty-six nations.

12

"Your President Is Dead"

SAN Francisco has been a beginning place for countless artists and the end of the road for countless politicians;
somehow no politician has ever leaped from San Francisco to
great national fame, and of the many who came here in pursuit of their own rainbows, not a few lost their way. The year
1920 was a good case in point.

Senator Hiram Johnson, San Francisco's favorite son,
climbed aboard a special train in June, 1920, accompanied by
a dozen crateloads of chilled California poppies, and set out
for Chicago in pursuit of the Republican presidential nomination. The 100-degree heat of Chicago wilted the poppies
and Johnson's presidential drive, and one week later, he returned, glum and empty-handed. The convention had nominated a nobody named Warren G. Harding.

"Harding," said San Francisco Fire Commissioner William
C. Mikulich, a Republican delegate with Johnson, "is what we
in San Francisco call a trimmer. He takes no stand on anything. But he's just the kind of candidate who gets elected.
All he needs is the G.O.P. on one breast and the American
flag on the other."

That was the first blow to San Francisco's pride in the summer of 1920. The second came when the results of the
United States Census were released. Los Angeles had passed
San Francisco in population, 575,480 to 508,410; San Francisco was no longer the biggest city west of the Mississippi.
San Francisco had grown a healthy 21 percent since 1910,
but Los Angeles had exploded with an outrageous 211 percent increase in population. The *Examiner* published maps
trying to prove that, block for block, San Francisco really had

more people, but a weary city official admitted that people were beginning to choose to live in Oakland or San Mateo and work in San Francisco. "We are the office," he said. "But the workshops and sleeping quarters are elsewhere."

But first city or not, San Franciscans did have something to be proud about that summer: Their city had been selected as the site of the Democratic National Convention, the first great political convention to be held on the West Coast.

Reporters and local residents crowded the lobbies of the hotels to watch the arrival of the Democratic notables from all over the country. Train after special train was arriving in town, and the lobbies were soon filled with men in straw boaters and baggy white Palm Beach summer suits, wearing sunflowers on their lapels, carrying tiny Confederate flags, and speaking in lazy Alabama drawls or the harsh accents of New York's East Side.

The Palace Hotel was the headquarters of the convention, and there were the headquarters of the leading candidates: William G. McAdoo, the secretary of the treasury and the son-in-law of President Wilson; James Cox, the governor of Ohio; A. Mitchell Palmer, the attorney general; Senator Robert Owen of Oklahoma; and no less than twenty-seven other candidates. There at the Palace to watch the circus of candidates were three of America's most unlikely journalists; Damon Runyon, Irvin Cobb and Ring Lardner.

"You pick a nice spot to do a bit of standing round," Runyon wrote, "and almost immediately you are dislodged by the violent impact of some prominent gentleman." He described being knocked from the cigar counter by the postmaster general and from the cashier's counter by the director of the mint.

Cobb struggled into the lobby after a taxi ride. "Something seems to tell me that if I am not killed in one of San Francisco's taxicabs, I shall be killed under one," he wrote. "The youth who has been driving me about is a lineal descendant of Ben Hur." Cobb inspected the crowd in the lobby. "The Cox rooters from Ohio have arrived on a special train," he wrote, "and are active. They came three hundred strong, but it was not so noticeable after they had had a chance to bathe."

Lardner said, "The idea now seems to be that the only

chance the Democrats have got to win this fall is to either nominate a woman or else get a man with as cute a middle name as Mr. Harding's, which as everybody knows is Gamaliel." He then proposed himself as a candidate, insisting that his middle name was "Worm."

Lardner then set off up the street to the St. Francis to locate the most famous Democrat at the convention, William Jennings Bryan.

Three times the Democratic nominee and three times defeated, Bryan, "The Boy Orator of the Platte," had now declined to the level of a national joke to many, although the rural countryside still loved him as "The Great Commoner."

Stately and slow-moving, with just a fringe of hair left, Bryan settled himself at a table in the St. Francis restaurant and ate, as Runyon recounted with wonder, "part of this year's canteloupe crop, a boiler of coffee, a derby-hatful of oatmeal, and rosary of lamb chops."

When Bryan finished breakfast, he left a dime and a nickel as a tip, then changed his mind and went back to reclaim the nickel. Said the waiter who served him, "And he's the guy that never took a drink. I don't blame him, neither. Once he got through eating he wouldn't have no place to put it."

Ring Lardner pursued the Great Commoner upstairs and pounded on the door of his room.

"Who is it?" a voice asked. Ring Lardner identified himself.

"He's not in," Bryan said.

As the convention opened, no one seemed to have any idea what was going on, much less whom they were going to nominate for president. The Palmer forces tried to figure out what to do with the thousands of palm-leaf fans with their man's picture on it that they had brought with them in anticipation of tropical heat. "Mr. Bryan has just dealt a severe blow to the Owen boom," Irvin Cobb wrote, "by coming out for Owen." Delegations from all the candidates were trying frantically to locate the delegation from the Philippines, which was finally located, some weeks later, in Manila. And the delegates were not always getting along too well with the native San Franciscans.

One delegate from Oklahoma, an undertaker back home,

asked a hotel clerk, "Of course we've all heard about your sa-
lubrious climate, but I suppose people die pretty often, even
in California, don't they?"

"No," the hotel clerk said. "Only once."

Only one person remained calm amid the madness. On the
deck of the battleship *Mississippi,* anchored serenely in San
Francisco Bay, Assistant Secretary of the Navy Franklin D.
Roosevelt watched the city, waiting for his moment.

The convention finally opened in Exposition Hall with the
lusty singing of "Dixie," "The Sidewalks of New York" and
"California, We Love You." Then an immense colored portrait of President Woodrow Wilson was unveiled.

"The delegates cheered for sixteen minutes," Irvin Cobb
noted, "but an artist from Boston in front of me fell down
and had an epileptic fit lasting even longer. The color treatment is reminiscent of the best work of the man who used to
stripe band wagon wheels for Ringling Brothers."

Nevertheless, hundreds of delegates jumped from their
seats and began to parade around in Wilson's honor. The
President himself was not at the convention; after the defeat
of the League of Nations his popularity had plummeted, and
the Democrats in San Francisco, since they couldn't ignore
him, honored him as a great man who, of course, shouldn't
run again. But not all the delegates would agree to even this;
many delegates, including Charles Murphy, the boss of New
York's Tammany Hall, refused to get up for Wilson.

Suddenly there was a commotion near the New York delegation. A hand seized the New York banner, and as the surprised Murphy struggled to his feet, fists began flying. A policeman rushed over into the middle of the melee, but it was
too late. Franklin D. Roosevelt had carried off the New York
standard and was now, as Murphy and the Tammany Democrats hollered and swore, carrying it around the hall in honor
of President Wilson.

The convention then broke into several hundred noisy fac-
tions, pausing in their arguments only occasionally to sing
"Dixie" or "Over There," when the chairman yelled at them
to do something. Senator J. "Ham" Lewis, "The Human Geyser," delivered one of his celebrated afternoon-long orations
on patriotism and the future of democracy while the delegates snored, sang old Army songs and hit each other over

the head with sticks. When Lewis finished, the delegates took up the chant "Bryan, Bryan, Bryan," as they had at every convention since 1896. The Great Commoner, in his rumpled black coat, was soon standing transfixed by the spotlights, tears streaming down his cheeks, speaking for Prohibition.

"We must not be confused by the hurrahs of the wets," he shouted, his right arm raised. "It is better to have the gratitude of one soul saved from drink than to have the applause of the drunken world!"

The Democratic convention, not known for its temperance, cheered Bryan until the rafters shook and then voted down his proposal. Then they set about trying to pick a presidential candidate. While the convention organ intermittently thundered "I'm Always Chasing Rainbows," each of the thirty-one candidates was nominated with a long and fiery speech, followed by the delegates whooping, parading and singing the virtues of such colossal Americans as Agriculture Secretary E. T. Meredith and New Jersey Governor Edward Edwards.

"I foresee stirring scenes in the convention hall," Irvin Cobb scribbled in the gallery, "with the delegates joyously uprooting the state standards and parading about the floor, crying in mighty chorus, 'Who? Who? Who?'"

As the convention reached the point of voting, the floor of Exposition Hall began to take on the appearance of street brawl. Cox delegates and McAdoo delegates wrestled mightily with the Missouri standard, finally ripping it in two; the MISS went with Cox, the OURI with McAdoo. A group of women delegates, the first at any convention, began slugging each other with their handbags. The Palmer forces produced megaphones and began singing "Palmer's Style All the While" until the organist drowned them out by playing "Over There" once again. Over the heads of the battlers, J. "Ham" "The Human Geyser" Lewis delivered a few more thoughts about patriotism and the future of democracy.

Then the balloting began; first McAdoo was ahead, then Cox, then McAdoo again. Delegates swarmed in and out of the hall, arguing, shouting and searching for something to drink. Now Cox was ahead again. Irvin Cobb and Ring Lardner each received half a vote; Ring Lardner had to be forcibly restrained from rushing down to the floor to accept the nomination. William Jennings Bryan sat anxiously in his room at the St. Francis, hoping the convention would turn to him.

Finally, at one-forty in the morning, on the forty-fourth ballot, the convention chose Governor Cox. Cox, who was still in Ohio, was notified by telephone. For vice president, the convention chose Franklin D. Roosevelt of New York. The delegates remembered him for his seizure of the New York standard two days before. The exhausted but happy delegates stumbled out of Exposition Hall and made their way back to their hotels.

"The trouble with the Democrats," Irvin Cobb wrote as the last of the conventioneers filed out the hall, "is that there are too few of them in the country and too many of them in the convention."

Not everyone in San Francisco had been watching the convention. While the Democrats had been arguing, a limousine drove up to the entrance of the Fairmont Hotel and unloaded an important New York oilman and his wife and four sons after an excursion to Golden Gate Park. Walking into the lobby, the family was met by reporters who asked the boys how they had liked the city.

"We liked Golden Gate Park better than any other park we have ever played in," twelve-year-old Nelson Rockefeller said solemnly.

Nelson's father, John D. Rockefeller, Jr., was more interested in the doings of the Republican candidate, Senator Warren G. Harding. He now read in the *Chronicle* that Harding had made his first campaign speech.

"Americanism is the basis of all that has made our people and our country supreme," Harding had declared in his deep, rich voice. "It must not be forsaken in any respect. It is the soul of our life as a nation."

That was as specific as Harding ever got on any issue. He declined to take a position on women's suffrage, Prohibition or the League of Nations. Although he never left his front porch in Marion, Ohio, during the campaign, his story too would become part of the history of San Francisco.

Harding's one and only ambition was to be the best-loved president America ever had. He never claimed any intellectual pretensions; he was a simple small-town boy who had risen by being there when people had needed him. The politicians had haggled and fought in the 100-degree heat of Chicago and had torn every candidate apart; when they were done, Warren Harding was left. No one could think of anything bad to say about him.

In November, 1920, Harding, the spokesman for Americanism and "normalcy" (a slip of the tongue when he meant to say "normality"), defeated Governor Cox and Franklin D. Roosevelt by a landslide. He moved into the White House and threw open the gates to the public, shaking the hands of thousands every day. At the same time he began appointing his friends to public office. He named his brother-in-law superintendent of federal prisons. He made his local Marion banker governor of the Federal Reserve System. He appointed his family doctor chairman of the Federal Hospitalization Board and a general of the Army.

Before long a delegation of his government arrived in San Francisco and, surrounded by a sea of luggage, checked into the Fairmont Hotel.

Colonel Charles Forbes had been an old poker partner of the President's; his reward was an appointment as director of the Veterans Bureau. This trip was, Forbes declared, a search for suitable sites for veterans' hospitals. It was being paid for by the man with Forbes, Elias Mortimer, a lobbyist for a large contracting company that wanted the contract for the hospitals.

Thus far the trip had been a great success. They had gone swimming in full dress in one city in the Midwest, and in another Forbes had presented medals in the name of the President to bewildered people in the train station.

Now, when they opened the door to their suite, Forbes and Mortimer and their wives found a dozen bottles of California wine with a note attached from a local real estate developer, who offered some land he thought suitable for a hospital. The delighted Forbes agreed, called up the developer and bought the land, paying $105,000 for it, including a $25,000 fee for himself. The actual value of the land, the government later learned, was $19,000, and it was unsuitable as a building site.

Forbes checked out of the Fairmont and triumphantly returned to Washington. Unfortunately for him, stories of his journey had got there ahead of him, and federal agents were waiting for him.

A visitor to Harding's office who arrived early for an appointment found the President slamming a man against the wall and shouting, "You yellow rat, you double-crossing bastard! If you ever. . . ." He saw the visitor and stopped. "I'm sorry. You have an appointment. Come into the other room." When the visitor left, he found out that the other man had been Colonel Forbes.

"This is a hell of a job!" Harding complained to editor William Allen White. "I have no trouble with my enemies. I can take care of my enemies all right. But my ———— friends, my ———— ———— friends, White, they're the ones that keep me walking the floor nights!"

Harding's wife, Florence, whom he called the Duchess, was little solace to him. A cold, forbidding woman, she used her Secret Service agents to spy on him and to bring her astrologers for secret consultations. Her astrologer warned her, "He will not live through his term. . . . I see the sun and Mars in conjunction on the fifth house of the zodiac, and this is the house of death; sudden, violent, or peculiar death. . . ."

Forbes fled to Europe, and the counsel to the Veterans Department and then the assistant to the attorney general committed suicide. The easygoing Harding was being surrounded by a nightmare of scandal.

In desperation he decided to flee Washington. He announced a nationwide tour to promote U.S. membership in the World Court, hoping this would take public attention away from the scandal. Boarding his private railway car, Superb, with his wife and staff, he rolled out of Washington and across the United States, through Ohio, Kansas, Utah and Montana, Oregon and Washington. In Seattle he boarded a warship to sail up to Alaska to inspect the new cities there and then cruised south again.

Not far from Seattle a Navy plane circled the ship and dropped a message pouch on the deck. The coded message was rushed to Harding. No one knows what it said, but it is believed to have been word that further scandals had been uncovered; when he read it, Harding turned white.

The old Palace, not long before the earth-quake.
Wells Fargo Bank History Room

April 18, 1906, 3:30 P.M.—the Palace Hotel in flames.
Wells Fargo Bank History Room

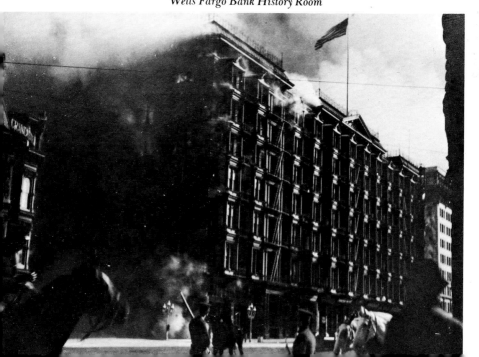

WEDNESDAY, SEPTEMBER 10, 1879.

MENU

SOUP
Chicken Okra
Consommé aux Macaroni

HORS D'ŒUVRES
Croquettes Lobster, à la Dartois

FISH
Boiled Sea Bass, sauce Hollandaise

RELEVES
Leg of Mutton, boiled, caper sauce
Lamb Pot Pie, Country style

ENTREES
Filet Beef, piqué, sauce Champignon
Chicken, sauté, à la Demidoff
Blanquette Veal, with Green Peas
Macaroni Spaghetti, à la Neapolitaine
Apple Charlotte, à la Parisienne

Boned Capon, Truffée, with Gelée

Punch à l'Ananas

ROAST
Spring Lamb, mint sauce
Ribs of Beef
Ham, champagne sauce

GAME
Saddle of Venison, sauce Venaison

Salad de Chicoree
Tomatoes   Cucumbers

VEGETABLES
String Beans
Boiled and Mashed Potatoes   Stewed Tomatoe
Beets   Lima Beans   Coarse Hominy
Green Peas   Boiled Rice
Cauliflower   Green Corn
Baked Sweet Potatoes

DESSERT
Pudding à la Parisienne
Peach Pie   Strawberry Tartelette
Bouchée à la Palermitaine   Cocoanut Cake
Crème de Nougat   Macedoine Jelly
Burnt Almonds
Biscuit Glacée, à l'Italienne

Fruit
Watermelons

Coffee.

An 1879 Palace menu.
Wells Fargo Bank History Room

Nob Hill, with the Fairmont at its summit, in 1905.
Wells Fargo Bank History Room

Nob Hill after the fire, with the Fairmont still standing.
Wells Fargo Bank History Room

President Truman outside the Fairmont—July, 1945.
San Francisco Chronicle

Fairmont lobby jammed with conventioneers.
Fairmont Hotel

Fairmont "plunge" becomes a cruise ship—1950.
San Francisco Chronicle

Cruise ship becomes tropical garden, complete with rainstorms.
Fairmont Hotel

The penthouse of the Fairmont, in 1940, now the home of Benjamin Swig.
Fairmont Hotel

Lobby of the Fairmont, about 1910.
Fairmont Hotel

Benjamin Swig.
Fairmont Hotel

Benjamin Swig's Fairmont tower.
Fairmont Hotel

Louis Lurie.
San Francisco Chronicle

In the middle of a speech in Seattle Stadium the next day, President Harding faltered in the middle of a sentence, dropped the manuscript and gripped the lectern with both hands.

Secretary of Commerce Herbert Hoover, sitting behind him, leaped to his feet, steadied Harding and then handed him the speech; the shaken Harding finished his address.

That evening, after another speech, Harding told his doctor he had violent cramps and indigestion. Blaming it on seafood the President had eaten, the doctor ordered his speeches canceled, and a telegram was sent to the Palace Hotel notifying it to expect the President immediately. Harding was rushed onto the Superb, and the train raced south.

Mayor Rolph, Dr. Ray Lyman Wilbur, the president of Stanford and of the American Medical Association, and a small silent crowd were waiting for the President at the Southern Pacific station.

The pale Harding stepped uncertainly down from the Superb, waved away a wheelchair and walked to a waiting car, squinting into the early-morning sunshine.

Helped upstairs at the Palace, he was put to bed in Suite 8064, overlooking Market Street. The Duchess took the room across the hall. Mayor Rolph ordered the streetcars on Market Street to cease ringing their bells when they passed the Palace, and the Ferry Building was illuminated with electric lights in tribute to the President.

The next day, July 30, 1923, he was much worse. He had a temperature of 102 and a racing pulse. "His acute illness came to a peak Monday night," Dr. Wilbur wrote, "with the rapid development of bronchial pneumonia." New York City schoolchildren were asked to pray for him, and the Pope called for prayers for his health.

Tuesday he seemed much better. "The fire is out," Dr. Sawyer, his old family doctor, announced triumphantly. The fever was down, and he was resting comfortably. The Duchess read him the morning papers. On Wednesday and Thursday his condition kept improving. Thursday night the Duchess read to him from the *Saturday Evening Post,* while he was propped up on pillows. When she finished, she put down the magazine and walked across the hall to her room.

The nurse, bringing him a glass of water, saw his face sud-

denly twitch. His mouth fell open, then his head fell to one
side, and his body slumped down on the pillows. The Duch-
ess, seeing what happened as she came back from her room,
ran into the corridor, shouting, "Get Dr. Boone!
Get Dr. Boone!" Postmaster General Hubert Work and
Herbert Hoover ran into the room, followed by Dr. Charles
E. Sawyer and Dr. Joel T. Boone, a Navy physician. The
Duchess was standing by the bed, sobbing, "Warren, Warren,
Warren." The President was dead.

Dr. Sawyer declared that it was a cerebral hemorrhage.
The other doctor promptly disagreed, and they stood
around the bed, arguing. Finally, they all signed a bulletin
saying, "Death was apparently due to some brain evolve-
ment, probably an apoplexy. During the day he had been
free from discomfort and there was every justification for
anticipating a prompt recovery." Mrs. Harding refused to
permit an autopsy.

Outside the door of the suite, Secret Service men massed
to keep back the crowd of reporters. The medical bulletin
was handed out, and a dazed Dr. Boone, still dressed for dinner, was saying, "All at once he went, just like that." He
snapped his fingers. "Something just snapped. That's all."

Within a few minutes the news had spread throughout the
hotel. The whole corridor outside the room was jammed
with people, as General Pershing and other members of the
President's party struggled to get through to the room. Finally, a squadron of policemen arrived, began to clear the corridors and then took up stations at all the stairways and elevators.

In the lobby the lights suddenly dimmed, and a voice announced, "Your President is dead." People having dinner
laid down their silverware, got up and hurriedly left.

A Pierce-Arrow hearse carrying a coffin and a car full of
undertakers drove up to the New Montgomery entrance at
the same time as newsboys arrived with special editions announcing Harding's death. Their shouts reached the windows of Suite 8064, and Mrs. Harding, hearing them, sent an
aide downstairs to buy copies.

In a farmhouse in Vermont, Vice President Calvin Coolidge was awakened shortly after midnight and told the news.
Kerosene lamps were lit, and his father, a justice of the

peace, held out the family Bible and swore him in as the President of the United States.

By midmorning Friday Suite 8064 was filled with sweet-smelling floral displays and crowds of people. President Harding was dressed in evening clothes, and his open coffin lay by the window.

"I want you to look at him," Mrs. Harding said. "He was magnificent in life, he is even more wonderful in death." She turned to the President's aides. "I will not break down," she said.

On the roof, workmen had lowered the presidential flag and had replaced it with an American flag at half-mast. Other workmen were hanging black crepe on the front of the building.

Late in the afternoon, a grim General Pershing led two soldiers, two sailors and two marines, with the coffin on their shoulders, down the corridor to the freight elevator, then downstairs, through the Palm Court and out onto New Montgomery Street, where the hearse and a line of black limousines waited. Preceded by a detachment of cavalry, cars carrying the governor, the mayor, General Pershing and Mrs. Harding and a band playing the slow strains of Chopin's Funeral March, the hearse drove slowly to the Third and Townsend Street Southern Pacific station. The coffin was placed in the windows of the Superb in view of the silent crowd outside. Mrs. Harding, as she was led to the train, was saying, over and over, "I will not break down." As the bunting-draped train pulled slowly out of the station, the crowd began to sing "Lead, Kindly Light."

After a slow train journey east, the worldwide tributes and a solemn funeral in Marion, Ohio, Harding's memory enjoyed a few years of honor. Ohio Northern University dedicated the Warren Harding College of Law, and a fund was raised for a statue of his dog. Then the skeletons began to fall out of the closets.

Harding's secretary of the interior, it was discovered, had built a magnificent ranch in New Mexico, financed by a paper bag full of money donated by an oil company. In return, the secretary had permitted the oil company to tap the naval oil reserves under Teapot Dome, Wyoming. The plans for the Harding Memorial had to be changed when someone pointed out that the marble tomb resembled a teapot. Then, in the final indignity, it was disclosed that, with the aid of the Secret Service, Harding had been meeting with a mistress in the closet of his office in the White House. This was too much for President Coolidge; he refused to attend the dedication of Harding's tomb.

As if Harding's memory had not been shattered enough, a charlatan named Gaston Means decided to trample the remaining pieces into the ground.

Means had once been hired by John Burns as an agent for his celebrated detective agency. In the days before the United States entered the war, the British had hired Burns to spy on the Germans in the United States, and the Germans had hired him to spy on the British. Burns simply assigned half his men to be for the British and the other half, including Means, for the Germans and directed them to spy on each other. Means rented an apartment on Park Avenue, put up a large picture of the kaiser and went into business.

Means showed particular talent, so after the war, when Harding chose Burns to head his new Investigation Bureau, Burns appointed him an agent. Means was nothing if not cocky; he immediately let it be known that he would sell the bureau's files to anyone who was interested in looking at them and boasted that he was able to fix the United States Supreme Court.

This was a little too much. J. Edgar Hoover took over the bureau, renamed it the FBI and threw Means into the penitentiary.

Sitting in his prison cell, Means had an inspiration. Calling in a ghost writer, he informed them that he, an important figure in the last administration and an intimate of Harding's, knew the *real* story of how Harding died in the Palace Hotel.

The result was a book entitled *The Strange Death of President Harding.* In it Means claimed to have been practically a resident of the White House (where he had never been) and a confidant of Harding (whom he had never met). He offered the intriguing theory that Mrs. Harding had poisoned her husband to save his honor from the unfolding scandals.

The book was an instant best-seller. Despite a vehement

denial by Dr. Wilbur in the *Saturday Evening Post* and the admission of the ghost writer in 1931 that the whole thing was a "colossal hoax, a tissue of falsehood from beginning to end," the story was readily accepted everywhere, quoted by Frederick Lewis Allen in *Only Yesterday* and cited by the San Francisco novelist Gertrude Atherton, and it is widely believed today.

Means finally outreached himself in 1932, when he confided to a rich widow that he could solve the Lindbergh kidnapping for a price. He took $100,000 from the woman and fed her hopes with daily reports of clandestine meetings with criminal gangs and promises that the baby would be released any moment. The baby was found dead, and Means was sent back to the penitentiary.

President Hoover was finally convinced to go to Marion to dedicate the tomb, but little could be done with Harding's reputation. At Northern Ohio University, the use of his name for the law school was gradually dropped, until finally workmen chipped his name off the façade of the library.

13

The Jazz Hotel

BY the 1920s the Palace had settled into the role of the Grande Dame of San Francisco hotels, tasteful, gray and respected.

"The Palace is stylish, perhaps," Almira Bailey wrote in 1921, "but principally it is select. It suggests to me women who wear suits of clothes, mostly dark gray, all wool and a yard wide . . . and who carry suitcases covered with foreign express tags . . . and the Palace suggests to me afternoon teas, and that peculiar composite chatter of women's voices which is more like the sound of birds in a flock." The Palace was still moving in the one-two-three waltz of the Edwardian era.

While black Pierce-Arrow limousines rolled solemnly up to the entrance of the Palace, glittering and low-slung Duesenbergs and bright-red Hispano-Suizas were growling up to the curb in front of the St. Francis and unloading the gayly dressed children of the Jazz Age at San Francisco's Jazz Hotel.

It had begun in 1913, when a group of fanatics seized the Rose Room of the St. Francis. Carrying large black cases, they had walked in, confidently arranged themselves around the stage, and unpacked from the cases strange gleaming joints of brass plumbing, which they fitted together.

When they were ready, they looked to their boyish leader for the signal to begin. He began tapping his foot on the stage and then nodding his head, and they leaned back and loosed a blast from the brass instruments which filled the lobby with an unearthly bass wailing and brought a startled

crowd rushing to the door of the Rose Room. The St. Francis
was hearing its first saxophones.

The leader of that band was twenty-five-year-old Art Hickman, and what he was doing was making jazz respectable.
His orchestra was to play its syncopated beat in the Rose
Room for seven years before he went on to greater fame in
New York, taking his orchestra to the Biltmore Hotel and the
roof of the Amsterdam Hotel. During his seven years he
helped promote musicians like Paul Whiteman, who then
was playing at the opening of the Winter Garden Ice Rink
(now Winterland, the home of Bill Graham's rock concerts),
and Ferde Grofé, a substitute piano player in North Beach
whom Hickman brought to his orchestra and who later won
fame by writing *The Grand Canyon Suite.*

Jazz had been around San Francisco a long time, mainly in
the crowded dance halls on Pacific Avenue, where saxophones had long been blaring and sweating drummers
tossed their drumsticks into the smoke-bleary air. It had
come out of ragtime, which, at the turn of the century, had
sparked popular music out of the languid one-two-three of
the waltz into the frantic one-two one-two of the two-step.

Ned Greenway had watched with dismay as the tranquil
rhythms of his circular waltzes and schottisches were rudely
disrupted by people doing tangos, ragtime and fox-trots.
Discreet placards were placed around the dance floor at the
Palace Hotel reminding dancers that such behavior was un-
acceptable, but it went on anyway.

San Francisco had suddenly caught dancing fever. The hotels began scheduling weekly and then daily dansants in their
ballrooms. Skirts rose to seven inches from the floor. Even
the sedate band in Golden Gate Park began slipping ragtime
numbers into its Sunday programs. New dances appeared
weekly; the Boston Dip, the Tipperary Trot, the New Twin-
kle, the Balboa, the Hesitation, the Liberty-Bell Trot, and the
Slow Fox—all were frantically stepped out in the ballrooms.

The newspapers were hard put to describe the craze. They
called it Zass at first. Then, in 1917, the *News-Letter* wrote:

> A strange new word has gained wide-spread use in the
> ranks of our producers of popular music. It is "jazz", used

mainly as an adjective description of a band. . . . The groups that play for dancing, when colored, seem infected with the virus that they try to instill as a stimulus in others. They shake and jump and writhe. The word is African in origin. It means "speeding up things." It is strict rhythm without melody. It is an attempt to reproduce the marvelous syncopation of the African jungle.

Jazz didn't win without a struggle. Mothers and fathers in the sedate East Bay were dismayed to see their children flocking onto the ferries to go dancing in San Francisco. Charles Keeler, director of the Berkeley Chamber of Commerce, warned the University of California Mothers' Club: "The students are subjected to the subtle insinuations of jazzy music. This vulgar 'syncopation' is the musical expression of barbarous and immoral races. The South Sea Islanders, among whom it got its start, are among the lowest living human types."

Theodore Alfred Appia, professor of eurhythmics at the university, thundered, "It is pitiful, disgusting and amazing to see college students and civilized people in public restaurants enjoying the excitation of their lowest emotions in this savage fashion. Jazz is pornographic."

Even then-Vice President Coolidge commented on it. "Home brewing, jazz dancing and risqué dresses," he said in his nasal voice, "are merely a passing whim of fashion."

But jazz had firmly grabbed hold of San Francisco. Hotel guests began carrying "jazz" baggage, wildly painted with polka dots, stripes and bright colors. Small boys hid in their bedrooms to read "jazz" magazines named *The Hot Dog, The Razzberry, The Flapper's Magazine* and *Jim Jam Jems*. And girls, to the horror of their parents, were bobbing their hair.

"Bobbed hair—and particularly this new method of shingling it," said the dean of a women's college, "is another defiance that the girls of today are hurling into the teeth of their elders . . . they've sneered at the delicate, feminine instincts that distinguished their grandmothers, and to back up their arguments about being the intellectual equals of men, they shave their necks. It's barbaric."

Anna Pavlova wistfully talked to a reporter about this new American girl: "She is so old inside, when her years are so

young. She has had everything that she has wanted. She has
seen everything. She is so blasé and so world-weary when everything should still be fresh and unspoiled. The war, it has
changed everything all over the world."

Evangelist Aimee Semple McPherson came up from Los
Angeles and made a last, desperate attempt to save the city,
speaking on "If Jesus Christ Came to San Francisco."

"If you would be healed," she cried, "go home and take the
jazz music off the piano, throw away your dancing slippers,
tear up your playing cards and theater tickets. Then, with
faith in your heart, come as sinners to be saved!"

But it was to no avail. In 1926 the white-haired Ned
Greenway died, and Paul Whiteman played to a packed Civic
Auditorium in front of a backdrop of a dozen brand-new
and gleaming Fords, the symbols of the Jazz Age. A Hollywood writer visiting San Francisco marveled, "I've never
seen anything like it. It's as if the entire city came from common parents, F. Scott Fitzgerald and Isadora Duncan."

The St. Francis was now the center of everything going on
in San Francisco. It became the home of the new motion-picture stars when they traveled up from Hollywood. Charlie
Chaplin, Douglas Fairbanks, Mary Pickford, Tom Mix, Ma-
bel Normand, Fatty Arbuckle, D. W. Griffith and Cecil B. De-
Mille all passed through the St. Francis lobby. The Palace
might entertain President Harding, but the St. Francis had
Sinclair Lewis and the Ringling Brothers, Isadora Duncan,
George M. Cohan, Trixie Friganza and Duke Kahanamoku,
the champion swimmer of the world.

Adding more color were the fairy-tale names in the register: Prince Tsai Hsun of China, Prince Fushimi of Japan, the
Princess Kauananakoa, the rajah and ramee of Pudukota,
the marquis de Polignac and princess von Hatzfeld. For a little balance there was the fiery evangelist Billy Sunday, William Jennings Bryan and Edsel Ford.

Society, too, moved into the St. Francis, and those who
wished to aspire to its higher reaches found that, with Ned
Greenway gone, they would have to deal with Ernest Gloor,
the headwaiter of the Mural Room.

The Rose Room had been redecorated with huge wall
paintings of allegorical Indians, Persians, Spaniards and Cal-
ifornians by Albert Herter, and it was below these paintings

that society took its place every Monday at noon for a luncheon and fashion show. The seating was as hierarchical as a meeting of cardinals, and it was all controlled by Ernest Gloor; he could raise anyone to the pinnacle of social eminence by placing them on the aisle or condemn them to the eternal torment of the back tables.

One could find in the Mural Room, the *Wasp* wrote in 1924:

> The quintessence of smartness, the epitome of everything and everyone who is deliciously unconcerned and worthwhile. One can munch and digest placidly to the accompaniment of beautiful women giving expression to their shimmering souls and temperaments. No disturbing intellectual thoughts or bolshevism here; no working class idlers to poison the atmosphere. Life has become fearfully and beautifully simple . . .
>
> At a nearby table one overhears the ambitious and thoroughly informed Mrs. Weatherby Worsted Witherington instructing her young, who gobble up her sophisticated bits of who's who and why's why with their avocados . . . while in the very center of the salon, surrounded by those who coach themselves all night in order to be near her in the day, is the important Mrs. McTomalby herself—she who forsook Paris, London and New York to lead the simple life in her Burlingame farm with its Versailles gardens, its English tudor castle and its famous collection of art treasures. . . .

So much for Monday afternoons. In the evenings the fashionable people drove up from their new Burlingame or even more exclusive Hillsborough mansions to attend the most fashionable of fashionable affairs of the 1920s, costume balls.

At the "Quatr'z Arts Ball" at the Fairmont in 1924, 3,000 people dressed as buddhas, mandarins, carrier pigeons and gypsies danced to four "jazzy" orchestras. "Mrs. Loller Jr.'s costume represented the California Poppy, with a yellow silk bodice studded with rhinestones and yellow ostrich plumes around the bottom of the skirt," the newspapers told a presumably entranced public.

The year 1925 exceeded even that with the "Gold Ball" at Mardi Gras. Dancers dressed as grapes, oranges, wheat kernels, Spanish senoritas, Indians and hula dancers. "Mrs. Horace Hill and Miss Marion Zeile were costumed as white leghorn chickens," the papers reported dutifully. "Mrs. Clinton LaMontagne was a State Highway Sign, in cloth of gold with a pointed hat, carrying a red signal light."

In November the public rooms of the St. Francis were occupied by the noisy rites that surrounded another San Francisco tradition, the dinners and reunions preceding the Big Game between the University of California and Stanford football teams. Dressed in the blue and gold or red that their alma maters required, the boosters of the two schools filled the café and ordered from football-shaped menus that listed and pictured the members of each team. Late into the night, the corridors shook with the Golden Bear Growl:

> Grrrrrrrrrr-rah! Grrrrrrrrrrrrr-Rah!
> Grrrrrrrr, rrrrrrrrrrrrr, rrrrrrrrah!
> We are the sons of California,
> Fighting for the Gold and Blue,
> Palms of Glory we will win
> For our alma mater true!

What was it that made the St. Francis so preeminently the hotel of the time? The size of the hotel, the biggest in town, had something to do with it, and certainly the location, in the very heart of the city. But also there was the remarkable staff. What other hotel in town could boast that the attendant of its Turkish bath was a veteran of Kitchener's Camel Corps or that its hotel courier had once shown the sights of Cairo to the visiting royalty of Europe? And what other hotel could boast that its chef had overthrown the king of Portugal?

Victor Hirtzler, the *chef de cuisine,* was a San Francisco legend comparable to Telegraph Hill or the Golden Gate. His arms folded across his chest and a black fez set rakishly aslant on his head, he commanded a kitchen that had no rival in the West and produced menus that were as legendary as he was, menus almost stunning in their lavishness.

The stories about Victor's early years are nearly all fantastic; Victor seldom bothered to deny a story if it added to his luster. It was said, for instance, that he was once a chef in the kitchens of the czar and tasted every dish before it was laid on the imperial table, a story which is interesting but not very probable.

This much is fairly certain: Victor was born in Strasbourg, France, and began cooking when he was thirteen. When the Germans besieged Strasbourg in 1870, he had to cook with horse flesh and cat meat as his ingredients; he learned to do it so well no one could tell.

After taking his formal chef's training in Strasbourg, he traveled throughout Europe, frequently cooking for royal families. It was on one of his travels that he overthrew the king of Portugal.

That king, Don Carlos, was celebrated for his extravagant tastes. For him Victor created an outrageously exotic dish he called La Mousse Faison Lucullus, a combination of Bohemian pheasant's breasts and woodcock flavored with truffles and a sauce of cognac, madeira and champagne. Don Carlos became immensely fond of the dish, which cost $180 a serving, so fond that he soon ate Portugal into bankruptcy. He was assassinated, and the monarchy fell; in 1910, the republic of Portugal was founded, and Victor always claimed the credit.

He was somewhat in disfavor with the royal families of Europe after that and emigrated to New York. There he became the chef of the Waldorf, and it was there that James Woods, the manager of the St. Francis, found him and convinced him to come to San Francisco.

The St. Francis kitchen would be envied by executive chefs today. With wages absurdly low, Victor was able to hire an enormous staff, including, his rivals charged, chefs direct from Europe who spoke no English and were unaware, largely because Victor didn't bother to tell them, that slavery had been abolished long before. They cooked for him with fanatical loyalty.

With this sort of staff, he was able to create remarkable and sometimes startling dishes some with names as imperial as their taste—Leg of Lamb Renaissance, Oysters Victor Hugo, or Filet of Sole Lord Curzon—or as surprising as Sautéed Barracuda or Reindeer Chop with Port Wine Sauce. Describing the last dish in his *St. Francis Cookbook,* Victor warned housewives faced with a newly purchased reindeer that their reindeer "should be hung up at least two weeks before being cooked, or the meat will be tough."

Victor selected his menus with the care of a composer writing a symphony, building to a staggering climax with the entrée and then gently carrying the astonished diner along through the dessert. This was a typical dinner menu:

> California Oyster Cocktail
> Oxtail Soup, English Style
> Frogs Legs, Jerusalem
> Filet Mignon, Bayard (on buttered toast spread with puree de foie gras, Madere sauce, sliced truffles, and garnishes of chicken croquettes)
> Flageolet Beans
> Sybil Potatoes
> Hearts of Lettuce
> Raspberry Water Ice
> Assorted cakes
> Coffee

Victor's fame was enhanced by the dishes which took his name—Celery Victor, Oysters Victor and Crab Cocktail Victor—and by those named after the hotel—Breast of Squab under Glass St. Francis and his remarkable Orange Soufflé, St. Francis, oranges stuffed with fresh fruit, maraschino, vanilla ice cream and sugared egg whites.

Victor had toppled a European dynasty; it was fitting that, coming to America, he should elect a president.

In the fall of 1916 America's voters were faced with a choice between President Wilson, who had barely won a three-way race for the office in 1912, and the Republican challenger, the bearded Governor Charles Evans Hughes of New York. The race was exceptionally close; as election day approached, both candidates were touring the country on campaign trains, seeking votes.

Hughes came to San Francisco and was honored at a banquet at the Commercial Club, hosted by Republican Committeeman Charles Crocker, of the family that owned the St. Francis. Crocker engaged Victor to prepare the banquet and ushered Hughes to the head table.

Twenty minutes after the banquet began, just as dinner was about to be served, the waiters, members of the culinary workers union, walked out on strike, leaving Victor alone in the kitchen with his staff. Hughes wondered if the banquet should be called off, but the furious Victor would hear nothing of it; food was more important than politics. Taking off his hat and apron, he personally carried the trays of food to Hughes' table and exhorted the kitchen staff to serve the rest of the guests.

Victor saved the dinner but lost the presidency for Hughes. When San Francisco union leaders heard that Hughes had broken a picket line to eat dinner, they printed thousands of handbills denouncing him as antilabor and had them handed out at the docks, factories and workshops all over the city.

When Hughes went to bed election night 1916, the returns showed he was beating Wilson and would be the next president. When he woke up the next morning, he found he had lost California by the razor-thin margin of 3,673 votes, easily accountable to the San Francisco union campaign against him, and by losing California he had lost the election. It had been an expensive banquet.

If Victor was disturbed by what he had done, he didn't show it. He cooked breakfast for Wilson when he came to the St. Francis in 1919.

Up on Nob Hill, LeRoy Linnard, the new manager of the Fairmont, watched the frantic activity inside the St. Francis enviously. The St. Francis attracted the most expensive cars; the St. Francis attracted the most colorful guests; the St. Francis had opened the third electric grill in the nation and had provided the banqueteers of the San Francisco Real Estate Board with 700 telephones on the banquet table, so they could talk to their brother realtors at another banquet in New York. Every time he picked up the newspaper he read about the St. Francis. Linnard decided to do something to make the Fairmont better known.

His first idea was to conquer the air waves. In March, 1922, he hired a seventeen-year-old electrical wizard named Charles Maass to wire together San Francisco's second radio station. Maass was given a tiny room under the roof, and soon he had filled the room with a phonograph, a fifty-watt transmitter and an upright piano. Owners of primitive crystal sets all over the Bay Area bent close to their sets and heard his voice: "Hello! Hello! Hello! This is the broadcasting station at the Fairmont Hotel in San Francisco. The first selection for this evening's concert will be the Railroad Blues, by the Benson Orchestra. Just a moment please. All right, here we go!"

It was primitive; he had to stop every fifteen minutes and listen for two minutes, according to government regulations, in case anyone wanted to answer, but it was a tremendous success. Soon the Fairmont station was joined by half a dozen others, including one at the Palace, and the newspapers began printing program schedules and diagrams of how to build crystal sets.

But it wasn't attracting new customers to the Fairmont. Linnard decided to try something more dramatic.

LeRoy's father, D. M. Linnard, who had bought the Fairmont a few years earlier, owned six other hotels in southern California: two in Los Angeles, three in Pasadena, and one in Santa Barbara, including the famous Green and Huntington hotels in Pasadena. It was always a problem to get guests from Linnard hotels in Southern California up to the Fairmont without losing them to other hotels along the way.

Most passengers traveled between the cities on the Southern Pacific's Lark or Daylight or took the more leisurely overnight cruise on the steamships *Yale* or *Harvard,* dancing to orchestras in the cafés through the evening. Now Linnard had an idea; he would fly the guests over the heads of his competitors and set them down practically at the door of the Fairmont. Inspired by the brilliance of his idea, he set about rounding up the state's first airline.

The same week that Charles Maass was broadcasting from the Fairmont roof, the *Chronicle* carried an announcement that the hotel was beginning the first scheduled air service between San Francisco and Los Angeles:

> Eight big aerial stages will maintain the service, equipped with Hispano-Suiza motors, carrying two or four passengers, in addition to the pilot, and more will be added to the line as the call for service may demand. Today's trip, more

in the nature of a demonstration, will include the entire commissioned fleet flying in formation over the cities between San Francisco and Los Angeles.

Early in the morning of March 27, 1922, Linnard's miniature air force was lined up on the pavement of the Marina airfield. The passengers, bundled up like the pilots in leather flying coats, helmets and goggles, stood around the seven biplanes (the eighth was in the hangar with a dismantled engine) saying good-bye to their friends and having their pictures taken in various poses of bravado by a newspaper photographer with his bulky Speed Graphic. Those first passengers included San Francisco County Supervisor Warren Shannon and his wife and daughter; two representatives of the Chambers of Commerce of Salinas and Santa Maria; Foster Curry, the operator of the Camp Curry resort in Yosemite Valley; and S. D. Adkisson, the assistant manager of the Fairmont, whom Linnard had sent along to represent him.

The tiny Imelda Shannon, the supervisor's daughter, nearly invisible inside her huge flying coat, christened the first plane. Prohibition having recently begun, she cracked a bottle of grape juice over the propeller. The spectators applauded, Mr. Shannon was handed a letter from Mayor "Sunny Jim" Rolph to deliver to the mayor of Los Angeles, and the passengers were boosted into the cockpits.

At 9:38, one by one the seven biplanes rolled down the runway and lifted into the air, flying out over the blue waters of the Golden Gate. The great red bridge was still seventeen years in the future. Then they turned south, and, circling for altitude, disappeared over the hills.

One plane, the one carrying assistant manager Adkisson, was back on the runway a few minutes later. The pilot had felt the engine running roughly and turned around. He and the mechanics tinkered with it, and he took off again, but he still wasn't satisfied. He landed for a second time, and the plane was rolled back to the hangar.

An hour after taking off, the line of silver biplanes passed over the farm town of San Jose, heading toward Gilroy. A few minutes before eleven a second plane's engine began to shake and sputter. The pilot waved to the others that he was all right and spiraled down, landing in a field just outside town.

The regular flights were scheduled to take five hours, allowing for two leisurely food and rest stops along the way. For this first flight, however, time had been allotted for ceremony. Shortly before noon the five remaining planes came in low over the lettuce fields and touched town at Salinas airfield, where they were met by a committee of city officials, Chamber of Commerce boosters and uniformed American Legionnaires. After an hour of handshaking and lunch, they climbed back into the planes and were off again.

They passed over King City at 1:35 and climbed over the rolling brown hills of central California, passing over Paso Robles at 2 and the halfway point of the trip, San Luis Obispo, at 2:30, losing altitude as they neared Santa Maria, the next scheduled stop. The engine of another plane started to sputter, and the pilot, as soon as he touched down, hurried to look at it. The mechanics shook their heads and told him he'd have to wait until the next day. As the second plane made its approach, the pilot saw someone, evidently unaware of the little rules of the new business of aviation, walking across the runway. He veered to the side and landed in a freshly plowed field. When he climbed from the cockpit and inspected his plane, he found his propeller sadly bent. He would have to wait until the next day.

The remaining three planes landed at Santa Maria for more handshaking and speeches. Then, after bidding farewell to their stranded fellow passengers, they gamely climbed back into the cockpits and were off into the air at 4.

They rose over the dark hills, and suddenly, they were next to the Pacific again, flying above the dark thread of the Southern Pacific's coast line. At 4:50 they flew over the green palms and white hotels of Santa Barbara.

In his office at the Fairmont, LeRoy Linnard looked at his watch and waited for word from his fliers. At Rogers Airport in Los Angeles officials from the Chamber of Commerce and Linnard's hotels there looked at their watches and waited. It was beginning to get dark, and the lights were coming on along the new palm-lined streets.

Then they heard a faint hum, and saw, tiny and silver, three biplanes dimly sparkling in the last light. One by one the planes circled down, and one by one they landed and rolled to a stop. The weary but smiling passengers climbed out of the cockpits and shook hands once more. It was 5:40 P.M., eight hours after they had taken off in San Francisco. LeRoy Linnard, whose tiny airline would soon be swallowed up and made a part of the growing commercial airlines, had succeeded in the first scheduled airline flight between Los Angeles and San Francisco, a route which today is the busiest single air corridor in the world.

No New Year's Eve, in San Francisco's noisy and glorious cavalcade of wild New Years, was more poignant than New Year's Eve, 1919, for San Franciscans believed it would be their last. The Eighteenth Amendment, enacting Prohibition, had passed, and future years would have to flow in on a river of grape juice, and every real San Franciscan knew that nothing, especially not a New Year, arrived on a river of grape juice. They were determined to make their last their best.

"By 10:00," the *Examiner* reported, "Market Street, ankle deep, looked like a snowstorm of confetti had fallen upon it. Sidewalks were crowded to the curb and a solid string of automobiles, laden with noisy happiness, crawled up and down the streets.

"Hotels were filled to overflowing with revellers from outside town and from Washington and Oregon who wanted to be in on the wake. . . ." At the Palace the crowds were shoulder to shoulder in the main corridor and the restaurants. "The crowds got their first thrill when a man in a dress suit and silk hat pulled a small barrel of wine from an automobile at the New Montgomery Street entrance and began rolling it through the lobby toward the cafe."

At the Fairmont, Rudy Seiger led his Fairmont Orchestra, dressed in Scottish kilts, in a mournful march through the lobby. Midnight was brightened by Miss Billie de Rex, the "eccentric dancer," who performed, to the delight of the crowds, her own opinion of Prohibition.

Thirty-six hundred people were seated at the tables of the St. Francis, watching the bellboys in masquerade costumes and listening to the nine orchestras that walked from room to room, playing "every kind of music from Javanese to good old American."

At midnight the mournful howls nearly drowned out "Auld Lang Syne." San Franciscans took their last gulps of champagne and looked grimly ahead to the future.

The greatest experiment of that dizzy age of experimentation was a complete and tremendous flop. The Women's Christian Temperance Union and the associations of church women had sat by simmering while jazz and bobbed hair and cigarette smoking had danced wickedly in. Now they saw their chance to strike back. Marshaling every fundamentalist and teetotaler and Southern Baptist they could gather in Midwestern legislatures and with a big hand from the Midwestern immigrants in Los Angeles, the only large pro-temperance town outside the South, they shoved through the Eighteenth Amendment, prohibiting the manufacture, sale or transport of intoxicating liquor.

Prohibition went into effect on January 17, 1920. On the sixteenth the San Francisco County Women's Christian Temperance Union, the Church Federation and the Epworth League held a coffee-and-doughnut Victory Celebration and Prayer Service at the First Congregational Church. Outside the church, trucks and wagons loaded to the railings with cases of liquor hurried from house to house, trying frantically to beat the deadline.

At midnight a great howl of sorrow rose from all over San Francisco. A few minutes after midnight Charles Callihan, the bartender of what was now a "former saloon" on Sixth Street, sadly closed the door and told his customers, "Well, fellows, we've got by for quite a while and this is the end. Here are two drinks of gin. Who wants to buy them?" Two men stepped to the bar, whipped out badges identifying them as federal Prohibition agents, and arrested Callihan, making him San Francisco's first Prohibition martyr.

One by one the great taverns closed or changed to tamer pastimes. The Odeon and the Portola-Louvre became cafeterias. Jule's and Techau's Tavern became dairy lunch bars. Cliff House tried to make it as a coffee shop, but finally had to close down completely.

The magnificent Palace Bar, with its dark and cozy paneling and its Maxfield Parrish painting, became an ice cream parlor. PALACE BAR TO BE ICE CREAM SHOP, the *Chronicle* headlined. YE GODS !

Almira Bailey, previously barred by the men-only rule there, visited the bar to see the Maxfield Parrish. She found the rail removed and the bar surrounded by a temporary wall that looked like a coffin. The former bartender was cleaning up.

"I asked him why they didn't remove the bar entirely and he said with unsmiling naivete that they were 'waiting to see,' and that they had saved the rail 'in case.'" They would have to wait thirteen years.

The new Prohibition agents were nothing if not zealous. The San Francisco office hired fifty new officers a few days before Prohibition went into effect. "They don't wear uniforms or badges," the office proudly announced. "All are ex-service men and members of the American legion."

Two agents went to Techau's Tavern and ordered a $15 meal, producing their own bottle of wine to accompany it. When their bottle was empty, they badgered the waiter to bring them another bottle. He did, and they promptly arrested him and the owners of the restaurant. A raid on the baggage room of the Argonaut Hotel netted thirty trunkloads of bottles and led to the arrest of nearly all the bellhops and porters.

Speakeasies and blind pigs, with their tiny peepholes and passwords, flourished in basements all over town, and stills were set up in cellars, in attics, even in the parks. Not much could be said for the quality of the product: San Franciscans were served gin made of crude oil, denatured alcohol, formaldehyde, peppermint and embalming fluid. A typical newspaper story of 1922 ran: "Inspector Roberts said yesterday that a seizure was made on Larkin Street that was the most vile concoction ever analyzed by chemists of the department. Camouflaged as whiskey, it was really a nauseating combination of alcohol, coloring matter and refuse."

The greatest indignity was when San Francisco had to welcome a guest. Marshal Ferdinand Foch, the hero of the Marne, came to San Francisco on his triumphal tour of the United States in 1921. After the guests at the Palace banquet for the marshal had waved their tiny French and American

flags while a glee club sang "Over There" and "Madelon,"
and Mayor Rolph, the commander, and then the vice commander of the American Legion had each mispronounced
the marshal's name, the toastmaster declared, "I want to say
that Ferd Foch is the eatingest marshal of France I ever saw."
Then they all raised their glasses to the gray-haired old soldier and drank a toast of vintage California water.

The experiment came to an end with a blast of the whistle
of the Ferry Building at 2:31 P.M., December 5, 1933. The
last required state, Utah, had voted to repeal. A chorus of
cheers rose as a convoy of fourteen Italian Swiss Colony wine
trucks rolled out of a warehouse and down Market Street to
the Civic Center to present the first legal bottle of liquor to a
smiling Mayor Angelo J. Rossi.

A few hours before the whistle blew, federal Prohibition
agents looking through a boardinghouse discovered a tiny
beer still hidden in the attic by a sixty-seven-year-old shoe-
maker, a widower who lived in the house with his eleven-
year-old nephew. The agents smashed the still and the beer
bottles and arrested the man. To their eternal credit, the
U.S. commissioners decided against pressing charges, in the
last dismal act of San Francisco's dry experiment.

14

The Orgy

WHISPERS and pointing fingers stirred the lobby of the St. Francis one autumn afternoon in 1921. The loungers and guests looked at the crowd around the registration desk and recognized a familiar figure signing the book. He turned, smiled at them, and then, followed by the bellhop with his luggage, went up to his suite, Rooms 1219, 1220 and 1221.

His name was Roscoe Arbuckle, but millions of Americans knew him as Fatty Arbuckle. Then at the peak of his fame, he was as well known to them as Charlie Chaplin or Tom Mix. Audiences roared as the baby-faced plump actor puzzled and blundered through a hundred comic film adventures, throwing pies left and right. "He had satanic marksmanship with pies," film critic James Agee wrote. "He could simultaneously blind two people in opposite directions." They called him The King of Fun-Makers.

Like Chaplin and Fairbanks and Pickford, his favorite hotel in San Francisco was the St. Francis; the hotel returned the compliment by listing him in their advertising brochure, along with General Pershing, William Jennings Bryan and Henry Ford, as a regular guest.

San Francisco had gone crazy for movies. First shown before the earthquake as a novelty between acts in the vaudeville theaters, they had nearly pushed vaudeville and even the legitimate theater out of town.

That week Wallace Reid was scowling in *The Hell Diggers* at the Orpheum. (The *Chronicle* modestly changed the title to *Hill Diggers* to protect its readers.) Douglas Fairbanks was flashing his smile and leaping from balconies in *The Three*

Musketeers at the Strand, William S. Hart was facing the out-
laws in *The Whistle,* and Tom Mix won the approving cheers
of boys as he rode his horse Tony across the screen in *Hands
Off!* at the Wigwam.

Behold the Man, the life of Christ, which, the ads said, had
taken eight years to film, was listed at the Rialto, but the management bought space to explain apologetically that their
projectionist had accidentally incinerated two reels, so they
were showing Viola Dana in *Life's Darn Funny* instead.

D. W. Griffith's *The Clansmen,* better known by its subtitle,
The Birth of a Nation, was to open, but it was being restrained
by protests by black organizations.

The Haight Theater was showing *The Travelling Salesman,*
which starred Fatty Arbuckle romping through "many mis-
adventures in a hick town," with his "Feminine fun accom-
plice," Betty Ross Clark.

Meanwhile, the real Arbuckle was relaxing in his room. He
checked in on September 3, and two days later, at one in the
afternoon, he was sitting in the parlor of his suite in his bathrobe and slippers, when there was a knock and the door
burst open. Nine of Arbuckle's friends from Hollywood
charged into the room, carrying bottles of gin smuggled in
paper sacks, and announced to Arbuckle that he was going to
have a party. Arbuckle laughed and shrugged and called
down to room service for food, a Gramophone and a stack of
records.

Soon they were all drinking, talking and listening to the
music. Among the guests were two young women from Los
Angeles who had driven to San Francisco the day before with
Arbuckle's agent. One was an unsmiling showgirl named
Maude Delmont, and the other was a pretty dark-haired
model and film actress named Virginia Rappe.

Miss Rappe, the other guests soon noticed, had drunk too
much. She had had three gins with orange juice, and she
seemed to be acutely uncomfortable. After a while she left
the room. A few minutes later Arbuckle apologized and disappeared into his bedroom.

The guests were surprised when Arbuckle came out of his
room and announced that Miss Rappe was very sick and
needed help. Several of them went with Arbuckle into the
bedroom, where they found the girl, her clothing disheveled

and in a stupor, lying moaning, on the bed. They tried to talk to her and then carried her to the bathroom, filled the tub with icy water and plunged her in. When this had no effect except to make her moan more, Arbuckle called the desk downstairs.

H. J. Boyle, the assistant manager, a doctor and a house detective knocked on the door a few minutes later. Arbuckle explained that the girl was sick, and the four of them carried her down the hall to Room 1227 and put her to bed. Arbuckle arranged with Boyle to pay for the extra room and then returned to his suite, where the party had ended. Arbuckle dressed, went to dinner and then to a personal appearance at a theater. The next morning he returned to Los Angeles. That seemed to be the end of the story.

It wasn't. On Friday, September 9, Arbuckle got a telephone call at his home in Hollywood. A reporter from the San Francisco *Chronicle* was on the line, and he asked if he could get a statement from the actor. Arbuckle was puzzled.

Hadn't he heard? the reporter asked. Virginia Rappe had been taken to the hospital on the eighth, the day after Arbuckle returned home. This morning she had died. Maude Delmont had told police that Arbuckle had assaulted and raped Virginia Rappe during the party.

GIRL DEAD AFTER WILD PARTY IN HOTEL was the headline on the front page of the *Chronicle* the next morning. S.F. BOOZE PARTY KILLS YOUNG ACTRESS was the *Examiner* headline.

"Arbuckle took hold of her," Maude Delmont told the army of reporters that flocked to the police station, "and said, 'I've been trying to get you for five years.'" Then he dragged her into the bedroom and slammed the door. An hour later there were screams, and Maude Delmont had kicked on the door until Arbuckle opened it. He was wearing Miss Rappe's Panama hat, and he slurred, "Get her dressed and take her back to the Palace. She makes too much noise." Inside they found Miss Rappe moaning "I'm dying, I'm dying, he killed me." After the cold bath had failed to revive her, they called the manager. The official cause of death was listed as peritonitis, a rupture of the bladder.

Seeing the coming storm, Arbuckle and his attorney left by car for San Francisco Saturday morning. Sensing another kind of storm approaching, the managers of the Haight,

New Fillmore and New Mission theaters told their projectionists to keep the Arbuckle films in the cans and show Mary Minter in *Sweet Lavender* instead.

Arbuckle drove into San Francisco at 8 P.M., parked and waited outside the Crocker Bank at Market and Montgomery, where he was met by San Francisco police detectives. They drove him to the Hall of Justice, booked him on the charge of "murder of a motion picture actress," and led him past the photographers to Cell 12 of felony row.

His lawyer had warned him to expect the murder charge, telling him that it would be changed to manslaughter, which it was, but neither Arbuckle nor his attorney anticipated what the San Francisco newspapers had in store for them.

The front-page headline on the *Chronicle* was black and forbidding: ARBUCKLE IS CHARGED WITH MURDER.

Miss Rappe, Captain of Detectives Duncan Matheson explained to reporters, "without a doubt died as a result of an attack by Arbuckle. That makes it first degree murder," he said, "without a doubt."

"I desire to state to the people of San Francisco at this time," District Attorney Matthew Brady declared, "that I will spare no effort to punish the perpetrator of this atrocious crime, although I know that I will be opposed by the cleverest lawyers which money and fame can purchase."

Then, the papers began on Arbuckle.

ARBUCKLE NEVER AIDED HIS FAMILY, STEPMOTHER SAYS, announced the *Chronicle*. They admitted a few days later the story was false.

The *Examiner* turned to poetry.

> Dead, in misery and disgrace
> Dead, in shame and humiliation,
> Dead, in agony and despair,

sang Annie Laurie, the grandmotherly, white-haired mudslinger in residence of the paper. "Who was this man, Arbuckle, who gave this party, anyhow?" she demanded. "The tales of his sickening orgies have spread from one coast to the other. Everybody who knows anything about him or his kind at all ought to know what a 'party' given by him would mean."

The editors of the *Examiner* labored to find more vivid adjectives to describe the party for each successive edition. On Tuesday it was "an orgy"; on Wednesday it was "a wild orgy"; on Thursday it was "the wild Arbuckle orgy"; on Friday they abandoned all restraint and termed it the "bestial, sordid, revolting tragedy." Their reporters sought every possible angle. One day they quoted police saying it had been "the prettiest party of women ever involved in a criminal case"; another day they wrote of "the life, and the laughter, and the liquor; the drama behind closed and locked doors; the climax of a fatally injured girl writhing in agony . . ." and each day they printed at least three photographs of Virginia Rappe, along with cartoons of Arbuckle as a sinister spider in the middle of a web.

One story was datelined Thermopolis, Wyoming, under the headline COWBOYS MOB ARBUCKLE FILM: "A mob of 150 men and boys, many of them cowboys, entered the Maverick Theater here last night . . . and shot up the screen and seized the film, taking it into the streets and burning part of it." It was a wonderful story and, as the *Examiner* admitted a few days later, totally untrue.

The *Chronicle* was not to be left behind. They headlined:

FATTY ARBUCKLE INVOLVED IN ORGIES IN LOS ANGELES, SAYS OFFICIAL

MANY GIRLS ARE RUINED AND FORCED INTO DRUG HABIT AT MOVIE PARTIES

The "official" interviewed by the *Chronicle* was one Captain J. H. Pelletier, executive secretary of the Los Angeles Moral Efficiency Association. He refused to give details but hinted darkly of Hollywood parties where guests had drunk, taken drugs and "danced nude."

Arbuckle, shown the newspapers, asked an *Examiner* reporter who came to his jail cell, "I don't understand why some of the papers are rubbing it on me this way. How are the L.A. papers? Are they as rough as the ones up here?"

The publicity was having its effect. Arbuckle's films had already been withdrawn from San Francisco theaters; now they were quickly banned in Los Angeles, Porterville, Fresno, Redwood City, Palo Alto, Billings, Butte, Oklahoma City, Toledo, Omaha, Detroit and Chicago.

When Arbuckle's trial opened on November 14, eighteen grim members of the Women's Vigilant Committee sat in the front row. Behind them, eating sandwiches and cake, were eleven members of the Mothers' Club of Lowell High School. There were other delegations from the Housewife's League and the Federation of Women's Clubs. The Reverend W. K. Guthrie of the First Presbyterian Church sat in the press box as a special correspondent for the *Examiner*. Outside the courtroom, hundreds of young women clamored to get in.

One person conspicuously absent from the courtroom was Maude Delmont. Before the trial began, District Attorney Brady had realized that no other witnesses backed up her story, and most, in fact, contradicted it. Arbuckle had never grabbed Miss Rappe, had never dragged her into his room; there had been no screams, and he had never drunkenly worn her Panama hat. Reporters tried to find her, but she had vanished.

But Brady persisted. He still had two witnesses who claimed Miss Rappe had said, "I'm dying, I'm dying, he killed me," and he brought them to the stand. Arbuckle's defense attorney, Gavin McNab, called witnesses who swore that Miss Rappe, when she had got drunk before, had behaved in the same way that she had at the Arbuckle party, and that being plunged into the cold bath, as much as anything, had shocked the girl and led to her death.

Before a packed courtroom Arbuckle himself finally told his story. He had gone into his room to change clothes, he said, and he had found Miss Rappe deathly ill in the bathroom. He carried her to the bed, but when he returned, she was moaning and tearing her clothing, so he had called the other guests and the manager. Brady, cross-examining him, was unable to shake his story.

The case was given to the jury on December 4. The next day the *Examiner* reported, with considerable annoyance, AR-BUCKLE TRIAL ENDS IN DISAGREEMENT. Although the jury foreman had called Brady's case "an insult to the intelligence," two jurors refused to accept Arbuckle's innocence. "I STOOD FIRM BECAUSE I FELT HE IS GUILTY," the *Examiner* quoted one of them saying in large headlines. "Forty-four hours of persuasions, arguments and threats had no effect on the convictions of Mrs. Helen M. Hubbard, the woman who hung the Arbuckle jury." A new trial was set for January, and a weary Arbuckle, released on bail, returned to Los Angeles.

Two weeks before the second trial began, the powerful Women's Christian Temperance Union called for a nationwide ban of Arbuckle's films. Afraid of this pressure, which by now was felt by the whole film industry, the Motion Picture Producers Association hired the rigidly conservative Postmaster General of the United States, Will Hays, a personal friend of President Harding's, to create an office for the censorship of motion pictures.

The second trial was a replay of the first. Once again Miss Rappe's health before the party was debated. Then the prosecution's case suffered a major blow when McNab compelled one of the two witnesses of the "I'm dying, he killed me" moan of Virginia Rappe to admit that she remembered hearing the words only when District Attorney Brady threatened to imprison her until she did. For the second time the case went to the jury, and once again the jury couldn't agree. A third trial was set for March 23.

By the time the third trial opened the *Examiner* had got bored with the whole affair and had moved on to bigger things. It was necessary to turn back to the finance and business section to find out that, midway through the trial, the last and crucial prosecution witness to the "I am dying" remark admitted tearfully that she had been locked away in the home of the deputy district attorney for safekeeping after the party, and while there, the deputy district attorney's mother had grilled her until she was ready to admit almost anything. With that the prosecution's case sagged and fell in. The deputy district attorney began denouncing the defense as "buzzards, skunks, snakes and blackguards," and District Attorney Brady left the courtroom.

Defense attorney McNab closed calmly. "We do not know how Miss Rappe was injured," he said. "We argue only that other possibilities exist, of such strength that they are sufficient to establish a reasonable doubt of the defendant's complicity."

Then he turned to the grim delegates of the San Francisco Vigilant Committee in the audience and called them "the stone-faced women who haunt the courts, clamoring for blood, more blood."

On April 13 Annie Laurie wrote in the *Examiner* about the latest fashions in gowns. That same day the Arbuckle jury deliberated for precisely two and one-half minutes and reached the unanimous verdict that the actor was innocent. Photographers leaped forward to take pictures of the happily smiling Arbuckle.

His joy was short-lived. Five days after the verdict he was stunned to learn that Will Hays, the new film czar of the Motion Picture Producers Association, had conferred with theater owners and announced that "at my request, they have cancelled all showings and all bookings of the Arbuckle films, to give the matter the consideration that its importance warrants." The San Francisco Women's Vigilant Committee sent a telegram of congratulations to Hays.

In December, 1922, after legal pressure by Arbuckle's attorneys, Hays reversed his decision and allowed Arbuckle's films to be shown. The comedian hoped that laughter would make the public forget, but the public remembered the lurid tales of orgies, of a drunken Arbuckle staggering from the bedroom wearing Virginia Rappe's hat. They didn't laugh.

On January 14 Arbuckle announced he was giving up acting. The comedian who had been as famous as Chaplin, Fairbanks and Pickford became part of the vaudeville circuit, traveling from town to town to throw pies and grin before crowds of the morbidly curious.

Then he tried directing films, under the ironic name Will B. Good. He was working on a film when he died suddenly of a heart attack in 1933.

Maude Delmont surfaced briefly in Fresno, where she was charged with bigamy. Then she submerged once more and wasn't heard from again.

One by one the principals in the story died, but as the years passed, the story curiously grew. What had really happened at the party? A story gained wide circulation of bizarre sexual experiments using icicles or ice cubes or, as one version has it, a Coke bottle, yet there is no evidence one way or the other. The newspapers certainly didn't talk about it; in the 1920s they refused to even print the word "rape." The transcript of the trial, which might have given the answer, was destroyed in 1972 after sitting in the basement of the Hall of Justice for fifty years.

There might or might not have been an orgy in Room 1220 before Virginia Rappe and Fatty Arbuckle went into the bedroom. What happened in Room 1220 was overwhelmed by the madness that seized San Francisco afterwards, spread to Hollywood and then moved around the world.

What became known as the Hays Office expanded to be the moral overseer of the entire film industry and the father of today's X-R-PG-G rating system. Its censors made life in Hollywood nearly impossible for writers like F. Scott Fitzgerald, and once they ordered Walt Disney to erase the udder of an animated cow.

15

New Lights on the Hill

AS the Jazz Age moved toward its frantic conclusion, a new constellation of light appeared in the sky over the summit of Nob Hill, announcing that San Francisco had a brand-new hotel. Built on the dark granite foundation of the Mark Hopkins mansion and taking his name, its pale filigreed walls and château roof loomed over the Fairmont and the downtown district.

The Mark Hopkins was the creation of a boyish-looking spectacled man with a shy smile named George Smith. Smith had taken his degree in mining engineering at the University of California and then had moved to the silver fields of Nevada, where he discovered his particular talents lay in organizing money, not mining machinery. Before long he was secretary to the governor of Nevada and head of the State Industrial Commission, and he had accumulated a sizable fortune.

In the early twenties he brought his money to San Francisco and plunged into the booming real estate market. First he bought apartment houses, fixed them up, and sold them; next he leased a hotel, the Biltmore, on Taylor Street; and in 1923 he built a hotel, the fashionable Canterbury. Then, determined to conquer the field, he set his eyes on the little San Francisco Art Institute on its granite foundation across the street from the Fairmont.

Mark Hopkins had never lived in the mansion that stood on the site until the earthquake. The master financier, who helped build the domineering Southern Pacific Railroad, lived in a small house down the hill and died in a private railroad car on a siding near Yuma. His wife, Mary, an avid reader of Sir Walter Scott's romantic novels, had built the extravagant mansion with a built-in pipe organ, oak paneling inlaid with ebony, arcaded living room and cuckoo clock exterior, on a solid granite-block foundation planned and laid by the railroad's engineers.

When Mary Hopkins died, she willed the house to her new husband, Edward Searles, an interior designer who had planned the furnishings of another castle she had built in Massachusetts. Searles donated the house to the San Francisco Art Institute, whose paintings and sculpture crowded the halls and galleries until the fire. When George Smith arrived and bought the lot, the institute was housed in a new and more modest frame building. His workmen tore it down and began putting up the steel skeleton of a new hotel.

Completed in December, 1926, the Mark Hopkins was half skyscraper and half château, after New York's Waldorf-Astoria. Nineteen stories high, its two wings gracefully outstretched like arms, it was thin enough that each room had a window and a view.

Its lobby made the display of European opulence then demanded of hotels. The floor was buried under a hand-woven Austrian carpet, the walls were covered with tapestries, and heavy Spanish furniture was scattered around the room. The lobby opened into a sunlit marble patio covered with a skylight and adorned with statuary and a tiled fountain afloat with wax posies. There were two great halls under the back of the hotel: the Peacock Court, decorated with colorfully realistic murals of the bird, and the Room of the Dons, painted with murals of California's mythical Amazons by Maynard Dixon and Frank Van Sloun. An imitation of the St. Francis' Mural Room, the room caused George Smith's publicist to rhapsodize, "For the first time in the history of art in the world, two great artists have worked together, and produced nine masterpieces which will live forever."

Elsewhere, the Mark Hopkins' designers had touched other stylistic bases. The Spanish Room, a small restaurant, offered the atmosphere and decor of a medieval castle; upstairs, in the Students Room, students from the Art Institute had been permitted to exact their revenge on the hotel by painting their notion of modern art on the walls.

On opening night thousands walked through the lobby

and public rooms and admired the town's newest hotel. Fifty
guests at the opening banquet believed that the silver spoons
were meant to be souvenirs and took them home; the banquet was interrupted three times by firemen who had mistak-
en the smoke from the kitchen blowing past the red beacon
on the roof for a major inferno; but throughout it all George
Smith beamed happily, especially when he unveiled the
greatest attraction of all, Victor Hirtzler, brought out of re-
tirement in France by Smith to be the assistant manager in
charge of catering.

Soon the child of the Jazz Age would be sobered by
depression and war, but this night the hotel was dazzling and
innocent, rocking with music and laughter, as if it knew it
was meant one day to be San Francisco's most famous hotel.

16

The Strike

ON November 9, 1932, a large banner floated over the factory of Consolidated Chemical Industries near the Bayshore Freeway. It read: "Re-elect Hoover; Protect This Plant and Your Position."

That same day, a large advertisement appeared in the San Francisco *Examiner;* it was a reprint of a Republican ad from the election four years before, headlined "A Chicken in Every Pot." Underneath the old Republican promises, it said, "Let's not be scared, clubbed, intimidated. Elect Franklin D. Roosevelt President of the United States."

San Francisco, like every other American city, was split down the middle in 1932, or, more accurately, split between top and bottom. In the sitting rooms, restaurants and ballrooms of the Fairmont, Mark, St. Francis and Palace, well-dressed men and women talked about Herbert Hoover and reassured themselves that prosperity was just around the corner; the President had just assured the nation of that in a rally at Madison Square Garden, where he had appeared on the same platform with Calvin Coolidge. But a few floors below them, in the steaming basements and laundry rooms and kitchens, the dishwashers and maids and engineers and truck drivers were wearing Roosevelt buttons and talking New Deal.

On September 22 a band outside the ferry building had struck up "Happy Days Are Here Again," and a crowd had closed in on the open car driving slowly out of the building. While a wedge of policemen tried to push a path for the car through the milling sailors and workers, Mayor Rossi had scrambled over the side of the flag-draped car and dropped in next to the governor of New York.

"I'm happy to welcome you to San Francisco!" Mayor Rossi yelled above the din.

Franklin Roosevelt grasped his hand and tossed back his head. "And I'm sincerely happy to be here," he said pleasantly. Soon the car was moving slowly down Market Street behind the band. The crowd at the Ferry Building fell in behind the car to form a noisy and unruly parade all the way to the Palace Hotel.

The next afternoon Roosevelt stood before the businessmen members of the Commonwealth Club in the Palm Court of the Palace, speaking in the cadence that would be so familiar for the next thirteen years. "Definite leadership, constructive leadership, truth-telling leadership, courageous leadership," he promised, "and with that leadership, the guarantee of a New Deal."

Now it was Tuesday, November 9, and the campaign was over. Senator Hiram Johnson, a Republican, was voting for Roosevelt in the Mark Hopkins Hotel. Roosevelt posters covered the fences and walls south of Market Street. And at the Ferry Building, a small crowd had gathered.

An open limousine rolled out the doors, and the crowd clapped politely. Herbert Hoover, the President of the United States, smiled faintly and nodded to acknowledge the applause. The car drove slowly down Market Street, where thin crowds watched, mostly in silence. A few clapped; from the back of the crowd there were a few boos.

Hoover was completing a cross-country journey to his home near the Stanford University campus in Palo Alto. That night, while a crowd of reporters waited outside on the floodlit lawn, he would receive the telegraphic bulletins of his stunning defeat.

Now, riding through San Francisco, he seemed hurt and bewildered; he had been raised to high office on his reputation as the Great Humanitarian, as the organizer of war relief for the Belgians and Russians; he had thousands of letters and embroidered food sacks made by peasants to thank him; now he was being jeered by a group of unemployed workers on the steps of the Public Library; they were holding him personally responsible for the Depression. Hoover looked straight forward and ignored them.

On the steps of City Hall he was met by Mayor Rossi and cheered by hundreds of children released from school for the occasion. He told a funny anecdote of how, as a Stanford student, he had once driven his car into a lamppost on Market Street and said how happy he was to be back in California; then, when the crowd clapped, he walked back to the limousine for the drive to Palo Alto.

On the highway to Palo Alto, the advance car of the President's party slowed and stopped at the municipal park in San Mateo. The advance man got out and looked around. Where was the crowd? Where are the city officials to greet the President? he asked. There aren't any, someone told him. Silently, he got back in the car. A few minutes later the President's limousine and escort cars drove through San Mateo, passing the park without stopping.

It was a whole new world. The heady champagne of the Jazz Age had gone flat. The bottom had fallen from under the stock market, out from under prices, out from under everything, and Montgomery Street wizards who had owned millions of dollars' worth of paper one day found they owned nothing but paper the next.

Suddenly, everything was tougher. Jobs were harder to get and paid less. Perhaps they were echoing the way men were talking in the new gangster films, or maybe it was the other way around, but men seemed to talk more roughly and act more roughly; their illusions were gone. The gowned and white-tied Fitzgerald heroes gliding through the lobby of the Plaza were replaced by Sam Spade, in *The Maltese Falcon,* invading the lobby of an imaginary San Francisco hotel called the St. Mark to crack a murder. There were breadlines in Franklin Street, blue NRA eagles in the windows of the shops and WPA musicians playing concerts in Union Square. Down on the waterfront, the white-capped longshoremen were walking the picket line, led by a lean Australian named Harry Bridges.

On July 3, 1934, five cargo-laden trucks, escorted by police squad cars, drove at top speed through the longshoremen's picket line at Pier 38. They were battered with volleys of bricks and stones. Two days later the police retaliated, fighting the pickets with tear gas and nausea gas and clubs all along the waterfront. Outside the International Longshoreman's Association headquarters on Steuart Street, the police opened fire with guns; two strikers, longshoreman Howard Sperry and cook Nick Bordoise, feel dead on the sidewalk. Within hours, the spot where they fell was marked with flowers, a small American flag, and the chalked words "Police Murder."

The longshoremen gave Sperry and Bordoise a huge funeral, following the hearse down Market Street by the hundreds, carrying American flags and many wearing the uniforms they had worn in the war. At midnight on July 15 the culinary workers walked off the job. The next morning the streetcars stopped, and trucks stopped all deliveries. Grocery stores quickly sold out of food, and gasoline stations went dry. By the seventeenth 127,000 workers were participating in a general strike, and the streets were nearly empty. The strike ended three days later, and although technically it had been a failure, the workers were jubilant; they had felt their power for the first time.

It was inevitable that the unionizing fever that gripped San Francisco in the early 1930s, following the passage of the Wagner Act, which required employers to negotiate with unions, would reach the hotels. Down in the basements of the hotels laundry workers were being paid less than $20 a week. Kitchen helpers were paid $47.50 a month, plus meals, for a six-day eight-hour-a-day week. Whenever possible, the hotels would hire Filipino workers who spoke little English and would willingly work ten- and twelve-hour days. Into the steaming, subterranean world of the hotel basements came union organizers, wearing the white or blue or red buttons of their unions.

Waiters had been organized since 1901, and cooks had followed shortly afterward. Bartenders and bakers and waitresses all had their own unions, and in 1937 a union was organized to include maids, desk clerks and bellhops. But in the hotels, none of these unions were recognized by the employers; a worker wore a union button at the risk of losing his job.

The cooks union had called the first strike against the hotels in 1925; although they stayed out for four and one-half months, the strike finally broke and most of their members were fired and replaced with nonunion workers. In 1934 all the union culinary workers in the hotels walked out again, demanding a five-day week and higher wages; again the strike was broken, and most of the union men were fired.

In April, 1937, representatives of the hotel owners reluctantly sat down with the union leaders to discuss the threat of another strike. Spurred by the enthusiasm of the general strike, the hotel unions could now claim large numbers of workers in every department. They demanded recognition from the hotel owners, permission for their business agents to talk to their workers, signs posted that it was all right to join the union, hiring from union hiring halls and a five-day forty-hour week. The owners, led by George Smith of the Mark Hopkins and Robert Henderson of the St. Francis, refused.

At five in the afternoon of May 1, the desk clerks closed the registers on the desks of the St. Francis, the Palace, the Mark Hopkins, the Fairmont and the other eleven hotels rated Class A. The cooks laid down their ladles, waiters and waitresses took off their aprons, porters and bellhops set down the luggage they were carrying, and they all walked out of the hotels. They returned a short while later, this time wearing red and white ribbons proclaiming AFL PICKET, and began to walk in lines in front of the hotel entrances. As soon as they walked out, it was announced that the other unions of the San Francisco Labor Council would support them; the musicians, bakers, drivers, chauffeurs and butchers all refused to cross the picket line.

At the St. Francis the assistant manager explained to a circle of angry guests that they would have to make their own beds. A puffing Oliver Hardy had to carry his own bags up the stairs to his room, and other administrators were put to work answering the telephone. At the Palace the elevators stopped. Three hundred guests on the top floors were moved to the first and second floors. At the Fairmont there was no heat or ice, the new swimming pool closed, and the assistant manager was handed an apron and sent to the kitchen to cook for the remaining guests. George Smith himself was running the elevator at the Mark Hopkins. Angry and bewildered, nearly all the guests, unable to get clean towels or room service, checked out and left the hotels silent and ghostly. Private guards stood at the entrances, watching to see that the strikers didn't try to enter. The only trouble that day came when groups of Stanford students, arriving at the Palace for their annual Barn Dance, found it canceled because of the strike; they heckled the pickets until the pickets chased them off.

The strikers were in a good mood, expecting a quick victory. "Scramble your own eggs, folks, and eat raw meat," some of them yelled good-naturedly at some guests going into one hotel. "It's good for you." "We are convinced the hotels cannot hold out another twenty-four hours," Walter Cowan, the president of the joint board of culinary workers, announced. But the hotel owners were determined, and their doors stayed closed.

"We are prepared to hold out as long as two months if necessary," Cowan now announced. The strikers settled in for a long siege. They established cafeterias and kitchens for their members, parties for their children and coffee stands for the pickets on the line. For Mother's Day they voted to allow florists to cross the picket line to deliver corsages to the elderly women still in the hotels. When a rumor came that a hotel was trying to reopen, carloads of pickets, followed by squad cars full of police, would rush to the hotel, bringing the number of pickets from a dozen to more than 200. None of the hotels tried to reopen.

The hotel owners had long been looking forward to the business they would get from the Golden Gate Bridge Fiesta at the end of May, when the great red span, under construction since 1933, would be thrown open. Now they faced the fiesta through locked doors. They published advertisements reading: "The unions are endeavoring to impose upon us conditions which in our opinion would destroy the splendid reputation for outstanding hotels which this city has earned."

Walter Cowan replied, "We are just as anxious to end this difficulty as you are. Our jobs are at stake."

The fiesta went ahead, without the hotels. President Roosevelt touched a key that set off cannon at the Presidio, Mayor Rossi used a torch to cut through a silver chain, and formations of planes from the Pacific Fleet buzzed over the bridge as it opened for the first time. Five thousand cars lined up to cross the first day. Pullman cars were lined up at the stations in Oakland and San Francisco to house the overflow of guests.

As May turned into June and the hotel owners made no new offers, the strikers got angrier. A ball bearing was shot through the window of one of the smaller hotels, acid was poured on the carpet of another, and two nonunion plumbers were jumped by eight men and beaten as they walked away from a struck hotel. Near the Hotel Gaylord, strikers saw twelve men in full dress suits walking toward the hotel; thinking they were waiters coming to break the strike, the pickets gave a yell and chased the men down the street, cornering them in a garage until they were rescued by police. The shaken men turned out to be Shriners coming back from an initiation; the embarrassed strikers apologized.

Yet compared with the other strikes going on in the country at the same time, the hotel strike was remarkably tame. That same week at the Republic Steel Plant in Youngstown, Ohio, four strikers were killed and eighty-eight wounded in open battle between strikers and police, hired guards and soldiers. The plant owner hired airplanes to drop food to strikebreakers working inside the besieged plant, and the strikers outside tried just as earnestly to shoot them down.

As it turned to July and got soggy hot, the city started planning for the visit of a celebrity. AMELIA EARHART DUE IN S.F. NEXT WEEK, the *Chronicle* reported. The aviatrix and her Navy navigator were in New Guinea, getting ready for the hop to Howland Island, then to Honolulu and at last to San Francisco. The San Francisco city fathers moaned that with the hotels on strike there would be no place to give her a banquet; she would have to be honored in Oakland. What sort of honor was it to have Oakland give you a banquet?

The strike remained deadlocked, but the Amelia Earhart Welcome Home banquet site problem was solved: She disappeared. EARHART AND AIDE DOWN IN MID-PACIFIC—FATE IS MYSTERY, the *Chronicle* reported. "Fuel Gone, No Land in Sight, Said Last Radio from Amelia: Plane Can Float, Asserts Expert."

While the Navy was trying to find Amelia Earhart, the unions, exhausted and nearly bankrupt from the two-month-old strike, decided to make their last, best offer. If the hotels would recognize them and let an arbitration panel of union, employer and government officials decide about hours and wages, they would end the strike. It was a great concession by the union; they knew they were likely to lose before an arbitration board. But the hotel owners, feeling they had finally beaten the unions, decided to go for all the cards and try to crush the unions completely; they refused the offer.

The next day the union launched a final, desperate assault. As long as the forty Class B hotels stayed open, they knew, there would not be too much pressure on the hotel owners to settle the strike. Trying to close the Class B hotels would utterly ruin the unions and stretch their manpower to the limit, but they had to do it if they wanted to win.

Harvey Toy was the manager and owner of the Class B Manx Hotel on Powell Street, the president of the San Francisco Hotel Association and a self-described enemy of the unions. A big, square, scowling man with glasses, he was standing in the lobby of his hotel, leaning on his crutches from a recent accident, when there was a tremendous commotion outside on the sidewalk. Stepping to the door to look out, Toy found dozens of men in white hats, suits and red AFL PICKET ribbons climbing out of cars in front of his hotel, forming into lines and marching in a chain, chanting, "Unfair!" Immediately he was on the phone to the police, but the police were already arriving; two squad cars parked in front of the hotel and reserves on horseback arrived to control the curious crowd, now in the thousands, that was blocking Powell Street, trying to find out what was going on. His lobby was jammed now with strike supporters, bewildered guests and people trying to escape the madness on the sidewalk outside. Toy was on the phone to a newspaper. "My hotel is running," he shouted. "A lot of rowdies came into the hotel and created a disturbance. I asked the police to protect my property and the rowdies were thrown out bodily."

Outside, the strikers were handing out streamers to anyone who would take them. The strikers were shouting, "Unfair!" at Toy, and the reporters who had arrived were shouting "Unfair!" at the police for not letting them into the lobby. One reporter, Kevin Wallace of the *Examiner,* was particularly abusing the police for not letting him do his duty. "That's the spirit, sonny," a picket, an "underfed man who looked something like Abraham Lincoln," told Wallace and handed him a streamer. Somehow Wallace wedged himself past the police into the lobby and charged up to the first man he saw. "Where is the manager?" he demanded. "We wish to complain to the manager!"

"I *am* the manager," the man snapped. "Harvey M. Toy, at your service." Then Toy looked down and saw the banner in Wallace's hand. "Officer, show this gentleman the egress," he said to a policeman standing next to him. Wallace was shouldered out, and Toy was left to explain to a group of tourists from Alabama why their luggage couldn't be carried upstairs, while a photographer from the *Examiner* took his picture. Outside, the picketers were war-dancing on the sidewalk.

Seventy-one of his seventy-five employees had walked out. Toy, furious, hoisted a banner over his hotel proclaiming THIS IS FREE AMERICA. When the picket lines marched out front, Toy, puffing furiously on his cigar, would hobble to the entrance; if he was particularly annoyed, he would throw water balloons at the strikers. The picketers jeered him loudly and pushed up against him when he came outside; if anyone came too close he would seize them and put them under citizen's arrest; one striker put him under citizen's arrest for hitting her with his crutch. An increasingly angry Toy called for citizen vigilantes to defend his hotel if the police "cannot control the situation," an appeal that was denounced by the unions and even the other hotel owners. Contributions began to come in to the union headquarters, as news of the statement spread, from unions as far away as Maine and Alaska.

The unions won their desperate gamble. Faced with the closing of nearly all of the city's hotels and the loss of their business to Oakland, the hotel employers accepted the union offer of recognition and arbitration, eighty-seven days after the strike had begun. For the first time the workers had won, and the unions were firmly established in San Francisco's hotels. Wrote a jubilant culinary worker in the union's magazine, "Yes sir, no sir, please sir, were just about all the words these poor devils knew when they came out on strike. But now they're learning, how they are learning!"

17

Treasure Island

TWO oddly matched, giddy women rambled along the stalls of Fisherman's Wharf, collecting armfuls of French bread and cartons of shrimp and lobster which they tossed into the back seat of an open car. In the evenings they haunted odd ethnic restaurants down strange-smelling alleys, ordering bizarre dishes and spending hours at the table, talking, eating and drinking. Then they did the circuit of all the French restaurants, the Italian restaurants, the German restaurants, anywhere that served food.

In 1935 Alice B. Toklas recalled these adventures with Gertrude Stein in her cookbook:

> In San Francisco we indulged in gastronomic orgies. Sand dabs meuniere, rainbow trout in aspic, grilled soft-shelled crabs, paupiettes of roast fillets of pork, eggs rossini and tarte Chamborde. The tarte Chamborde had been a specialty of one of the three great French bakeries before the San Francisco fire. To my surprise, no one in Paris had ever heard of it.

How did one outdo a turtle race? This was the problem that was being worried over in salons and parlors up and down the Peninsula one week in the 1930s.

As the twenties had been the decade of the costume dance, the thirties were the decade of the party. Following the earthquake, society had taken shelter at their friends' country houses south of San Francisco, in the rolling hills of San Mateo and Burlingame, waiting for their mansions to be rebuilt. To their surprise, they found they liked it; they could walk through the trees, they could drive their motorcars along the ocean, and they could play polo to their heart's content. Many of them decided to stay, and the affluent suburb of Burlingame was born. The sleepy landscape began to bloom with stucco and chicken-wire Tudor mansions, Moorish castles and Florentine villas.

Then they settled down in the cathedrallike sitting rooms of their palaces and waited for something to happen. Something was always happening in the hotels in the old days; one simply had to walk down to the lobby of the St. Francis, and the next moment he was as likely as not whisked into the back seat of a Hispano-Suiza along with three debutantes and a case of champagne and roaring off to Del Monte or Lake Tahoe.

But nothing was happening in Burlingame. What good was it to have, as William Bowers Bournes had on his estate, acres of gardens, a half mile of yew trees, a Georgian mansion, a private ballroom and chandeliers that had been borrowed from the Palace of Versailles, unless you could show them off? The residents of the Peninsula realized they had to do something, and something extravagant, to lure people down from the city, or they would die of boredom. So it was that, while men in evening dress and women in long gowns cheered lustily, a small pack of very worried turtles scrambled across the floor of a Burlingame mansion.

How did one outdo a turtle race? One socialite tried a Roman feast, dressing the guests in togas, reclining them on couches and feeding them with grapes and roast pig. The avante-garde yawned; that was nothing new. Malcolm Douglas Whitman tried hanging his ballroom with huge comic strips and inviting the guests to dress as Popeye, Little Orphan Annie and Dick Tracy. That was a little better, but it still wasn't drawing them down from the city in droves. Neither did the stunt of another socialite of hiring a skywriter to draw "I love you" in the sky for his wife over his backyard; the San Francisco elite scoffed, pointing out that Ned Greenway had outdone that years before by hiring an aviator to sprinkle Cliff House with champagne.

Desperate, the Burlingamites resorted to gimmicks; at the 1937 wedding reception of Isobel McCreery and Augustus Taylor, Jr., two policemen shoved their way to the front of the room, handcuffed the groom and, while the guests screamed, dragged him toward the door. Reaching the door, the policemen turned and began to sing; they had been hired to enliven the reception.

But the social elite of San Francisco were unmoved. It was all too, too common, too much trouble to take their Rolls-Royces out of the garage for such a long drive. The Burlingamites realized that since the elite of San Francisco wouldn't come to them, they would have to take their parties to San Francisco. But how to do it so that they would take notice?

The Venetian Carnival at the Fairmont was an early effort. With the addition of striped poles, gondolas and singing gondoliers, the swimming pool of the Fairmont was transformed into the Grand Canal of Venice (as much as a swimming pool could be transformed into the Grand Canal; the gondoliers soon wearied of singing "O Sole Mio" as they poled in circles), and the guests strolled into the ballroom, decorated as the Doge's Palazzo.

But the city's real elect barely batted an eye; anyone could come up with a few gondolas and a few tons of pasta.

Then, one day, while gazing at the Pacific Fleet anchored off the Embarcadero, one of Burlingame's bright set thought: How about a battleship? Why didn't they have a party on a battleship? His friends were skeptical; whom did he know who owned a battleship? But nothing deterred a resident of Burlingame when he had an idea for a party. He called old friends and classmates to see what they could do, and before long he proudly announced to his friends that he had borrowed a battleship; to be precise, the USS *Pennsylvania,* the flagship of the Pacific Fleet.

The party was held in August, 1933. Motor launches carried the delighted guests out to their battleship. Ascending the ladder to the deck, they found the entire ship strewn with marigolds. Hedges hid the antiaircraft guns, waterfalls cascaded from the bridge, rock gardens decorated the walkways, and entire flower beds had been dug up in Golden Gate Park and temporarily transplanted onto the main deck. Musicians played atop the gun turrets, the guests fed themselves at long tables, and everyone had a marvelous time, except possibly Admiral Chester Nimitz, who looked uncomfortable, wondering how his guns would be able to fire through the hedges.

That did impress San Francisco; there was almost universal agreement that it had been one of the best battleship parties of the season. Who could outdo it?

Elsa Maxwell, with her reputation as one of the nation's leading party givers at stake, tried. She announced that she would give a barn dance at the St. Francis Hotel in 1938.

When the guests, suitably dressed in jewels and overalls, arrived, they found the ballroom of the hotel transformed into a replica of a barnyard and country store. There were live goats, a horse, two pigs, a donkey and a live cow. A country music band played between the waltzes, and Elsa Maxwell proudly showed off her special touches, a well full of beer and a life-size mechanical cow whose teats, when squeezed, spurted streams of champagne.

In November, 1937, the second great bridge, connecting Oakland and San Francisco, opened, and in January, 1939, the last ferries between the two cities stopped running. The rows of passengers behind their peach-colored editions of the *Call-Bulletin,* the contract bridge games, the men in their overcoats drinking Acme Beer, the cheers on Big Game Day and blizzard of white straw hats thrown into the Bay on the first day of fall were suddenly just memories. So, too, were the little kits of pajamas and toothbrushes the hotels would give commuters who had missed the last ferry.

The visitors continued to come from all over the world. Gertrude Lawrence left her room at the Mark Hopkins early one morning and soon was bouncing over the Pacific on a fishing boat, exuberantly singing "The Flat Foot Floogie." On stages downtown, Katharine Cornell was playing Juliet and Helen Hayes the young Queen Victoria.

In March, 1936, eighty-year-old George Bernard Shaw sailed into the Bay on the British steamer *Arandora* and immediately began to fence with reporters. "I want my breakfast and I'm going to take two or three hours," he told them. "No movie photographers? What a backward place, San Francisco. Only four papers in San Francisco? How frightfully one-horse. By the way, what was that beastly thing with the two poles?" The reporters told him it was the Golden Gate Bridge.

After breakfast, Shaw was ready for more. "Of course I'm a communist," he announced. "I can tell you that, now that my immigration papers are all right. Franklin Roosevelt is only an amateur communist. By the way, I don't approve of anything that happens in the world."

"How would you go about making a better world?" a reporter yelled.

"You'll have to read all my works to find out," Shaw replied. "But the world has never taken my advice, and has always been sorry twenty years after."

"Do you think America was wise to . . ." A reporter began.

"No," Shaw said.

Franklin Roosevelt visited the city in July, 1938, in a way characteristic of the hurried pace of the thirties. His train arrived at 9 A.M. at Crockett, and he climbed into the back of an open limousine for a hurried tour of Mare Island Naval Station. Then, at 11:05, he passed under a huge banner reading "Welcome" on the Golden Gate Bridge and entered San Francisco. Without stopping once, Roosevelt's car, with a squad of white-hatted Secret Service men on the running boards, rushed through the city at thirty miles an hour; Roosevelt waved his hat and grinned at the crowds that lined the streets from the Marina to the new Civic Center, down Bryant and onto the new bridge.

While the President was rolling through the streets, Oscar, the chef of the Fairmont, was busily assembling a glorified box lunch of chicken with mushrooms, potatoes and peas, with a Secret Service man looking over his shoulder. It was a far cry from the banquets San Francisco had traditionally given visiting Presidents, but then these were new times. The chicken was carried to a waiting truck, and escorted by police motorcycles with sirens screaming, it was driven onto the Bay Bridge at nearly the same moment as President Roosevelt. It arrived in front of him at the table in the Treasure Island Administration Building just as the President sat down at a banquet for 1,000 Democratic leaders.

After eating the chicken and addressing the Democrats, Roosevelt was back in the limousine and driving to Oakland, where he boarded the USS *Houston* and steamed in a circle around the Bay, looking at the great gray battleships of the Pacific Fleet, most of which would be sunk at Pearl Harbor in three years. Then he was back at the Oakland pier, getting back on his train, and with a whistle he was off to another part of the nation.

San Francisco refused to stoop under the weight of the breadlines and hard times. Despite the gloom at home and the news of approaching war from Europe, the city decided to overwhelm its and the nation's sorrows with one great fling of pageantry, another great fair, this time on a newly created strip of land in the center of the Bay called Treasure Island.

The walls and towers that rose there were made of wood planks covered with stucco, but you could never convince the thousands of visitors of that. The massive walls of the Court of the Moon, the huge Arch of Triumph, the statue of Pacifica and the Tower of the Sun, topped with a twenty-two-foot gilt Phoenix, seemed as awesome and permanent as the Pyramids. Critics might deride the blocky style of the buildings as "WPA Egyptian" and describe the statue of Pacifica as an "overgrown automobile radiator ornament," but the crowds came anyway, to stroll down the flower and statuary-filled Court of the Moon, to gape at the fountains and exhibition halls, and to watch Billy Rose's Aquacade.

"I'm yours for a song, for a song of romance," Morton Downey would croon, and the dozens of swimmers would link themselves together and splash in elaborate circles. Eighteen-year-old swimming star Esther Williams would smile above and below water and cavort with Johnny Weissmuller, the champion swimmer of the world, and for the finale, Fred Waring's Glee Club would sing "Yankee Doodle's Gonna Go to Town Again," while the entire cast donned red, white and blue swimsuits, seized flags and turned the pool into a watery Fourth of July parade, to the applause of the audience.

If that was too serious for the visitor, there was a fiendish machine called the Giant Octopus, or the Flying Scooters, or Sally Rand's Nude Ranch, where a dozen young ladies dressed in cowboy hats, boots, scarves and nothing else pretended to brand cattle and drink coffee behind large windows. For the more artistically bent, the Hall of Fine Arts displayed Botticelli's "Birth of Venus," brought from Florence, and Salvador Dali's "Construction with Soft Beans, a Premonition of Civil War." Next door there was a genuine artist to stare at, Diego Rivera, scowling, munching on a loaf of french bread and dabbing paint on a huge mural for San Francisco City College.

For the visionary, there were glimpses into the future. A smiling woman pressed 200 shirts a day with an electric iron in the General Electric Pavillion, and U.S. Steel offered a miniature diorama of a futuristic San Francisco in 1999 that promised that the city would be dominated by gleaming clusters of sixty-story skyscrapers in the financial district. On one side of the island, show was combined with practicality as Pan American Airways constructed a landing ramp for its great Boeing B-314 flying boats, the four-engine China Clippers that flew in each week from Manila, promising to open the Pacific to peaceful commerce.

The fair brought the world's celebrities to San Francisco. A look into Izzy Gomez's saloon on Pacific Street revealed not only the 300-pound Gomez preparing his steakburgers and beakers of red wine, but, in a corner, sipping his wine, Somerset Maugham. A stroll through the lobby of the Clift Hotel could bring one close enough to overhear Bertrand Russell talking to a reporter.

"Hitler is as mad as Napoleon was mad," Russell was saying. "I applaud Chamberlain for his honesty, love of humanity, and his courage in being duped." He paused, thoughtfully. "When I consider what clever men do," he said, "I think it's well to be stupid."

At the Mark Hopkins Eleanor Roosevelt dashed into the lobby, just back from her visit to the fair. "It's really perfectly beautiful," she called to the reporters. "The wonderful towers and buildings and colors and water effects and the flowers and the birds. The President will be so happy to hear about it, and will want more than ever to come West as soon as possible."

Someone asked about the world situation. "The situation seems more tense to me today than it did in September," she said. "Of course, things are always tense when one country swallows another."

In a corner of the International Hall on Treasure Island a Czech official was sadly untacking and taking down the word "Czecho-Slovakia" from the back of his display of shoes, glassware and cutlery. Before he left, he lowered the small Czech flag to half-mast. His country was no more, having just been swallowed by Germany.

A man who was shortly to lose his country for the second time was living in his private railroad car at the Southern Pacific station at Third and Townsend. Ignace Paderewski had a grand piano in the car, but he never practiced anymore; he saved his strength for concert appearances. He was playing Chopin that night at the Opera House. Looking neither right nor left, speaking to no one, the seventy-eight-year-old Pole walked stiffly from the railroad car to a waiting limousine. This was to be his last concert tour.

While Paderewski walked, a smiling, jovial German sat in the corner of the Mural Room of the St. Francis, hoping that someone would come up and say hello to him. Captain Fritz Weidemann, the Nazi consul general to San Francisco, had come bouncing into the city on March 7 and had almost immediately discovered that no one wanted to talk to him or have anything to do with him. At parties he was left standing alone; hardly anyone showed up for his receptions; he was left to driving around the city in his Mercedes and talking with the members of the anti-Nazi Abraham Lincoln Brigade who showed up to picket his office.

Salvador Dali, too, showed up in San Francisco. Reporters seeking to interview the world's foremost surrealist found him warming his stockinged feet in front of an unlit fireplace and gazing wistfully at an upside-down clock on the mantel of his room at the St. Francis.

In rapid French, Dali explained to the reporters that he was planning a party entitled "Surrealistic night in an Enchanted Forest." "I have ordered three goats, one giraffe, two thousand pine trees, five thousand gunny sacks, four thousand pounds of old newspapers, four truckfuls of pumpkins and one wrecked automobile," he insisted. "Please, do not take lightly the cause for which this party is being given. Europe's émigré artists need help. One of the guests is coming attired as a tidal wave."

Dali adjusted his black bathrobe and white stocking cap and began explaining his art.

"Freud probed the soul with words," Dali explained. "I use paint."

This discourse was interrupted by the arrival of the photographer from the San Francisco *Chronicle,* who was carrying a lobster, a head of cabbage and a plate of stewed calf brains. Dali shrieked with delight, rushed over to the photographer, seized the lobster, clamped it on his head, and leaped up onto the mantel.

The photographer frowned and shook his head; this was supposed to be his photograph, not Dali's. He gestured toward the bathtub. Dali, realizing he was in the presence of another artist, shrieked again, seized his wife, and plunged into the bathtub. He made sure the lobster was squarely on his head, held the cabbage in one hand, and, for good measure, pulled on a pair of emerald-green goggles and then struck a pose.

"Feed your husband the brains," the photographer instructed Dali's wife. She smiled. She didn't understand English. The photographer gestured frantically, pantomiming eating.

"Ah! Ah!" shouted Dali and his wife, and she began spooning the brains into his mouth. The photographer snapped the picture.

But Dali, Lord Russell and Mrs. Roosevelt were ignored when Hollywood came to San Francisco. A special train pulled into the Southern Pacific station, and before it had jerked to a stop, it was surrounded by a mob of screaming, shoving teenagers and their mothers, reporters, photographers, city officials, fair officials, and publicity men. The crowd practically screamed their names in unison as they stepped down from the train:

"Don Ameche!"

"Sonja Henie!"

"Cesar Romero!"

"Douglas Fairbanks!"

"Loretta Young!"

"TYRONE POWER!"

And behind the cavalcade, beaming proudly as his stars were nearly squashed by the onrushing crowd, came Darryl F. Zanuck. One of the lesser celebrities on the train struck up a conversation with one of the reporters as they were shoved out of the station by the crowd. "I'm working on a screenplay about Napoleon," he told the reporter, struggling against the mass of elbows and autograph books. "He was a fascinating man, but he had a terrible Zanuck complex."

The stars were herded through the fair, dined in the Palm Court of the Palace and put on the train back to Hollywood, but there were many more in San Francisco to satisfy the public's celebrity lust. Boris Karloff lurked on the upper floors of the Sir Francis Drake, Cary Grant was entertaining friends in his room at the St. Francis by burlesquing scenes from Noel Coward's *Private Lives,* and the two greatest detectives of all time were sleuthing about the city: Sidney Toler, who, by squinting his eyes and applying a false mustache, became Charlie Chan, was roaming the fair as the star of *Charlie Chan on Treasure Island* and at the Mark Hopkins, the tall, angular features of Basil Rathbone, the very image of Sherlock Holmes, strolled the hallway, practicing his reading of Byron's *Manfred* for the San Francisco Symphony.

One celebrity came and went without any fanfare at all. John Steinbeck phoned ahead to restaurants, warning them that he wouldn't come if they let reporters know he was there. He soon hurried south to Los Angeles, unseen and uninterviewed, to sign the contract for the filming of his latest book, *The Grapes of Wrath.*

In one exhibit hall on Treasure Island, Emory Hoffman had reason to keep Steinbeck in mind. As secretary of the Kern Country Chamber of Commerce and representative of the growers who were portrayed as oppressors in *The Grapes of Wrath* he cheerfully explained that Steinbeck was misinformed or worse and invited the visitors to see a short film on the joys of being a migrant worker, entitled *The Plums of Plenty,* shown three times a day at the San Joaquin Valley Exhibit.

Some people had a hard time enjoying the fair. At one table of the Persian Room, which then was trying to be a West Coast version of New York's 21, Martha Raye was amusing herself by throwing sugar cubes across the room. At another table, financier Louis Lurie, who had an interest in nearly every enterprise in the city, lamented, "I took an interest in the hot dog concession at the Fair on the condition that the operators would not discuss the hot dog business with me. Well, from that moment until five seconds ago, I've heard nothing but hot dogs."

On the first day of September, Fritz Weidemann parked his Mercedes, instructed his secretary that he was too busy to see reporters and locked himself in his office. A few hours later, the voices of the paper boys could be heard all through downtown San Francisco: "Warsaw bombed! Germany invades Poland! Britain ready to act! France mobilizes! Ultimatum sent to Hitler!"

That night at the fair, Jack Benny concluded his act in the

Hall of the Western States. When the laughter and applause had subsided, the loudspeakers in the hall were plugged into the radio for a special broadcast from Washington. The familiar voice of President Roosevelt filled the hall: "Tonight my single duty is to speak to the whole of America. Until four thirty this morning I had hoped against hope that some miracle would prevent a devastating war in Europe and bring to an end the invasion of Poland by Germany. . . . At this moment there is being prepared a proclamation of American neutrality. . . ."

Even as the German blitzkrieg thundered across Europe, San Franciscans kept their eyes on their fair, watched the lovely pastel lights of Treasure Island by night and the banks of flowers in the daytime. Surely this was the future, not what was happening in Europe.

When 1939 ended, San Francisco refused to relinquish its fair; the buildings were cleaned and repainted and opened again as "The Fair in Forty," and once again the bands marched through the courtyards, the fountains gushed, and thousands crowded the Hall of the Western States to see Edgar Bergen and Charlie McCarthy or to hear Kay Kyser and his Kollege of Musical Knowledge sing:

Down by the river in an itty bitty poo
Thwam thwee little fishies and a momma fishie too;
Thwim! said the momma fishie, tho they thwam,
And they thwam, and they thwam, all over the dam!

The night of September 29, 1940, the new cocktail lounge on the top floor of the Mark Hopkins was more crowded than usual; everyone was crowded on the east side of the room, watching the blue and mauve lights that bathed the buildings of Treasure Island and the crown of searchlights that fanned out from the Tower of the Sun. Suddenly the brilliant lights of Treasure Island went dark; the fair was over. Many in the Top of the Mark began to cry.

By November, 1941, most of the fair buildings were closed up and empty, and plans were being made to tear down the Tower of the Sun, but the China Clippers were still stopping at the island. On November 8 a small crowd of reporters was waiting in the Pan American reception room when the clipper, large American flags gleaming on its wings and fuselage, skimmed across the water, taxied to the ramp and, with the help of mechanics in bathing suits , was moored to the shore. The door opened, and a small man in a black suit and homburg, carrying a briefcase, stepped ashore and fought the wind to the reception room. His name was Saburo Kurusu, and as a special envoy of the government of Japan he was en route to Washington to try to revive the faltering discussions between his country and the United States.

Reporters quickly surrounded Kurusu as he entered the lounge. "Do you hope for a peaceful settlement of the Far Eastern problem? one asked.

"If I had no hope, why should I have come such a long way?" Kurusu answered.

"Do you bear proposals or questions to Washington?" another asked.

"All ambassadors have some instructions," Kurusu said. State Department officials escorted Kurusu away from the clamoring reporters to a car to take him to the airport to continue his trip east.

The discussions in Washington, as the daily headlines in San Francisco announced, did not go well; neither side would yield. On November 22 Saburo Kurusu spoke via transpacific telephone to the onetime guest of the Fairmont, Admiral Isoroku Yamamoto, in Tokyo. They used a code in which "matrimonial question" meant the negotiations and "Miss Umeko" meant Secretary of State Cordell Hull.

"How did the matrimonial question go today?" Yamamoto asked.

"There wasn't much that was different from what Miss Umeko said yesterday," Kurusu said. "Does it seem as if a child will be born?"

"Yes, the birth of a child seems imminent," Yamamoto said. "It seems as if it will be a strong, healthy boy."

The United States Army signal corpsmen tapping the telephone looked at each other and wondered what that meant.

18

"Is the Ocean Ours or Theirs?"

IT was 11:20 A.M. on a sleepy Sunday morning. Some of the hotel guests were still asleep, after staying up late to see Katharine Cornell in Shaw's *Doctor's Dilemma* at the Curran. Others were lazily listening to jive on KSAN. Around their beds many of the guests had scattered the pages of the Sunday paper. Dick Tracy, they found, had finally cornered the Mole in his hiding place under an old boiler. Skimming the movie section, they found the St. Francis Theater showing *Shadow of the Thin Man* with William Powell and Myrna Loy, and Tyrone Power and Betty Grable in *A Yank in the RAF* at the Uptown. At the bottom of the pile the front-page headline announced, FDR SENDS NOTE TO EMPEROR OF JAPAN—CRISIS NEAR BREAKING POINT.

The music on the radio stopped suddenly, and a voice broke in: "We interrupt this program to bring you a special news bulletin. President Roosevelt said in a statement today that the Japanese had attacked Pearl Harbor, Hawaii, from the air. The attack of the Japanese also was made on all naval and military activities on the island of Oahu. No further details were given immediately. At the time of the White House announcement, the Japanese ambassador Kichisaburo Nomura and Saburo Kurusu were at the State Department."

San Francisco had become, without warning, the front line of a war. That afternoon cars approaching the Golden Gate and Bay bridges were stopped by soldiers with rifles and fixed bayonets who peered into the trunks and back seats for explosives. Police cars stopped in front of the NYK Shipping Line office and took the local manager of Mitsui Lines away, under arrest. Twenty-two police and four FBI agents surrounded the Aki Hotel on Post Street, in Japan Town, and arrested the manager, ten other men, two women and three young girls.

That night, for the first time, there were no lights on the Golden Gate Bridge. Policemen shuffled nervously along the waterfront, carrying unfamiliar machine guns.

The next morning black headlines in the *Examiner* confirmed the news. US AT WAR! appeared in huge letters. PARATROOPS LAND IN PHILIPPINES. JAPS BOMB HAWAII, INVADE THAILAND. RAIDERS FLY FROM HIDDEN AIRCRAFT CARRIER—GUAM IS SURROUNDED, WAKE FALLS, some of which was true. Strangely, there were no details about the damage at Pearl Harbor.

In the afternoon one could walk down the corridors of the hotels and hear the unbroken voice of Franklin Roosevelt coming from radios in every room, followed by the applause of Congress: "Yesterday, December seventh, nineteen forty-one, a date which will live in infamy, the United States of America was suddenly and deliberately attacked by the naval and air forces of the Empire of Japan. . . ."

That night Mayor Rossi ordered all neon lights extinguished. The city sat anxiously in the darkness, under a clear, moonlit sky, not knowing what to expect next; their minds were full of the newsreel clips they had seen of London shaking under German bombs. Shortly after 1 A.M. the sound of airplanes was heard overhead and then, while people held their breath, grew more distant and went away.

The next morning the headline announced: JAPAN PLANES NEAR SF. "There was an actual attack," an Army general was quoted. "I don't know how many there were, but there were many. Some of them got in the Golden Gate, turned and headed southwest."

That settled it for many San Franciscans. That night hundreds slept in tunnels and under bridges, despite the cold, and others turned off all their lights and sat fearfully in the dark. Crowds downtown smashed store windows to turn off lights, radio stations were taken off the air, and soldiers shot at cars with headlights on. The next morning a nearly hysterical General John Dewitt, commander of the Fourth Army, ordered reporters and civil defense officials to the Supervisor's Chambers of City Hall and shouted at them, "You people do not seem to realize we are at war, so get this—last night, there were planes over this community. They were enemy planes! I mean Japanese planes! And they were tracked out to sea. We were in imminent danger of being bombed. You can thank God bombs weren't dropped! Don't be jittery, learn to take it. If you can't take it, get the hell out of San Francisco, now, before it comes. Remember that San Francisco is so full of military objectives that the whole city is a military objective. And remember that we're fighting the Japanese, who don't respect the laws of war. They're gangsters."

That day the civil defense officials tried to make up for lost time. "If planes come over, stay where you are," the city's director of civil defense advised. "Don't run. Do not scream. The chance you will be hit is small." The *Chronicle* ran columns of advice on what to do during air raids: "Play a FINE SPRAY ONLY on bombs. A JET or SPLASH of water will make them explode." Lumberyards began to advertise blackout screens: "You can black out easier with plywood. Used extensively in England and other European countries. Can be salvaged after emergency for cutouts, furniture, walls, etc."

At night a warbling siren on the Ferry Building would announce a new blackout. Curtains were yanked together, shutters closed, and lights turned off; all traffic stopped on the bridges, and streetcars stopped in the street, their passengers waiting inside in the darkness.

Everyone looked nervously around for a gleam of light that might be giving him away; any flicker of light was instantly greeted with yells and curses. Then people sat back to listen for any sound of planes overhead. In the bars and restaurants, the hotels and nightclubs, in the dozens of buses and streetcars stopped in the darkened streets of the city, thousands sat, anxiously listening. Then one or two people would begin singing, and the others would join in. The dark figures of the police and air raid officials shuffling through the night could hear the singing floating out the doors of every bar on Market Street.

Each morning that December, when the sun rose, the painters would report for work on the Golden Gate Bridge, and each morning the guards posted on the bridge, nervous and unsure of what was going on, would shoot at them, thinking they were Japanese saboteurs.

Each morning the bundles of newspapers would thud onto the sidewalk next to the newsstands, and each morning the headlines would be worse. Wake Island fell at Christmas. Submarines were reported everywhere off the coast, and each morning Army officials swore that Japanese planes had been overhead the night before.

The newspapers tried hard to report some good news. Each day the *Chronicle* reported that the Japanese invaders of the Philippines had been hurled back into the sea, until one day perceptive readers noticed on a back page that somehow they had been hurled back into Manila and had captured it. The *Examiner* reported, in large headlines, the sinking of two Japanese battleships. When the battleships inconveniently reappeared a few days later, the *Examiner* had to sink them again with more headlines.

One morning the *Chronicle* revealed that the Oakland garbage scow *Tahoe* had rammed and sunk a Japanese submarine outside the Golden Gate. The owner of the scow proudly showed off the large dent in the front on his barge, but the Navy was skeptical. There were so many reports of Japanese submarines off San Francisco, and so many Italian fishermen from Fishermen's Wharf found their boats mistaken for submarines and fired on, that the Coast Guard, with humor rare for those days, suggested that fishermen fix their boats to look like Japanese submarines. A young *Chronicle* columnist named Herb Caen made one of the worst puns in history: "Guam with the Wind."

That New Year's Eve the streets were nearly empty. The traditional Ferry Building siren was kept silent in case of an air raid. Inside the Palace Hotel 3,000 people jammed the ballroom to dance to music of Henry Busse. At midnight they and the thousands in the ballrooms and restaurants of the other hotels paused, before they sang "Auld Lang Syne," and sang, as few of them had sung it before, "The Star-Spangled Banner."

The news in the first months of 1942 was hardly any better. The list of islands and cities lost continued every day: Hong Kong, Malaya, Burma, the Dutch East Indies, Singapore and Corregidor. The Pacific was turning into a Japanese sea, and San Franciscans began to feel more and more like the people in the foremost outpost. Only Hawaii and a tiny island called Midway were left now in the central Pacific between Japan and the Golden Gate.

"All the news is bad, but not all of it is true," President Roosevelt said. Often, however, the truth was worse than the news. The Defense Department at last released what it said had been the damage from the Pearl Harbor attack; the Navy had lost only one destroyer and one battleship, and that was an old one. But a man sitting at a table in the newly opened Officer's Club in the Fairmont knew the truth. He was haunted by it.

Outside the hotel a line of taxis waited, each with a "Remember Pearl Harbor" sticker on its windshield. At his table Husband E. Kimmel, wearing a starched white uniform, sat turning the pages of the official reports that had led to his removal as the commander of the Pacific Fleet. He should have known, the reports said; he should have known it was coming. He had been awakened that Sunday morning by an urgent telephone call from his deputy; rushing outside of his bungalow at Makalapa, he had been just in time to see the tiny Japanese planes circling Pearl Harbor and watch the torpedoes erupt against the Pacific Fleet's great battleships and watch them turn over, one by one, and sink.

Now San Franciscans felt they had one duty, and one duty only: to win the war. Any complaint, any protest about anything was instantly met with "Don't you know there's a war on?"

Hollywood was enlisted to keep the morale up on the West Coast. A series of benefits for the Red Cross, for Russian War Relief, for Navy War Relief, and especially to sell war bonds and stamps kept the Civic Auditorium filled. Charlie Chaplin spoke for the Russians at the auditorium and then went to Louis Lurie's apartment atop the Sir Francis Drake to send a telegram to President Roosevelt, appealing for a second front in Europe to take the pressure off the Russian armies.

Sailors wearing shore patrol armbands filled the lobby of the Fairmont, keeping the curious away from the rehearsals of the Navy Relief Show that night in the auditorium. Behind the closed doors of the rehearsal room, Al Jolson, Eddie Cantor, Milton Berle, Charles Boyer, Cary Grant, the Andrews Sisters, Groucho Marx, Desi Arnaz, Laurel and Hardy, Abbott and Costello and Bert Lahr practiced their parts in the show. James Cagney, dressed in a civil war uniform, practiced the song and dance from *Yankee Doodle Dandy* that would win him an Academy Award later that year.

At the Palace Hotel, Bob Hope practiced with his radio troupe, rehearsing their lines for their weekly show which they planned to broadcast from the Presidio. And all the hotel lobbies were filled with musicians carrying instrument cases, for the Golden Gate Theater was featuring the best bands in the nation—Tommy Dorsey, Ted Lewis, Duke Ellington and Count Basie—playing the smooth swing that largely supplanted the frantic jazz of the last decade. People liked to stand in the back of the darkened halls and sway to the rhythms now, not dance. The one exception was the most frantic of all musicians, drummer Gene Krupa, whose thunderous beats invariably brought audiences jumping to their feet. He had a special surprise waiting for him in San Francisco.

Matthew Brady, the nemesis of Fatty Arbuckle, was still, incredibly, the district attorney of San Francisco in 1942, and he still believed, evidently, that lecherous Hollywood was trying to seduce his fair maiden city.

Krupa finished his set and, while applause still rocked the theater, made his way backstage to his dressing room. There were several men, ominously dressed in slouch hats and raincoats, waiting for him. When the surprised Krupa asked who they were, they produced badges and identified themselves as federal narcotics agents. They laid hands on him and placed him under arrest.

Several hours earlier the prop boy of the Golden Gate Theater had emerged from Krupa's room at the St. Francis carrying a small bag. Before he had got out of the hotel, he had been surrounded by more narcotics agents and arrested; they took the bag and opened it and found what they suspected: marijuana cigarettes.

"It's not a novelty for me," Krupa told a reporter as he was escorted to jail. "I've been accused of being a dope fiend. I suppose it's the way I play the drums, the energy I put into my work."

Krupa was lucky. Despite Brady's efforts to have the "dope fiend" locked away for the rest of his life, the judge gave him only ninety days in jail for corrupting a minor, saying, "It would be too severe to send an addict to prison."

Brady had just about come to the end of his usefulness. The local Democratic machine made him a judge, replacing him with Edmund G. Brown, who eventually became governor of California, as did his son in 1974.

Meanwhile, the Russians were still busily trying to promote the second front. They sent the Don Cossack Choir to sing in the Civic Auditorium, only to have them defeated, not by the German Army, but by Alfred Frankenstein, the music critic of the *Chronicle,* who thought they were awful. The Russians, however, were persistent; again and again they sent the Don Cossacks, only to have them slaughtered in print by Frankenstein. Finally, they tried a new tactic; they sent a woman sniper.

Lieutenant Ludmilla Pavlichenko was everything one expected of a woman sniper; when she arrived at the Palace Hotel, she wore a frumpy khaki uniform, boots and eight medals, including the Order of Lenin. She was, her proud escort announced, twenty-six years old, a former student at Kiev University, and she had shot 309 Nazi soldiers.

Naturally. the reporters were intrigued. "What about the second front?" one of them asked.

"You tell me," she snapped.

"What do you think of women's fashions in America, particularly women's underwear?" another reporter asked.

"I am not at all interested in your questions. You have what you have here, you must like it. Therefore, I do not comment. Besides, I am not interested."

"How did it feel to kill three hundred and nine Germans?"

She smiled. "By killing poison snakes, I saved many Russian lives."

But the overriding feeling of those first few months was uncertainty and fear, fear that often turned to hatred. Some of it was simply silly: Sailors stoned a Sukiyaki sign on Grant Street, and hostile glances turned toward anyone in North Beach who said the name Roberto, because, as Herb Caen explained in his column, "Roberto" was not a name at all, but a Nazi code word standing for Rome-Berlin-Tokyo. The editor of a local Italian newspaper accused Mayor Rossi of gestures that looked like Fascist salutes during a speech, which the mayor furiously denied.

At Fisherman's Wharf the FBI posted notices that no one of Italian, German or Japanese citizenship could go near the waterfront. Most of the Italian fisherman found themselves unable to use their fishing boats.

"I try, try, try to become a citizen," one fisherman, Luciano Mantiscalco, pleaded. "But my head, she is too hard." He was fifty-eight, he explained to a reporter, and he had twelve children, including a son in the merchant marine, a son in the Navy, a son in the Army and a daughter driving an ambulance. "Can't learn, can't write. Can't write, can't get papers. I can fish good as anybody, can't write. My head she too damn hard!" He thumped his head with his fist.

In the Top of the Mark one night a group of women were admiring the constellations of lights of the new military installations around the Bay.

"Yes, the view from here is terrific," one of the women said, "but the real time to come here is late in the afternoon. Why, with a pair of field glasses, you can see all kinds of military secrets going on."

J. Edgar Hoover, seated at the next table, turned around and glared at them but said nothing.

The Japanese went quietly. On April 7, 5,000 of them, both American and foreign-born, waited outside their homes in Japan Town for the buses that were going to take them to Tanforan Racetrack, where they would live until camps were built in the desert for them. While they waited, they played cards, and the teenagers danced to swing music on the radio. Each of them had a name tag around his or her neck. One boy, Keith Miyamoto, wore a red, white and blue suit. Finally the buses came, and soldiers with clipboards began ordering the people aboard. While they patiently waited for their place aboard the bus, they could have read about themselves in one local magazine:

> It is well known that many a Japanese servant or humble employee of any kind in the past has been an important man in the Japanese Army or Navy . . . he will do anything for the sake of his government . . . he will violate his private

The Mark Hopkins Hotel, 1927.
San Francisco Chronicle

Living room of Daniel Jackling's apartment at the Mark Hopkins, now the Top of the Mark.
San Francisco Chronicle

The Royal Suite of the Mark Hopkins.
San Francisco Chronicle

The St. Francis Hotel in 1904.
Wells Fargo Bank History Room

San Francisco in flames, as seen from the roof of the St. Francis.
Wells Fargo Bank History Room

General Douglas MacArthur arrives at the St. Francis and is greeted by Dan London.
San Francisco Chronicle

MacArthur enters the St. Francis lobby.
San Francisco Chronicle

The St. Francis and its tower.
St. Francis Hotel

**Salvador Dali, wife, and lobster
in a St. Francis bathtub.**
San Francisco Chronicle

The St. Francis with its new tower.
St. Francis Hotel

The Jack Tar Hotel.
Jack Tar Hotel

The Hyatt Regency Hotel.
Hyatt Regency Hotel

The Hyatt Regency interior.
Hyatt Regency Hotel

and other Hollywood and theater stars sang for the soldiers. Isaac Stern played for the sailors at Treasure Island, and Igor Stravinsky was conducting his own compositions at the Opera House. There was a place where classical musicians in uniform gathered to play Bach and Brahms together and a special USO for black soldiers and sailors. For the officers there were clubs at all the hotels.

What did a soldier or sailor do his last day before sailing? If he was with his family, chances are he would have a quiet dinner with them and then a long walk or a look at the city from Telegraph Hill, walking slowly, saying very little.

If he was alone or with ship or barracks mates, he went to Playland-at-the-Beach to ride the Diving Bell, the Motor Boats, or the Big Dipper. Then he might go downtown to one of the city's flourishing nightclubs. At Joe DiMaggio's Yacht Club on Fisherman's Wharf, he could watch and listen to the rumba rhythms of Chuy Penita's Latin Orchestra, or he could step across the street to the Copacabana, where Juanita Rios looked sultry and sang and Lolita and Ardo clung to each other and rumbaed from one end of the dance floor to the other. Closer to the center of town, in Chinatown, the Wongettes, "those dancing Chinese cuties," might be prancing at the Chinese Sky Room, while down the street, at Kubla Khan, the petite Chinese exotic dancer Noel Toy performed her "Pants Dance of the Nations," removing one by one panties decorated with the flags of eight of the United Nations, with an appropriate dance for each. Nearby, in the Forbidden City, for some odd reason Charlie Low and his Chinese singers wore cowboy hats and chaps, twirled lariats, stomped across the floor in square dances and sang "Home on the Range." A few blocks away in North Beach, Tani, the Tahitian Tornado, danced at the Hurricane, and at Finocchio's, bewildered soldiers and sailors, who most likely didn't know what they were in for, watched female impersonators dance a gay floor show while Mrs. Finocchio beamed at "my boys!"

Then they might go to the hotels. In the Rose Room of the Palace hundreds crowded around the dance floor to listen to the music of Henry Busse's orchestra and the singing of Betty Brownell. More servicemen jammed the Mural Room of the St. Francis, watching the antics of an enormous woman in a flowered muu-muu who belted out songs, joked and called herself Hilo Hattie, between the songs of Harry Owens and his Royal Hawaiians.

Then there would be the cab drive up the hill for the inevitable final destination, as the clock crept toward the midnight curfew. The cabs stopped at California and Mason, and the soldiers and sailors joined the long line that led into the lobby of the Mark Hopkins and up to the elevators marked "Top of the Mark."

Downstairs in the Peacock Court Dorothy Lamour might be singing "The Moon of Manakoora," but the servicemen wanted to go to the top, to take a last look at the city.

The nineteenth floor of the Mark Hopkins had once belonged to the Copper King, Daniel Jackling. When George Smith built the Mark, Jackling had left his enormous suite at the St. Francis and had designed the floor at the Mark Hopkins precisely to his taste, with a grand piano, an immense library, high ceilings to house his art collection, dark wood paneling, and spectacular views of Marin, Oakland and San Francisco. In 1936 Jackling moved to a more traditional estate down the Peninsula. George Smith decided to convert the apartment into the first "Sky Room." Clearing out the walls, he had enormous picture windows and a bar installed and opened it, complete with an orchestra, Don Francis and his Franciscans. It proved so successful the orchestra was kicked downstairs and room made for more tables.

By the middle of the war 30,000 servicemen a month were coming to the Top of the Mark for their final view of the city. Fliers went to the bar and asked for the squadron bottle, getting a free drink by signing their name and squadron number; the person to finish the bottle bought a new one for his squadron mates who would follow him. Every table was crowded with young sailors and soldiers, sometimes with their families, sometimes with girlfriends, drinking slowly and watching the lights of the city with intense interest, trying to see it all and remember it all.

One night in June, 1943, two people seated at a table at the Top of the Mark were paying little attention to the view. Their eyes were fixed on each other, and they were talking intensely, in low voices.

None of the people surrounding them there knew it, but

the man would soon be instrumental in ending the war. He was Dr. Robert Oppenheimer, the director of the research at an installation on a remote mesa in New Mexico where scientists were trying to develop a new kind of bomb. He had come to San Francisco and Berkeley frequently to recruit new scientists, and each time he had met with the woman; but now the research had reached a critical stage, and this would be his last trip here. He couldn't tell her what he was doing, how long he would be gone or if he would ever see her again.

Her name was Jean Tatlock. She was ten years younger than Oppenheimer. The daughter of an English professor at Berkeley, she had been an ardent supporter of the Loyalists in Spain, a contributor to the farm workers in California and an occasional member of the Communist Party. While the tall, lean Oppenheimer read no newspapers or magazines, didn't listen to the radio and didn't even have a telephone and considered politics a needless distraction, she was concerned for every cause and chided him for his indifference. Since they had met in 1936, they had considered themselves engaged twice, but they were really too much alike, too melancholy, too intense, for either of them to be able to lean on the other. Oppenheimer had married someone else, but he still came back to see Jean. He looked at her with his pale-blue eyes, his perpetually puzzled expression. Her eyes were green and equally puzzled.

They rose from the table and walked slowly to the elevator. She would drive him back to her apartment on Telegraph Hill, where they would spend the night, and in the morning she would drive him to the airport.

Unknown to the two of them, a man had been closely watching them as they had sat in the Top of the Mark. Now he too rose, followed them downstairs and, when he reached the lobby, went to a telephone. As soon as the couple left, he telephoned Boris Pash, the chief of counterintelligence for the Ninth Army.

Seven months later Jean had heard nothing from Oppenheimer. She had become more and more depressed and had gone to psychiatrists for care, but nothing would relieve her. She locked the door of her apartment, filled the bathtub and placed cushions on the floor beside it. Then she swallowed a handful of pills and began writing letters. When the drug began to take effect, her writing trailed off into a scrawl. She put down the pen, leaned forward and plunged her head into the bathtub.

The last page of her letter, unaddressed, read, before it trailed off: "I wanted to live and to give and I got paralyzed somehow. I tried to understand and couldn't. At least I could take away the burden of a paralyzed soul from a fighting world."

Back at the Top of the Mark the bar was closing; it was midnight. The older patrons looked out at Treasure Island, still brightly lit, and remembered how it had been. Where the swan boats had once pedaled across the Lagoon of Nations, there were now the lights of a Navy hospital; where the Court of the Moon had been, there were now the glowing windows of barracks; and where Saburo Kurusu's flying boat had landed, there were now the dark silhouettes of warships riding at anchor.

Downstairs in the hotel, and in the St. Francis and Palace and Fairmont, men set to sail the next morning were unable to sleep.

Some took off their clothes and ran shouting through the corridors. Others brawled with other soldiers and sailors in the hall, slugging and shoving, until the fights were broken up by military police and the hotel staff and they fell into bed, exhausted. For others, the YMCA Canteen kept a wedding chapel.

The next day the Top of the Mark had a different clientele. In the northwest corner, which the staff called the Weepers' Corner, mothers, fathers, wives and girlfriends watched the troopships steaming slowly past the green-brown hills of the Golden Gate out into the Pacific.

By April, 1945, the hammer had swung clear across the Pacific. Japanese suicide planes were desperately trying to stop the American fleet anchored off Okinawa. Admiral Yamamoto was dead, shot from the sky by American P-38s.

In San Francisco everyone had become accustomed to news bulletins, but this one, on the afternoon of April 12, hit them like a blow: "We interrupt this program to bring you a special bulletin: President Franklin D. Roosevelt died unexpectedly today at 4:35 P.M. of a cerebral hemorrhage." Later that day stunned and weeping San Franciscans heard a new voice on their radios, the high-pitched and strange voice of their new President, Harry Truman, telling them, "I ask only to be a good and faithful servant of my Lord and my people."

San Franciscans particularly felt the loss of Roosevelt, because he was to have come to the city in two weeks to open the first meeting of the United Nations. Now the future of the world organization, put together after an arduous series of meetings, seemed in doubt.

The idea of the United Nations had come at the first meeting of Roosevelt and Churchill on board the cruiser *Augusta* in a lonely Newfoundland harbor in 1941. They had issued the Atlantic Charter, pledging an international organization to end war. There had followed more conferences at Casablanca, Quebec, Moscow, Cairo and Teheran, where Stalin, Roosevelt and Churchill met for the first time, and then a meeting at Dumbarton Oaks, near Washington, in August, 1944, where the foreign ministers hardened the idea into a set of principles and a charter. Stalin, Roosevelt and Churchill had met one last time at Czar Nicholas' summer home near Yalta and approved the arrangements, and San Francisco had been selected as the site of the first meeting.

Late in April the delegates began arriving, and banks of foreign flags unfurled over the entrances of the hotels.

At the Top of the Mark an elegantly dressed man with a clipped mustache sat alone at a table before opening time, sipping tea and reading a newspaper. He was Anthony Eden, the British foreign minister. Some days he was joined by Clement Attlee, who would shortly surprise the world by replacing Winston Churchill as prime minister. Elsewhere in the Mark Hopkins was Moses Grant, the representative of Liberia, a delegation of Syrians, whose country was fighting France for independence, and T. V. Soong, the delgate of Chiang Kai-shek's China. A representative of Mao Tse-tung's army in the mountains of Yenan was politely informed that he was not welcome at meetings.

Twenty-seven flags flew over the St. Francis. Iran, Canada, Turkey, Egypt and France, represented by Charles de Gaulle's foreign minister, Georges Bidault, were there. Bidault was established in Suite 1219–1221, the scene of the Arbuckle scandal. There were also a host of Latin American nations, watched over by a young undersecretary of state for the Americas, Nelson Rockefeller, who occupied the most expensive suite in the hotel.

But the stars of the St. Francis were the Russians, who occupied the entire tenth floor. They had come on their own ship, the *Smolny,* and immediately proceeded to seal off their floor from the rest of the hotel. Guards were posted at all the stairways and elevators; everyone's security cards were checked two and three times; the wires on all the clocks were cut to keep them from being bugged. The Russians themselves, led by the dour ambassador to the United States, Andrei Gromyko, and the even more dour people's commissar for foreign affairs, V.M. Molotov, usually wore plain military tunics and boots and the Order of Stalin on their lapels and spoke to no one. The staff, who began to refer to the floor as the Frozen Wastes, wasn't even sure how many there were; rooms would be vacant one day and occupied the next. Manager Dan London once ventured through their floor and recalled, "As I walked I could hear the click of door locks opening behind me, and had the feeling of many eyes upon me. When I turned abruptly around, a wave of doors would quickly close." After hearing these stories, San Franciscans were delighted to learn that the Russians had secretly applied for extra ration coupons to buy shoes.

If the Russians at the St. Francis were the most mysterious, the Arabs at the Fairmont, led by the then-Prince Faisal of Saudi Arabia, were easily the most colorful. Hundreds of spectators gathered in the lobby to see them come and go in their flowing robes, with jeweled daggers swinging from the waists of their bodyguards. "You should see me on a horse!" one of the bodyguards called to the spectators. One reporter, uncertain of the spelling of the prince's name, boldly stepped up to him and asked him to write down his name. Faisal smiled, wrote with a flourish and swept off; only then did the ecstatic reporter find that the prince had written his name in Arabic. The reporters closely observed every habit of the Arabs, noting that they were extraordinarily taken with fried chicken and green apple pie and that they despised American coffee, which managed to violate every point of the traditional Arab code that coffee be "black as night, sweet as love and hot as hell."

The Yugoslavs, the Norwegians and the Belgians also lived in the Fairmont; so did the venerable South African prime minister, Jan Christiaan Smuts, a veteran of the Boer War, and the Czech foreign minister, Jan Masaryk, the son of the first president of his country, who was himself to become a martyr fighting against a Communist takeover, pushed out a window into the courtyard below.

Serenely established on top of the Fairmont, in the ten-room penthouse belonging to Mrs. James Flood, was the secretary of state of the United States, the silver-haired, dark-browed former chairman of the board of U.S. Steel, Edward Stettinius.

The Palace Hotel, meanwhile, had been taken over by the 2,500 reporters who had come to cover the conference. William L. Shirer, Lowell Thomas, Drew Pearson, Raymond Swing and H. V. Kaltenborn marched in and out of the lobby. Hedda Hopper wandered in and out under her outrageous hats, and in a corner, slouched against a pillar, with a New York police press card tucked in the band of his hat, Walter Winchell barked machine-gun bulletins into a telephone. Nearly lost in the confusion was a young reporter for the Hearst papers, just out of the service and working on his first job. His name was John Fitzerald Kennedy.

It was the largest gathering of nations the world had ever seen; fifty nations were represented by five prime ministers, thirty-one foreign ministers and innumerable diplomats of lower rank. To keep them happy, San Francisco had organized an enormous army of greeters and translators and drivers to show them the city and explain to them the peculiar ways of Americans . The Army drove them to Muir Woods, and the Navy flew them in blimps around the Bay, and no party was complete unless it could offer at least one delegate expounding on the future of Europe or Asia. Anthony Eden was most in demand, Molotov was impossible to get, Georges Bidault was worth a lot of points if you could get him in your living room, and so was Field Marshal Smuts; but most people had to settle for a second or third deputy minister and hope that he would end up prime minister someday and remember them. Groups of tourists and schoolgirls swarmed through the lobbies, looking for someone they recognized. Inevitably they would give a big cheer for the tall, dapper man with the homburg and rolled umbrella who they thought was Anthony Eden but was actually Dan London, the manager of the St. Francis. London would smile and wave and thank them in an English accent.

From the day Stettinius and the foreign ministers of the large nations opened the conference, their voices booming over loudspeakers to the crowds gathered outside the Opera House, the conference faced an unprecedented collection of problems. First of all, there were the colonial nations, like Syria, that wanted immediate independence; the Syrian delegates nearly rioted on the top floor of the Fairmont, trying to get upstairs to see Stettinius in his penthouse. Secondly, there was the matter of what group of people would represent a government. Poland, for instance, was represented by two governments, a pro-Western government in exile in London and a pro-Soviet government in exile in Moscow. The Russians solved this problem by occupying the country, inviting the London Poles to come share in the government and then arresting them all for "diversionist activities against the Red Army."

When the arrests were announced in the middle of the conference and the cries of outrage threatened to bring down the entire United Nations, Molotov showed how much he had learned from American politics. He called a press conference in the Colonial Ballroom of the St. Francis, and then, while hundreds of reporters jammed the room, shouting "Poland! Poland!" he blithely ignored the entire issue, speaking about international understanding and brotherhood and speculating that there would be peace if the war ended. The other delegates were satisfied, Molotov was pleased, the reporters were bewildered, and the conference went on as if nothing had happened. That was international politics.

After endless conferences behind lines of white-helmeted military police in the offices of the Veterans Building near the Opera House, and private meetings between Eden, Molotov, Soong and Stettinius in the penthouse atop the Fairmont, the conference finally, several weeks behind schedule, arrived at a charter. Germany had abruptly surrendered in the middle of the conference, sending Eden, Molotov and Bidault hurrying home; in the early days of June the last details were settled by their deputies.

No one was entirely satisfied with the work. The small nations, particularly the Latin Americans, felt the big nations had too much power; the big nations didn't feel they had enough; and no one was sure how, if someone wanted to start a war, this assembly of diplomats could stop it. But surveying the war-wrecked world around them, watching the loaded gray troopships sail out the Golden Gate, they knew they had to do something, and San Francisco was the starting place.

On June 25 a silver C-54 touched down at Hamilton Field, taxied over to a row of waiting automobiles and stopped. The door opened, the military officers waiting below saluted, and Harry Truman, the President of less than a hundred days, stepped uncertainly down the ramp.

He looked, on that visit, like a small-town merchant on his first trip to the big city, wearing a bow tie and a wide-brimmed white hat with the brim turned up. He grinned and shook hands with the waiting dignitaries and then climbed into the back of an open car for the ride over the Golden Gate Bridge into San Francisco. Curious crowds lined the streets for a look at their new President as his car made its way downtown and then up Nob Hill to the Fairmont.

The people watching weren't quite sure what to make of him as he rode by; their eyes were still filled with the grand gestures of Roosevelt, his tossed head, his confident wave, his reassuring voice on the radio. Until that stunning moment when they heard that Roosevelt was dead, most of them had never heard of Truman; by now they had heard his flat Missouri accent on the radio, had seen pictures of him in a loud Hawaiian shirt and a baseball cap and had read what he told reporters after Roosevelt's death: "Boys, if newspapermen pray, pray for me now." No one expected much from Truman. He surprised them.

The people of San Francisco didn't know it then, but Truman, sitting in his new office in the White House, had faced Molotov and Gromyko and had told the veteran Communists the United States and Britain had kept their part of the Yalta agreement, and Stalin had better do the same. We are, Molotov replied. Not in Poland, Truman had said, and he had demanded to know what the Soviets thought they were doing by arresting the London Poles. "I have never been talked to in my life like this," Molotov had protested, and Truman had replied, "Carry out your agreements, and you won't get talked to like this."

Truman had one more secret in his mind, the knowledge that the world's first atomic bomb was being assembled in a remote New Mexico base and would be tested in three weeks.

None of this was evident that afternoon, as Truman was shown to his room, a two-bedroom suite on the fifth floor overlooking Powell and Sacramento streets. From his room Truman could see the loaded transports sailing out into the Pacific, and he could remember the predictions that he had been given about Operation Olympic, the invasion of Japan planned for November 1. A million American casualties were expected, and MacArthur predicted the war might continue in the Japanese countryside for ten years. San Francisco was preparing for the expansion of shipyards and barracks that would be needed to house the thousands of troops passing from Europe to the Japanese Theater of Operations. From his window Truman could see the lights of the dockyards shining through the night.

The next afternoon Truman stood on the stage of the Opera House in front of the massed flags of the United Nations and a line of soldiers, sailors and marines . As the delegates from other countries lined up with him, he leaned over and signed his name in a blue leather book embossed with the gold symbol of the world entwined by olive branches, making the United States a charter member of the United Nations.

Three weeks later, early in the morning in the desert near Alamogordo, New Mexico, Robert Oppenheimer watched the eruption of the first atomic bomb. As the great mushroom cloud billowed skyward, he turned to the awestruck men with him and quoted from the Bhagavad-Gita:

> If the radiance of a thousand suns were to burst at once
> into the sky, that would be like the splendor of
> the mighty one.

I am become death
the destroyer of worlds.

At Potsdam, President Truman, meeting with Churchill and Stalin, was handed a message: "Operated on this morning. Diagnosis not yet complete but results seem satisfactory and already exceed expectations."

On August 6 Senator Hiram Johnson, now seventy-nine, the slayer of Wilson's League of Nations, died of a cerebral thrombosis in Bethesda Naval Hospital. The same day a single American B-29 dropped Oppenheimer's bomb and destroyed the city of Hiroshima.

Headlines and news bulletins tumbled over each other the next few days, climaxing with the sudden blast of all thirty of San Francisco's air-raid sirens at 4:04 P.M. on August 14, 1945. The Japanese, the wire machines typed, had accepted the American terms of surrender.

The city went mad. Hundreds of phone books were shredded and hurled from office windows, along with wastebaskets full of trash and buckets of water; thousands swarmed out onto Market Street into the crawling jam of cars and streetcars honking their horns and ringing their bells. Sailors and soldiers tossed away their caps and seized the hats of hapless civilians and began a parade down the middle of the street, walking along the roofs of the streetcars, breaking the windows out of cable cars, tearing the fenders off buses and building bonfires in the street. Others, mainly servicemen who now wouldn't have to fight, crowded the liquor stores. It took sound trucks and 2,000 military police to finally restore order on Market Street.

It was over, but it wasn't over; there was more to come. Some remembered the words of Eduard C. Lindeman of the American Civil Liberties Union at a conference on "Whom to Hate and How Much" held at the St. Francis Hotel in 1942.

"If we become haters," he said, "and the war is over, and there is no Hitler to hate, we are going to hate each other."

19

MacArthur

IN April, 1951, San Francisco greeted its last hero. The city had poured out into the streets to welcome Grant, Admiral Dewey, Teddy Roosevelt, Wilson and Pershing, Lindbergh and FDR. Now, in one last romance with greatness, they came out, 600,000 strong, to see Douglas MacArthur.

The world seemed to be breaking apart in those grim postwar years. Russia seemed to have become our implacable enemy, Eastern Europe had gone Communist, China had fallen to Mao Tse-tung, Greece was torn by civil war, and Western Europe was in ruins and calling for aid. At home Americans, confused, sought solace in a nostalgia craze, dancing the dances and wearing the clothes of the 1920s. They looked desperately for someone to blame for what was happening to their once-orderly world and for someone to lead them out of their troubles. In April, 1951, they found them both, in the persons of President Truman and General MacArthur.

The seventy-one-year-old general had been an Army officer for forty-eight years. He had been the youngest Army general at age thirty-eight, commanding the Rainbow Division in France in 1918, he had been Chief of Staff, and he had commanded the Army in its drive across the Pacific to Japan. He had a gift for the memorable phrase ("I shall return" and "There is no substitute for victory") and for memorable appearance, invariably dressed in a battered khaki raincoat, gold-braided cap, aviator sunglasses and long-stemmed corncob pipe. But he had two failings: He was vain, referring to himself always as MacArthur, and he believed that he, not President Truman, should decide foreign policy in the Orient.

Now MacArthur was commanding the first United Nations peace-keeping army in Korea. At first, his bold plans worked. He surprised the North Korean army invading South Korea by circling behind them and landing marines at Inchon, driving them in disarray back to the Chinese border, but then he himself was surprised when the Chinese sent 300,000 soldiers across the border, driving his men into a retreat back through the bitter-cold snowy valleys. The war slowed to a stalemate.

The impatient MacArthur, without consulting Truman, called for an invasion of mainland China by Chiang Kai-shek's troops on Taiwan and called reporters into his office in the Dai-Ichi Building in Tokyo to tell them, "If the U.N. merely blockades the Chinese coast and smashes their railway system, the Chinese will quickly be reduced to impotence." The commander of the American Legion promptly agreed and said he thought, for good measure, the Japanese and Germans should be rearmed to fight the Russians. The San Francisco *Examiner* also agreed, running a cartoon of MacArthur heroically wrestling a Russian bear, nipped at by hounds labeled "Disloyal officials," "U.N. Meddlers" and "Fellow Travelers."

When he read MacArthur's statement, Truman was furious. A few weeks earlier he had summoned the general to a meeting at mid-Pacific on Wake Island. When MacArthur had arrived, he had ordered his pilot to circle, trying to make Truman's plane land first so the President would have to greet him coming down the ramp. Truman saw the trick and ordered his pilot to circle until MacArthur's plane landed or ran out of gas and crashed. After a few minutes MacArthur gave up and landed, but he refused to greet Truman when he got off his plane.

Shortly after the Wake Island incident, Truman had sent MacArthur the secret terms of a peace proposal he was giving the Chinese. MacArthur promptly called in reporters and gave them copies, explaining dramatically how *he* would only offer the Chinese annihilation unless they gave up.

Now, with MacArthur's demand for an invasion of China, Truman came to an end of his patience. With the support of the Joint Chiefs of Staff, he sent a telegram to MacArthur in Tokyo firing him, and read a statement to reporters: "With deep regret I have concluded that General of the Army Douglas MacArthur is unable to give his whole-hearted support to the policies of the United States and of the United Nations."

The *Examiner,* and millions of Americans, who had almost religious confidence in the man with the pipe and braided cap, reacted with a thunderclap of outrage. TRUMAN OUSTS MACARTHUR IN QUARREL OVER KOREA—A TRAGIC DAY FOR AMERICA, roared the *Examiner.* "It is a victory of the politicians who have been consistently wrong over the strategist and statesman who has been consistently right." Then the paper unloaded invective on President Truman, quoting a San Franciscan calling him "that jackass" and another saying, "The commies must be laughing at us. It is unbelievable that one man can be that stupid."

The *Examiner's* outrage was widely shared. Flags were lowered to half-mast in Oakland, the San Francisco office of Western Union turned down dozens of telegrams to the White House because the language was too abusive, and Lieutenant Governor Goodwin Knight of California called the President the "Missouri dunderhead." Senator Joseph McCarthy speculated that Truman made the decision while drunk, while an *Examiner* columnist suggested he had been drugged by his advisers.

MacArthur himself, in Tokyo, took the news serenely. He had something else to look forward to: a triumphant return to the United States and, in sixteen months, the nominating conventions for the presidency of the United States. Two hours after his firing was announced, he received a telegram from Mayor Elmer E. Robinson of San Francisco, begging him to make his first landing in that city "so that its citizens may pay you homage," an invitation to address a joint session of Congress and a call from Dan London, the manager of the St. Francis, inviting him to stay at his hotel. MacArthur accepted them all.

As the day neared for MacArthur's return, the nation's pulse seemed to move faster, and city after city begged for his presence. President Truman was booed when he appeared at Washington Stadium, and the mayor of San Francisco urged its citizens to hail the returning general with church bells, factory whistles and ship horns. The *Examiner* pictured him wreathed with flags, with light glowing from his head, and hymned, "Let the gladness that is in our hearts be shown to him, that he may know the happiness we wish for him. All America rejects the act of dismissal that has brought General MacArthur home and despises the little man responsible for that act."

At the St. Francis on the night of the general's arrival, Dan London inspected the two-bedroom suite which had been readied for MacArthur and his wife. For Arthur, the general's thirteen-year-old son, who had never been in the United States, London had brought in a new round-screened television set. Outside, a workman fastened the letter *M* to the door. In front of the hotel the general's flag of five white stars on a red field floated over the entrance. One hundred police struggled to keep back the crowd that had already gathered in Union Square, finally calling for help from military policemen and servicemen in uniform in the crowd, who locked arms to keep it back from the entrance. The tiny girls of St. Mary's Chinese Drum Corps checked their costumes and held onto their glockenspiels.

The *Examiner* had an extra edition on the newsstands, picturing MacArthur holding an olive branch, with a halo over his gold-braided cap, and praising him with these words:

> We thank thee, Heavenly Father,
> For General Douglas MacArthur
> He is God's gift to America.
> Where is there an arch high enough to
> Welcome you, hero of humanity?

All along the route, veteran policemen, who had seen the crowds that had met Roosevelt and Admirals Nimitz and "Bull" Halsey, watched the hundreds of people pressing up to the street with amazement.

At 8:35 P.M., MacArthur's plane, the *Bataan*, touched down at San Francisco Airport. The plane rolled over to the terminal, where it was suddenly bathed in a harsh white light for the television cameras. Then the door opened, and 10,000 people began cheering as Mrs. MacArthur, smiling, appeared in the door, and then the general, in his khaki overcoat and braided cap, holding his son by the hand. He descended the ramp, while 200 military policemen and a double line of police tried to keep back the crowd. A military band struck up "Some Enchanted Evening," and guns began to fire salutes, while MacArthur smiled and shook hands with Mayor Robinson and Governor Earl Warren; then the police lost control of the crowd, and only the gold-braided cap could be seen.

It took the general's car two hours to get to the St. Francis. Its presence was heard before it was seen by the great waves of cheers that surged ahead of the car and echoed through the stone canyon of Post Street. The St. Mary's Chinese girls started bravely hammering on their glockenspiels, but the music was drowned out by the tremendous roar as the car turned the corner. The crowd pushed against the backs of the police and soldiers holding arms around the entrance, and Dan London, standing by the entrance canopy, saw a snow of white descending around him. He looked up and saw with horror that the guests had shredded pillows and were pouring feathers out the windows. Then the car was at the entrance, surrounded by the crowd and lit by TV lights, Dan London was seizing MacArthur's hand as he stepped from the car, and the gold-braid cap was moving toward the door.

MacArthur, his wife and son and Dan London, accompanied by military aides and a photographer, marched through the roped-off lobby into the elevator and upstairs to his suite, where they stopped and watched the first television set the MacArthurs had seen.

The crowds were out early the next morning, packed onto the Market Street sidewalks. The police watched with awe as they kept coming, until they filled the side streets, balconies and roofs. Looking down from a rooftop, senior officers estimated that there were more than 500,000 people along the route and jammed into Civic Center Plaza. Overhead an *Examiner* helicopter circled, taking pictures. People in the front rows held tiny flags and looked anxiously down the street.

There was a distant coughing of motorcycles, and as the cheering of the crowd rose, a phalanx of police bikes roared

past, closely followed by a truck, a car jammed with TV and
newsreel cameras and then the city's 1934 Lincoln open limousine, decorated with an American flag, and in the front
seat, Arthur MacArthur, wearing a baseball cap, and in the
back, a smiling General MacArthur, flanked by Governor
Warren and Mayor Robinson.

The crowd screamed, many burst into tears, and women
rushed forward to toss flowers into the open car, until it was
nearly filled to the windows. Then, when the car had passed
and the roaring had moved down the street, hundreds
crowded around the display window of Sherman and Clay's
music store to watch the picture of the general's car on the
tiny screens of the store's new TV sets.

They saw the tall figure of MacArthur saluting in front
of the City Hall during the playing of "The Star-Spangled
Banner." Then the thousands in the Civic Center Plaza
heard Governor Warren's voice booming over the loud-
speaker: "Isn't it great to have General MacArthur home today?" The roar of cheers shook the government buildings
and echoed down the side streets. After short speeches of
welcome, the crowd hushed and heard the deep, measured
voice of MacArthur, saying, "I have no political aspirations
whatsoever. I do not intend to run for any political office and
I hope that my name will never be used in a political way.
The only politics I have is contained in a simple phrase
known well by all of you . . . 'God bless America.'"

San Francisco's cheers were still sounding in his ears when
MacArthur's car left the Civic Center Plaza and drove to the
airport. The *Bataan* took off once more and carried him to
Washington, where he stood before a hushed Congress, telling them, "I now close my military career and just fade away,
an old soldier who tried to do his duty as God gave him the
right to see that duty. Goodbye." In the wild cheering and
applause that followed, an awed Congressman turned to a
reporter and said, "We heard God speak here today, God in
the flesh, the voice of God."

MacArthur, of course, had no intention of fading away.
He went on to New York for an even greater reception there
and meetings with Republican leaders and William Randolph Hearst, the publisher of the *Examiner* and the other

Hearst papers around the country, and then he began a series of speeches to state legislatures, blasting the policies of President Truman.

Americans didn't like their gods to dabble in politics, at least not so openly. Slowly, but perceptibly, the fever died down; the moment had passed . The nation had emptied itself of its passion and now settled down to serious matters.

MacArthur was at the Republican convention in Chicago sixteen months later, delivering the keynote address, but he was out of uniform now, without his gold-braided cap and raincoat. The television cameras showed him as an ordinary mortal. By the end of his speech the delegates were talking to one another, and his voice could hardly be heard.

MacArthur returned to his hotel suite in New York and waited for the convention to call him. The *Bataan* waited on the runway at LaGuardia Airport, its engines running, to fly him to Chicago to accept the nomination. But the call never came. As MacArthur watched on television, the convention nominated Eisenhower. The *Bataan* was rolled back to the hangar, and MacArthur and his era began to fade into memory. Disillusion had flooded in. Never again would San Franciscans pour into the streets for a man. Never again.

20

Zen and Château Lafite Rothschild

IN February, 1950, Jane Russell, the buxom star of Howard Hughes' western epic *The Outlaw,* reclined on a sofa in her suite at the Mark Hopkins and told intrigued reporters what she thought about the world.

"The H-bomb?" she said. "Most unfortunate. But necessary, perhaps. But unfortunate."

That could be said about a lot that was happening at the Mark Hopkins, and in San Francisco in general, in the 1950s.

As the end of the war approached, San Franciscans began to look forward to an imperial future. What London had once been, what New York was, San Francisco was to be: the banking and administrative center for a whole corner of the world, the capital of the Pacific rim. Hadn't their city been the home of the United Nations, if only for a short while? Hadn't all eyes focused on the Golden Gate? Now China and Japan, Chile and Argentina would tremble at Montgomery Street's whim. The largest corporations in the city, the Bank of America, Crocker Bank, Wells Fargo Bank, Levi Strauss, Kaiser Industries, Del Monte, Bechtel and Pacific Gas and Electric sent representatives to a Bay Area council to plan the imperial city's future. They planned an expanded port, a new airport, a rapid transit system and a magnificent multi-skyscraper world trade center.

San Francisco became involved in the peculiar politics of the 1950s. In 1949 the Palace canceled a scheduled banquet of the Civil Rights Congress which had planned to raise funds for eleven Communist leaders jailed in New York. "We simply canceled the banquet," Edmund Rieder, the general manager, said. "The character of the organization is not the type we care to have at the Palace."

Two years later Senator Joseph McCarthy spoke in his rasping voice in the Palm Court: "Anyone who can add two and two must conclude that unless the course changes, in eight to ten years Communism will have created a red world. There can only be two reasons why we are losing; either because of fumbling, stumbling idiocy, or "—he paused, and his voice dropped—"or because it was planned that way."

In Washington, D.C., in Room 2022 of the Atomic Energy Commission Building, attorney Roger Robb stood next to a table piled with the transcripts of tape recordings, copies of classified government documents and old security diaries. Across from him, his eyes as pale and haunted as always, sat Dr. Robert Oppenheimer. Robb was demanding to know, over and over, why Oppenheimer had met with Jean Tatlock in San Francisco ten years earlier, when she had been a known Communist. When the hearing concluded, Oppenheimer would be stripped of his security clearance and denied access to the facilities necessary to his work.

Up at the Fairmont, General Dwight D. Eisenhower summoned the valet, Henry Kalfain, the same Henry Kalfain who had caught Franz von Papen in 1915. When Henry opened the door, Eisenhower greeted him in Turkish and rattled off a string of Turkish phrases. The commander of the North Atlantic Treaty Organization forces beamed and explained he had just been inspecting NATO bases in Turkey and wanted to try out what he had learned.

A few weeks later, when President Harry Truman walked with his entourage through the lobby of the Fairmont, someone yelled out, "We like Ike, Harry!"

Truman yelled back, "I like him too—in the Army!"

But California, like the rest of the nation, wanted Eisenhower in the White House. He was overwhelmingly elected in 1952 and then sought renomination in 1956 from the Republican National Convention, meeting in San Francisco.

President Eisenhower himself didn't need to come until the last day of the convention; his renomination was assured, so the Presidential Suite of the St. Francis was tenantless.

What little excitement there was was provided by Harold Stassen, the "Boy Wonder" governor of Minnesota, who was determined to dump Vice President Richard Nixon from the ticket and replace him with Secretary of State Christian Herter, the son of the man who had painted the murals in the Mural Room. From his room at the St. Francis, Stassen telephoned and wrote and pleaded with delegates, but to no avail. Richard Nixon, serenely established on the seventh floor of the Mark Hopkins, was unshakably on the ticket. Eisenhower didn't want any petty squabbling in the party, and he telephoned his managers in San Francisco and told them so.

So despite the Republicans' ingenuity in hiring the assistant director of Cecil B. DeMille's *Ten Commandments* to stage the convention, and despite the thunderous and endless and prearranged cheers of "Stick with Dick" from the galleries, ordered to reassure Nixon, the convention was a colossal bore. The most energy in town wasn't at the convention at all, but in the Venetian Room of the Fairmont, where Ethel Merman was belting out "There's No Business Like Show Business," in a voice that nearly blew out the walls.

Society, meanwhile, was devoting its attention to the opera. Since the opening of the Opera House in 1931, opening night at the opera had become the single most important date on the entire calendar.

Reservations for the pre-opera dinner in the Mural Room had to be made five months in advance. The dinner and wine order was made at the same time as the reservation; by the afternoon of the opening a long row of silver trays, platters and champagne buckets, each tagged with the name of a prominent San Francisco family, would be waiting in the kitchen of the St. Francis.

That afternoon the hairdressers would be frantically busy. Sometimes Antoine, the director of the most exclusive of the hairdressing salons, would leave his bedroom in Paris, with its Lalique glass coffin, and fly to San Francisco to direct the arrangements; he would be met at the airport and handed, as he demanded, an armful of white lilies; then he would walk purposefully through the terminal, drawing every eye. He habitually wore a snow-white suit with a red sash, and his black hair was dusted with blue powder.

While the hairdressers worked, the servants would be preparing the gowns and taking the diamond tiaras and emerald chains out of the safes and strongboxes. Dorothy Spreckels' servants would by laying out her $15,000 platinum mink coat. Dressing tables would be lined with bottles of perfume: Coax Me or Tabu or Tiger or Shocking or Shameless. The men's dressing tables would be fragrant with bottles of Sage Brush or Polo Field.

Then the procession of limousines would begin, first to the St. Francis, where the kitchen staff was placing the oysters on the half shell, crab legs Voltaire and breast of capon Muscotte on the silver platters. Two hours later, when the headwaiter signaled that it was time to end the dinner and be off to the opera, the limousines would line up like a great funeral procession at the door of the St. Francis, swallowing up the stream of men in white ties and gowned women ablaze with diamonds.

The opera itself served as a pleasant break before the next event, the post-opera dinner in the Peacock Court of the Mark Hopkins. Once again, the great funeral procession of limousines streamed by the Opera House and then wound its way to the top of Nob Hill. Inside the Mark, the tables were laden with chicken, welsh rarebit gala, poached eggs benedict, broiled club steak a la opera, peach melba, baba au rhum and decorated with golden candelabra, vases of flowers, and the chief embellishment, the star of the opera, whose presence at one's table was the chief goal of the evening. When the platters were clear, the champagne gone and the opera star either giddy or unconscious with exhaustion, the long procession of limousines appeared again, and the diamonds and emeralds once again began their journeys back to their safes and strong boxes to slumber until the next season.

In a dimly lit coffeehouse called the Trieste on Grant Street, several blocks from the tourist shops of Chinatown, a bearded man in a black sweater, worn Levis and sandals pulled a lever on an ornate bronze machine, and a thin stream of boiling espresso coffee spurted into a cup. In the background, someone pattered on a bongo drum while another bearded man read, in a low monotone, from Allen Ginsberg's latest poem, "Howl": "I saw the best minds of my generation destroyed by madness, starving hysterical naked. . . . "

This was North Beach, San Francisco's Greenwich Village,

in the 1950s. San Francisco had always been a haven for bohemians, but never like these. In old San Francisco, to be bohemian was to wear hobnail boots and a flannel shirt to the Palace Bar, as Joaquin Miller had done, or to lecture the patrons there on socialism, as Jack London had done; no one questioned whether it was all right to drink at the Palace Bar. But now a whole dark city had been created in the North Beach cellars and coffeehouses, an alien city of dim candles on bottles and Kerouac novels and Zen and discordant, eerie jazz.

At the hungry i, its owner, Ernest Banducci, adjusted his black beret and listened attentively to his new comedian, Mort Sahl. Wearing an old sweater and holding a newspaper, Sahl was delivering a rapid commentary on the FBI, jazz, President Eisenhower, sports cars and psychiatry. Lenny Bruce sat listening in the audience, knowing and hating the fact that audiences were comparing him to Sahl.

Just up Broadway and down half a block, the poet Lawrence Ferlinghetti sat at the counter of his City Lights bookstore, watching the customers sitting on the floor as they studied Kerouac's *On the Road,* a book called *Beat Zen, Square Zen and Zen* and his own *Coney Island of the Mind.* Local poets piled his desk with handwritten manuscripts.

Down Green Street at the Jazz Cellar, black-sweatered customers sat in the smoky haze, nodding at the eerie howling of the saxophone; another poet, Kenneth Rexroth, began a rhythmic reading of one of his poems, raising his voice and chanting the words with the music.

Above, on Grant Street and Broadway, Gray Line tour buses filled with guests of the St. Francis and Fairmont crawled along the street, slowed by the packs of black-jacketed motorcyclists who filled the streets and sidewalks, as the guests looked with horror at the bearded crowds and dark entrances of the bars and cellars.

One day in 1958 a private railway car slowly trailed into the Oakland station, attached to the rear of one of the Southern Pacific's crack trains. When it came to a halt, a Rolls-Royce pulled alongside. The door of the train opened, steps were put in place, and Lucius Beebe stepped imperially down to the platform. He had come to San Francisco, he announced, to eat.

It was the idea of *Holiday* magazine. It had previously hired Beebe, a columnist who wrote about food with the same lofty authority that St. Augustine used when writing about sin, to take a spendthrift's tour of New York; he had been assigned to dine at the best restaurants and spare no expense.

Now *Holiday* assigned Beebe to do the same thing for San Francisco. "Of all the cities in the U.S.," he wrote, "not excepting New York . . . not even excepting New Orleans . . . none has the associations of luxury that gather around San Francisco." Beebe set about to test the city's reputation.

First he established himself in the Presidential Suite of the Palace Hotel, strolling through its forty-foot drawing room to inspect, with some satisfaction, "the marble bathroom no larger than a skating rink." This, at $100 a day, should give him a comfortable base. He left his St. Bernard dog to take care of the railway car.

In the morning Beebe ate a modest breakfast of shirred eggs, chicken liver, broiled sand dabs and lamb chops with grapefruit, coffee and raisin toast while he planned his campaign. Dressing carefully, he wandered out of the Palace to see how much money he could spend.

He warmed up for dinner by having a modest $43 lunch of abalone steak and pineapple at the patio restaurant of the Canterbury Hotel, which kept him occupied until it was nearly time for dinner. Then he moved downtown to Ernie's for some serious eating. Alfred Hitchcock had admired the decor of Ernie's so much that he had it reconstructed on a sound stage in Hollywood, populated it with Jimmy Stewart and Kim Novak and used it as the set for his film *Vertigo*. Beebe ignored the decor and concentrated on a plate of Long Island duck à l'orange with asparagus, cracked crab and a chocolate soufflé for dessert, accompanied by a modest 1934 French wine. When he was finished, he looked with satisfaction at the check: $70.

The next day after breakfast Beebe aimed his Rolls-Royce at Bardelli's, an elegant luncheon restaurant on O'Farrell Street, where he wolfed down crab legs au gratin Mornay and Jerusalem pancakes in flaming brandy. The tab was a paltry $19.25; evidently he was saving his energy for dinner.

Beebe settled down at a table at the Blue Fox and was quickly deluged with flaming crepes suzette, flaming coffee, snails and tenderloin wrapped in bacon and mushrooms, artichokes and hollandaise. "The management adores serving anything resembling a major fire hazard," Beebe noted happily. Through the smoke of his dinner, he sipped a $20 bottle of claret. His check came to $61.

After dinner he felt lonely, so he visited the theater, saw Noel Coward in the leading role of his play *Nude with a Violin* and took Mr. Coward for highballs at the Terrace Room of the St. Francis. Then, looking at his watch, he realized he could still fit some eating in; he hurried to Grison's Steak House for a quick midnight snack of lobster, cherries jubilee and champagne, adding $25 to his bill.

The next morning Beebe realized he had better do some *real* eating or the editors of *Holiday* would be dissatisfied. He hurried to Julius' Castle on Telegraph Hill for a quick lunch of Rex sole meunière ($30.60) and sped through the streets to Alexis' Tangier on Nob Hill, across from the Mark Hopkins, where, by beginning with caviar and vodka, working up to chicken Kiev and Australian lobster tails sautéed with mangoes and curry in white wine and drinking an almost ridiculously rare champagne, he achieved a respectable bill of $86. That was a little better.

Sunday was his last day. Lunch was taken care of in the Palm Court of the Palace: an oyster cocktail, mignonettes of lamb on rice and, for dessert, small heart-shaped blobs of cream floating in an enormous bowl of fresh strawberries and red wine, with a bottle of Château Lafite Rothschild. The manager and chef watched approvingly over his shoulder as he worked through the meal. Then he was back in his Rolls-Royce and off to the Fleur de Lys on Sutter Street. Four bottles of wine waited for him on his table; he used them to help him through the broiled oysters Anna, the vichyssoise and the filets de boeuf Périgourdine with truffles and foie gras. Taking the last spoonful of cherries bombe and swallowing the last gulp of Château d'Yquem 1948, he leaned back heavily in his chair, and asked for the check—$81.50. With the $41.20 check for lunch, his bill for the day came to more than $120, besting the check for the first day. Triumphant, Beebe waddled to his Rolls-Royce; he had spent more than

$500 on food in four days, in addition to his hotel bill of $430. Now he could report to his editors at *Holiday* that his mission was accomplished.

One of the remarkable things about Beebe's expedition (besides the fact that *Holiday* was willing to pay for it) was that he didn't eat dinner at a single hotel—lunch, yes, but never dinner. It would have been unthinkable for a visitor not to eat at the old pre-earthquake Palace and unthinkable for anyone in the first decades of the century to miss Victor's cooking at the St. Francis; yet by the 1950s the hotels had vanished from the epicurean map of San Francisco.

Of course, the old chefs at the Palace and Victor had had some unfair advantages: Labor had been cheap and easily available (Victor's staff was evidently never informed that slavery had been abolished by the Constitution), and they cooked only one main course a day; if Victor felt like serving reindeer, then all the guests at the St. Francis ate reindeer, whether they liked it or not.

But there was no question that the food at the hotels declined as their restaurants became simply another item to be calculated into the balance sheets; it was difficult to stand in front of a grim-faced accountant with an adding machine in front of him and justify the purchase of reindeer or sand dabs. Furthermore, the hotels were dealing more and more now with corporate travelers passing through, who didn't care what they had for dinner as long as it was steak, well done. Fewer and fewer diners were willing to sit through great culinary extravaganzas orchestrated like Wagnerian operas; they wanted Muzak for the palate.

So it was string beans and lamb chops and not truffles and champagne that saw out the last great hotel chef, Lucien of the Palace, when he retired in 1954.

Lucien had been a potboy in the kitchen of an elegant restaurant in Lisbon at the same time that Victor had been undermining the Portuguese monarchy. Somehow he found his way into the French Army and then, after World War I, worked his way across the Atlantic as a saucier on the *Majestic*. He worked at a series of New York hotels, finally ending up at the Navarro, which was managed by Baron Edmund Rieder, soon to become the manager of the Palace. When he moved to San Francisco in 1942, Rieder brought Lucien along and installed him like a field marshal in the glass-walled office of the huge kitchen, overlooking a staff of 125. A banquet for 1,500 was nothing unusual; as Lucius Beebe observed, "The old baronial formula for preparing a banquet in Czarist Russia: 'Souse ten thousand ortolans, roast a herd of sheep,' is something he and the Palace would take in stride." Before long, lawyers, doctors, publishers and even the French consul were begging for tables, and the whole Palm Court would gaze in awe as Lucien went to work on one of his celebrated desserts; eight chefs would march out of the kitchen, surround the table of the diner, and each chef would make a separate sauce, until they were all poured together in eight cascades of cream, chocolate and brandy.

Such grandeur was too good to last; restaurateur Michael Romanoff confided to Lucien that he wanted to open a new luncheon spot for the movie colony in Hollywood and offered Lucien a regal salary if he would leave the Palace and come with him. After some hesitation, Lucien agreed, packed his utensils and flew to Hollywood.

A cloud of gloom descended over the Palm Court, and not least over the table of Baron Rieder; the Palace kitchen without Lucien was like the Vatican without the Pope.

Baron Rieder thought he knew something about human nature and something about vanity; playing on a hunch, he flew to Los Angeles and went to eat lunch at Romanoff's.

Sitting at his table, Rieder looked around him; the other customers were eating tossed salads, cottage cheese, and roast beef and drinking iced tea. There wasn't a truffle or a spreading of pâté de foie gras in sight. Using all his imagination, Rieder ordered the most elaborate, sophisticated meal he could, composing it like a symphony from the first overture of hors d'oeuvres to the last sip of brandy.

No sooner had the order gone into the kitchen than Lucien came flying out, surprised and delighted, to greet his old boss. He acknowledged sadly that he was not being challenged; he was a symphony conductor directing a high school band. Rieder offered his sympathy.

For the next few months, every time Rieder went to Los Angeles he stopped at Romanoff's, and his order was a signal to Lucien that he was there. It was getting worse, Lucien grumbled. Everyone in Los Angeles seemed to be dieting.

Rieder painted a picture of a San Francisco starved for one good truffle, desperate for a light soufflé.

It finally worked. One day the diners of the Palm Court were delighted to find the sole Dugléré and tournedos Rossini coming out of the kitchen and to watch the eight chefs again concocting the eight sauces. Lucien had come home to the Palace.

But once again, it was too good to last. Sheraton took the Palace, and there was no place for Lucien. The grand age of hotel dining rooms had come to an end.

21

Ben Swig's Tower

THE Mark was still as lively as it had been during the war. Carmen Cavallaro played *The Warsaw Concerto* on the piano, Rudy Vallee warbled "Your Time Is My Time," Carmen Miranda, dressed as an animated fruit salad, pranced through the Peacock Court, and down in the lower bar author William Saroyan pulled fried shrimp out of a greasy paper bag and popped them into his mouth. When the other patrons stared, Saroyan turned to them, held out the bag and demanded, "Wanna shrimp?" They quickly turned back to their martinis. Upstairs in his suite, Arthur Godfrey reached to the basket of fruit by his bed, took a peach and bit into it. He wrinkled his nose; it wasn't ripe. He hurled the peach out the window, only then realizing that his false teeth were still in it. Pulling on his bathrobe, he hurried down the stairs, through the lobby, out the doors and onto Mason Street, just in time to see the peach, and his teeth, flattened by a truck.

The corporate officials of the Bay Area Council were not amused; there was no room in their plans for quaintness; the Mark Hopkins might be fun, but it was certainly not the ultramodern hotel of the 1950s that was needed for the capital of the Pacific.

When the Mark Hopkins was built in 1926, gargoyles were an appropriate decoration for office buildings, and hotels tried to look like French châteaux. Their interiors resembled movie sets more than public rooms, under the theory then popular that, if a hotel lobby looked like the Hall of Mirrors at Versailles, the guest would feel more important. Therefore, George Smith had furnished the first Mark Hopkins lobby with a false wood-beam ceiling and ponderous Spanish furniture, striving to make his hotel look like a set from *Zorro*. Now, in the ultramodern 1950s, he had to catch up with the times. He announced to the press that he had hired Dorothy Draper to redecorate his hotel.

Today to mention the name of Dorothy Draper in the company of interior decorators draws approximately the same response as belching in the dress circle of the San Francisco Opera House. But in the 1950s, the era that gave us Howard Johnson's and the Edsel, her ideas were considered the unassailable summit of good taste.

In 1952 Hart Smith, George's son, who was in charge of the redecoration, stood next to Dorothy Draper in the Peacock Court and proudly told assembled reporters, "Only the name and theme of peacock luxury will remain when we're through. Everything in the Peacock Court and Lounge will be transformed. Modernized . New."

It certainly was. Dorothy Draper cast her eye around and went to work. She walked into the sunlit lower bar and ordered them to paint over the skylight. Sunlight wasn't modern. Following her directions, workmen moved into the Peacock Court and began painting it in a nightmare of bright blues, pinks and greens. As an enchanted Hart Smith watched, she moved hedges trimmed into peacocks into the room, a feather-colored carpet and bright-pink plastic chairs.

Then she turned her attention to the dark and tranquil Spanish Grill. That room, she decided, should become, for reasons obscure to everyone but her, a little bit of old Scotland. It was promptly blanketed in electric green tartans, brass mugs, pictures of men with bagpipes and ruby-colored plastic chairs and renamed the Kiltie Bar and the Lochinvar Room, to "recapture the romantic spirit of Scotland." Downstairs, she sensed challenges yet unmet. She created the Vienna Coffee House, a terrifying collection of vinyl walls, pink swivel chairs and phony windows overlooking Austrian palaces. Finally, she applied her attention to the lobby, transforming it into a faithful reproduction of the set of a Debbie Reynolds movie. Dorothy Draper collected her check and flew triumphantly back to New York, and George Smith bravely smiled and said he loved it. He now had a modern 1950s hotel.

In those years San Francisco was systematically savaged by the planners seeking that illusive regency over the Pacific. If a neighborhood stood in the way of an office building, the neighborhood had to go; bulldozers swarmed throughout downtown, chewing old buildings to kindling. The California Division of Highways laced the ruins with elevated freeways, and soon the electric railway tracks on one deck of the Bay Bridge were pulled up to increase the volume of automobile traffic into the city. Before long downtown parking spaces were as rare as diamonds, and nearly as expensive. The shadows of the new buildings began to darken the once-sunny streets. The planners of the Bay Area Council could walk through the financial district, look up, squint their eyes and almost, almost imagine that they were in New York.

But once, in 1947, San Francisco fought back. In January Mayor Roger Lapham, "the businessman's mayor," efficient, no-nonsense and incorruptible, delivered his annual message to the Board of Supervisors. After reviewing the police and fire departments and city administration, he came to the subject of the municipal railways.

"I am strongly urging the Public Utilities Commission," he said, "to get rid of our cable car system as promptly as possible. While I know there are strong sentimental reasons for keeping this old, ingenious and novel method of transport going, the fact remains that the sentimentalists do not have to pay the bills, and do not have to run the risk of being charged with criminal negligence in the very possible event a cable breaks and a car gets loose on any of our steep hills. They are old, outmoded, expensive and inefficient, and do not belong in any modern transit system."

Did this bombshell stir San Franciscans to righteous anger and furious action? No. "We'll Miss Them," the *Call-Bulletin* editorialized. That said something about how New-York-minded San Francisco had become.

But the cable cars did find one defender: Mrs. Hans Klussmann, a painter, the wife of a surgeon and the president of the San Francisco Federation of the Arts. She quickly wrote a letter pointing out that Mayor Lapham was wrong: The cable cars had fewer accidents than the buses, their cables never broke, they had an emergency brake that practically welded them to the street if they started to get away, and, most of all, they were fun, and people liked to ride them. So what if they lost money? For every dollar they lost, the city got back three from the tourists who came to San Francisco to enjoy their noise and color.

Mayor Lapham denied all this. He wrote back to Mrs. Klussmann:

> The horse car had to go, the cable cars have to go. Who knows but that we may soon develop, and even in San Francisco adopt, an atomic-energy propelled bus, and that even before the tears of the petition-signers are dried. San Francisco is bound to grow and develop. Waving petitions in the face of progress can no more stop it than could King Canute stop the waves by royal decree. Those of our citizens and visitors who take delight in bumping the bumps and riding the curves should find their enjoyment in the chutes, scenic railway or spinno-rocket at the beach.

"Mayor Lapham," Lucius Beebe observed, "is possessed of all the sentiments of a pismo clam."

Mayor Lapham went ahead with the plans to scrap the cable cars. Herb Caen reported one morning, ". . . the city has quietly tested a new, twin-engined bus that can stop and start, fully loaded, any number of times on the steepest hills." The April issue of *Bus Transportation* carried a full-page ad by the bus manufacturer, the Twin Coach company of Kent, Ohio, boasting, "Motor Coaches with a Future replace cable cars with a Past. . . . Dual twin coaches climbed to the challenge. They successfully combined unprecedented *performance* with much-needed *economy*. . . ."

But Mrs. Klussmann was not deterred. On March 4, 1949, she called the first meeting of a Committee to Save the Cable Cars at the Public Library and began circulating a petition.

Since their inventor, Andrew Hallidie, had ridden the first cable car down Clay Street at 5 A.M. on a foggy morning in 1873, those clattering antiques had gradually captured the hearts of their riders.

As they passed the petitions from hand to hand, San Franciscans passed on their favorite cable car stories: of the conductor who had rudely shouted, "Kowfodakuv!" each time his cable car swung into a curve, until one day he himself forgot to hang on and was flung off; of the late car on Powell

Street, whose conductor and grip stopped the car, collected change and bought hamburgers and coffee for themselves and the passengers; of the grip who played "Happy Birthday" on the bell, with all the passengers singing, for a lonely old woman; and of the day when somehow the cables had reversed and the cable cars began running backward, making the cars drive frantically for cover.

By 1947 most of the cables had been pulled up and buses put on the lines, but three lines remained, and Mrs. Klussmann was determined to keep them. As a Powell Street shoeshine man told Lucius Beebe, "When it's goodbye the cable cars, Mister, so quick it's goodbye San Francisco."

Each day the petitions filled with more names, and Mrs. Klussmann's crusade gained notice. The City of Paris department store put on a show of paintings and photographs of cable cars, and the Emporium began to sell cable car print dresses. Schoolchildren were asked to write essays about them, the symphony added *The Cable Car Concerto* to its repertoire, and a barbershop quartet, singing in harmony, rode the Powell Street car over Nob Hill.

Visitors were enlisted in the campaign: Katharine Cornell swore she would never play in a San Francisco without cable cars, thousands of tourists signed the petition at tables in front of the St. Francis, and Mrs. Roosevelt, intercepted on one of her periodic dashes through the lobby of the Mark Hopkins, agreed that they were an invaluable asset to the city.

Mayor Lapham wasn't interested. Under his direction, new double-engined buses, loaded with sandbags to simulate passengers, were tested on the hills.

Yet the campaign kept getting more and more attention, as stories ran in *Time* and *Life* and the cable cars were pictured on the cover of the *Saturday Evening Post.* Mrs. Klussmann began to receive letters from all over the country, showing her that the rest of the country liked the cable cars, even if San Francisco didn't.

"Tell them, the jugheads," a man in Clipper Gap, California, wrote, "that without the cable cars San Francisco would be just another Detroit, Pittsburgh or Des Moines."

Scorning Mayor Lapham's arguments for economy, the *Pacific Builder* editorialized, "Think of all the space and ink, time by typesetters and typists and other savings if we dropped the 12-letter name 'San Francisco' and used the 6-letter word 'Frisco.' "

In the distant Mojave Desert, the Chowchilla *News* thundered, "Cable cars are as much a part of San Francisco as the palms are a part of Chowchilla."

Mayor Lapham was stung that his friends not only weren't talking to him anymore, but were wearing cable car tie clasps and print dresses, but he refused to abandon his vision of atomic buses whirring up Nob Hill. Stubbornly insisting that he was right, he asked the Twin Coach Company to show conclusively that the bus was better than the cable car.

The Matterhorn-like slope of Powell Street to the summit of Nob Hill was selected for the demonstration. At the appointed time, the Twin Coach Company's most powerful dual-engine bus growled up to the curb at Powell and Sutter. The door hissed open, and a delegation of city officials, Municipal Railway officials, representatives of the Twin Coach Company and reporters stepped aboard. Photographers remained outside, gazing up the hill, ready to record the assault. From far down the street, the dinging of an approaching cable car could be heard.

A bus company officer gave the word, and the driver shoved the coach into gear and pressed down the accelerator; the twin diesels roared and breathed blue exhaust fumes as the bus began to crawl up the steep grade, leaving the photographers behind. It crawled steadily toward the summit; gravity pressed the passengers back in their seats as the bus tilted skyward.

Then the bus began to slow. The engines began to roar furiously, belching clouds of blue smoke, and the whole coach vibrated with the strain as the bus inched upward, then inched more slowly, then stopped, hanging on the hillside. The driver pressed the accelerator to the floor. The bus shook madly, and the engines screamed in anguish, but they were unable to gain another inch. Painful screechings ground from the engines, and the bus company engineers winced—their engine was strangling. Gradually the bus began to slip back, inch by inch, then foot by foot, its overloaded engines futilely trying to catch a hold on the steep slope. The representatives of the press looked at the representatives of the city, who looked at the representatives of the Municipal Railway, who looked at the representatives of the Twin Coach Company, who looked at their shoes, or at their watches, or out the windows of the bus.

Policemen cleared the traffic from the intersection of Powell and Sutter so the bus could roll back to where it had started. As it did, the clanging grew louder, and the Powell Street cable car appeared, rattling jauntily up the hill, the grip leaning back on his lever. The conductor and grip and passengers on the old wooden slat benches looked curiously at the exhausted bus panting in the intersection as they clattered past. Then the cable car tilted skyward and climbed up the slope, its bell ringing, until it leveled out at the very summit and came to a halt beside the Fairmont Hotel.

The war was by no means over, but it was downhill from there on. The petition gained enough signatures for an election, the election committed the city to keep the cable cars, and Mrs. Klussmann fought eight more battles in the coming years to prevent the city from circumventing or undermining the results of that election and won them all. While four-engine Lockheed Constellations flew high overhead, then new jet-engine Boeing 707s, then huge-bodied Boeing 747 jumbo jets, then, in 1975, the slim fuselage of a supersonic French Concorde, the cable cars continued to rattle precariously up and down Nob Hill, watched over by the vigilant Mrs. Klussmann.

While the struggle over the cable cars was going on down below, Ben Swig, the new owner of the Fairmont was puzzling about how to fit a four-masted clipper ship into the Fairmont swimming pool.

Benjamin Harrison Swig was the ultimate postwar man. "You've got to live modern," he declared. "You've got to think big to be big. . . . The whole San Francisco skyline is going to change. We're going to become a second New York."

Born in 1893 in Taunton, Massachusetts, Swig was a determined worker; without a college education, he worked his way to be the youngest treasurer of a bank in the United States when he was only twenty-three. Moving into the more profitable field of real estate, he became a land broker for Penney's, Woolworth's, Grant's and other nationwide chains, locating and buying sites for their stores all across the nation. In 1944 he journeyed clear across the country on the City of

San Francisco, only to have his projected deal fall through. It seemed a shame to leave San Francisco without buying something, so he bought a hotel; the St. Francis Hotel. It was a bargain. Plagued by wartime restrictions, the Crocker family had put the hotel on the market for $5,000,000; Swig bought it for $750,000, plus the mortgages. He put up only $20,000 of his own money. He sold it a year later for a profit of more than $1,000,000.

In August of the same year Swig, pleased with his first acquisition, inspected the Fairmont. Despite its magnificent exterior, wartime restrictions and age had worn down the Fairmont on the inside; the Linnards had been paying more attention to their dreams of a helicopter landing pad than they had to the plumbing, and consequently the pipes burst an average of fifteen times a day. Because of wartime rent controls, some of the elderly widows living there paid only $50 a month for their rooms. "She was nothing but an old ladies' home," Swig recalled. "You could shoot a cannon through the lobby."

He did nearly that. He bought the hotel, and as soon as the war ended and rent controls were lifted, he informed the little old ladies that henceforth they would be charged the same day-to-day room rate as any traveling salesman. Within a few months nearly all of them were gone.

Then he put all the old furnishings and fixtures on public auction, hired Dorothy Draper to redo the lobby and looked for a way to add zing to his hotel. New York had zing—why not San Francisco?

His search for zing led him to the Fairmont swimming pool. In 1929 the enterprising Linnards had roofed over the garden terrace behind the hotel and dug a swimming pool, which they named the Fairmont Plunge. The Plunge's first swimmer had been a young actress in a pea-green swimming suit named Helen Hayes; from the day she jumped in, the pool had been one of the Fairmont's most popular features, the scene of the Venetian Carnival and the rehearsal pool for Billy Rose's Aquacade.

But now, Swig reasoned, it was out of keeping with the modern hotel, to say nothing of unprofitable. While he was mulling over this problem , Swig learned that, rotting in the sun on a mud flat near Martinez, was the wreck of a four-masted lumber schooner called the *Tonga*. Swig began to think; if the Fairmont Plunge could be the Grand Canal in Venice for a 1930s party, why couldn't it be a tropical lagoon? At Swig's order, the wreck of the *Tonga* was purchased, sawed into pieces, trucked to San Francisco, carried into the hotel and reassembled around the swimming pool. It was decorated with life preservers, ropes and appropriate nautical touches, a bandstand was floated in the swimming pool, and it was opened as a nightclub. It was an instant success, crowded nightly with customers.

A few years later Swig was troubled again. The novelty of dancing on the deck of a lumber schooner was wearing thin; people were getting tired of nautical nightclubs. Swig decided to push the gimmick to the ultimate.

Truckloads of tropical foliage began arriving at the doors of the Fairmont, followed by trucks full of pipe and carloads of plumbers. When the new Tonga Room reopened a few months later, the old lumber schooner had been overrun by a tropical jungle. Waterfalls splashed in the corners, palm fronds decorated the floating bandstand, Chinese cooks worked in the kitchen, the staff was dressed in flowered shirts, and, thanks to the miracle of modern plumbing, tropical rainstorms showered down sixteen times a night. Ben had created a tropical paradise right in his hotel. Despite occasional breaks in the happy fantasy when tipsy patrons mistook the tropical lagoon for a swimming pool, leaped in and swam a few laps, the Tonga Room, like the SS *Tonga* before it, was a grand triumph.

But Ben Swig was still dissatisfied, and this was the reason. He was a very important man. On the wall of his office there hung or soon would hang photographs of Ben Swig with Harry Truman, Ben Swig with Adlai Stevenson, Ben Swig with Lyndon Johnson, Ben Swig with David Ben-Gurion, Ben Swig with Pope Paul VI. He owned a hotel in Colorado, a hotel in New York and a uranium mine in Utah; the grand piano Leonard Bernstein played at concerts of the Israel Philharmonic was a gift of Ben Swig; so was the Chrysler Imperial the president of Israel drove, and the Chrysler Imperial David Ben-Gurion drove. He owned gold mines in New Zealand, copper mines in Canada and apartment buildings and a department store in San Francisco. Three times he had been invited to dinner at the White House. Yet whenever Ben Swig stood proudly in front of the Fairmont and looked up, he saw the Mark Hopkins looking down. This infuriated Ben Swig. He became obsessed with the idea that he had to look down on the Top of the Mark.

It wasn't purely a matter of pride, of course; Swig was too good a businessman to let pride interfere with his judgment. Swig knew that a tower capable of looking down on the Mark would be a good investment.

Following the war, it quickly became evident to Swig and the other hoteliers in town that their old, traditional customers before the war, the elderly widows and the families on month-long vacations, weren't coming back; they couldn't afford to anymore. In their place came the corporate men, hurrying executives in tan raincoats and briefcases and flight bags, and the new lifeblood of hotels, conventioneers.

Conventioneers might clog the lobby, wear plastic name tags and bizarre suits, slap unwary guests on the back as they passed through, they might jam the restaurants and overcrowd the elevators and carve their initials in the closet doors and throw lamps out the windows, but the hotel accountants loved them. They bought entire blocks of rooms, sometimes the whole hotel, they could be scheduled years in advance, they ate and drank unbelievable amounts, and they paid their bills. The bellhops might grit their teeth every time a convention surged into the lobby; but the accountants smiled, and the accountants were running the business.

In 1950 Swig unveiled his plans for the ultimate convention-catching machine, a proposed thirty-two-story skyscraper attached to the front of the Fairmont, capped with a revolving drum containing a restaurant which was surmounted by a quaint replica of the Eiffel Tower.

"This will be a wonderful monument to San Francisco," Supervisor Ernest J. Torregano enthused. Others were less enchanted. "San Francisco doesn't need monuments," one witness complained at a Planning Commission hearing, "it needs good planning." The planning director agreed, calling it "an absurdity in zoning practice" which would turn the tranquil summit of Nob Hill into a commercial beehive. Most displeased of all, understandably, was George Smith, who pictured Ben Swig looking down on him and gloating. He and the Pacific Union Club, Grace Cathedral and the other neighbors of the Fairmont hastily organized the Committee to Protect Nob Hill, complaining that the tower would "destroy the character of the entire neighborhood."

But Swig was not easily stopped. He and George Smith met face to face at a Planning Commission hearing. After Smith had listed his complaints, Swig took the floor. If Nob Hill was such a peaceful residential neighborhood, he asked, why were there two gas stations, two parking lots, five garages, nightclubs and fifty stores there? Nob Hill was already commercial, he argued. "Just because the Mark Hopkins doesn't want a tower that might be bigger than theirs, are we going to stop progress? I think it will bring people in, and that will help the Mark Hopkins."

Then Swig produced the carrot and the stick. The stick was, Swig warned, that the American Medical Association, the elephant of conventions, would hold its conventions in Los Angeles instead of San Francisco unless the tower, with its additional rooms, were built. This argument, although it wasn't true, was persuasive. Then the carrot: Swig promised, that if he were allowed to build his tower, he would build a convention hall on the back of his hotel, featuring space for 5,000 delegates in two ballrooms connected by an electric sliding wall.

The city thought about the new convention center and counted the number of visitors, who, instead of trooping through Fisherman's Wharf buying postcards and cable car key chains, would go to Disneyland and Grauman's Chinese Theater if conventions started going south. They voted 4–3 to allow Swig to build his tower.

Just when George Smith seemed doomed to fall in the shadow of Ben Swig's tower, he received some unexpected help from Mao Tse-tung. Red Chinese armies swept across the Yalu River and forced the United Nations army in Korea to retreat, forcing the United States to restrict the use of steel to essential war projects. Ben Swig was unable to convince the government that his tower was necessary to win the war, and he had to drop the project.

It's possible there would still be no tower today were it not for the monster that decided to sit down next to Van Ness Avenue on March 28, 1960. Unleased by one Ed C. Leach, an enterprising businessman and former bellhop who evidently wanted to exact revenge against hotel owners everywhere, the monster was an enormous, glaring red, white and blue plastic and metal box with a gigantic revolving cap on top that announced with huge neon letters to everyone within miles that it was the Jack Tar Hotel.

There had been motels out in the countryside for forty years, and Kemmons Wilson and his mom, Ruby L. "Doll" Wilson, had opened the very first Holiday Inn in Memphis in 1952, but not until Ed Leach built the Jack Tar had one of these neon shoeboxes moved into San Francisco.

It was characteristic of the species that when the Jack Tar opened, it was reviewed not in *The Architectural Forum* but in *Popular Mechanics.* Resembling an oversized jukebox, the Jack Tar took pride that a guest could stay there without ever having to lay eyes on another human being. Upon arriving in the garage under the hotel, the guest announced to a closed-circuit TV camera that he wanted a room; a pneumatic tube whooshed him his key. When he wanted to leave, he returned to the garage and put his key and his money in the mouth of another tube, which whooshed it away.

In his room the guest found a dial to tune him into radio, television or Muzak and was reassured, in the shaky early 1960s, by the presence of an air-raid siren in every room. Somewhere downstairs, according to *Popular Mechanics,* there were hotel employees keeping track of the guests by rows of lights on a huge console.

We who might shudder at the Jack Tar and at the news that it was a colossal financial success from the day it opened must remember that, in 1960, the year that gave us rocket-ship tail fins on cars, this was what Americans wanted. On the success of the Jack Tar, the Hilton Hotel chain built its giant concrete icebox in 1964, adding a forty-six-story pinball machine in 1971. Holiday Inn joined the feast with no less than three of its giant shoeboxes and electric heaters, and the new Hyatt chain began plans for a huge concrete typewriter. A desperate Ben Swig, needing more rooms to compete with these new hotels that were making downtown San Francisco look like an appliance showroom, took his old tower plans out of the closet, erased the Eiffel Tower from the top, removed the revolving restaurant, shortened it two stories, and presented it to the city for approval.

Once again the Planning Commission screamed in outrage, not because of zoning problems, but because the tower was so ugly. Looking like a transplant from Las Vegas, the gold and white shaft was crowned by a wavy paper plate roof with a pop art steeple on top. On the side of the tower, an outside elevator slid up and down a ribbon of light, causing one critic to call it "an illuminated thermometer." It was "an architectural atrocity," George Rockrise, the head of the Planning Commission, complained, "nothing more than a sign, calling attention to the building and put up with malice aforethought." The Building Trades Council seemed to agree with Rockrise's description when they sprang to the defense of the proposed tower and opposed those who sought to "curtail and limit the electrical advertising industry."

Nevertheless, the tower was approved and built, and the name of the Fairmont Hotel became the Fairmont Hotel and Tower. From the day the tower opened in 1961, guests loved it. The hotel discovered that there was a noticeable increase in requests for room service and found that guests were spending all day in their rooms in the tower, gaping at the view. The Presidential Suite on the twenty-first floor provided the most prestigious view; furnished with marble coffee tables, silk wallpaper, two bathtubs with whirlpools and an antique French sideboard that opened into a cocktail bar, it was the home of Joan Crawford and President Lyndon Johnson when they stayed in the city, at the suitably towering price of $150 a day.

Above the Presidential Suite, at the very top of the tower, the elevator stopped at the Crown Room. There, at a small table by the window, served by waitresses in brief Georgian brocade costumes, powdered wigs and miniature crowns, Ben Swig could at last sit back comfortably and look down on top of George Smith's Mark.

22

Khrushchev

IN October, 1962, American missiles all over the world were armed and trained on targets in the Soviet Union, and fleets of B-52 bombers, loaded with nuclear weapons, circled over their bases on full alert. President Kennedy had come on television to tell the nation that the Russians must withdraw their missiles from Cuba or face the United States. In Moscow, Premier Nikita Khrushchev armed and aimed his missiles, and, for hour after hour, the world hung precariously over the abyss of nuclear war. Then, as everyone knows, Khrushchev backed down.

Historians have analyzed those tense hours and come to their conclusions why Khrushchev backed down, but I have my own theory. I believe Khrushchev didn't want to blow up San Francisco.

Three years earlier, on September 15, 1959, the bald five-foot-five Premier Khrushchev, wearing the Order of Lenin on his right lapel and the double red stars of a Hero of the Soviet Union on the other, had hopped down the ramp of his jet at Andrews Air Force Base, the first Russian leader to set foot on American soil. He arrived at one of the chilliest moments of the cold war, and it's difficult to imagine a ruder reception than he was given.

Khrushchev proudly carried with him a model of the Soviet Luna rocket that had just been landed on the moon. When he landed, he read in the papers that Vice President Nixon had belittled the Soviet achievement, saying, falsely, that the Russians had failed three times before they succeeded. At the dinner at the White House that night to welcome the premier, President Eisenhower observed that the United States was ruled by peace-loving people and thus would never start a war, implying that Khrushchev and the Russians were war-hungry madmen.

The next day, at a press conference, reporters pressed Khrushchev on the Russian suppression of the Hungarian uprising until he was close to fury. "We've got a lot of dead cats we can throw at you and they are fresher than any Hungarian dead rat," he snapped, a remark which his interpreter did not translate. "I have no intention of putting difficult questions to you," he said, and the translator picked up again. "I've come here with an open heart, not in a mood to relive old difficulties."

Yet the press insisted on hounding Khrushchev. The premier, a shepherd when he was a young boy, was referred to as "the former swineherd" by Bob Considine, a Hearst columnist. Annoyed by his reception in Washington, he went to New York, where the reception was even worse. Hecklers and pickets surrounded the Waldorf-Astoria, he was booed and jeered, and the New York churches had hired a skywriter to draw a cross in the sky over his car. Inside the hotel he was heckled from the floor as he tried to address a meeting of the Economic Club, until he stopped his speech and announced, "Gentlemen, I am an old sparrow, so to say, and you can't muddle me. I came here not to beg anything. I came here as a representative of a great country which has made a great October Revolution and no cries can do away with the achievement of our people. I will reply to the question when there are no interruptions." But the heckling continued, and the former factory worker and miner and long-time Communist waved his fist and said angrily, "You forget something. When our revolution took place, you sent your armies to crush us. It took you sixteen years to recognize something was going on in our country, something that had been born without your permission. If now you want to indulge in any such forceful measures in regard to us, I'm sure you're well aware what this might lead to."

On this threatening note, Khrushchev flew to Los Angeles. Arriving in the late morning, he was taken to a Hollywood studio to watch the filming of a scene from *Can-Can* and then to a luncheon, where he was introduced to Marilyn Monroe, Henry Fonda, Bob Hope, Gary Cooper and Frank Sinatra.

Then the problems began again. Spyros Skouras, a motion-picture industry leader, began describing his rise in the capitalistic system, saying in his speech, "I was a poor immigrant. . . ."

"*I* began working when I learned to walk," Khrushchev interrupted. "I was a shepherd boy, a factory laborer, I worked in the coal pits, and now I am the prime minister of the great Soviet state."

Skouras tried to continue, explaining that he hoped more American films could be shown in the Soviet Union. Khrushchev interrupted him again, leaning forward to shout to his minister of culture, seated at the far end of the banquet table: "Zhukov! How many American films have we chosen to show in the Soviet Union lately?"

"Ten," Zhukov replied. Khrushchev looked at Skouras.

"Zhukov! How many of our films have they chosen?"

"Seven," Zhukov said. Khrushchev looked at Skouras again.

But the worst was yet to come. Khrushchev was handed a note, which he read and then put away. Then he announced, "I cannot but express deep disappointment and surprise over something I have just learned here at the table." The audience leaned forward, afraid of hearing that war had just been declared.

"I as prime minister was given a definite program and a plan in advance of my arrival here," he continued. "But just now I was told I could not go to Disneyland. What do you have there—rocket launching pads? Your American security says it cannot guarantee my safety if I go there. Is there an epidemic of cholera there? Have gangsters taken control of the place? Your police are strong enough to lift up a bull; surely they are strong enough to take care of gangsters, if indeed gangsters have taken over." He shook his head. "I would very much like to see Disneyland. What must I do now? Commit suicide? This situation is inconceivable. I will never be able to explain this to my people. Come to my country. No foreign guest will be harmed in the Soviet Union. I thought I could come to this country in peace and not sit in a closed car in the smothering heat."

Presumably, Khrushchev was joking, but that night, at another banquet, his humor turned to anger. Mayor Norris Poulsen of Los Angeles commented snidely upon an old

Khrushchev statement, and the premier exploded, angrily threatening to take his whole party and go home. "What if Khrushchev had not been invited here for you to rub him in your salt, show him your might, make him shaky at the knees?" Khrushchev had replied, pounding the table. "It took us only about twelve hours to get here. Perhaps it would take less time to get back."

On that frosty note, Khrushchev boarded a special seventeen-car train for the trip from Los Angeles to San Francisco the next morning.

In San Francisco, preparations were under way for his arrival. The Royal Suite on the sixteenth floor of the Mark Hopkins had been selected for him, with its walnut-paneled living room, dining room, glassed-in terrace, marble fireplace and two bedrooms. Through the bulletproof glass windows he would have a clear view of Telegraph Hill and the Golden Gate Bridge.

Eighty other rooms were taken in the hotel for the security men, Khrushchev's family and the American and Russian diplomats traveling with him. Hotel employees busily arranged floral displays, baskets of fruit and bottles of Coca-Cola on the tables, while telephone company employees and Russian technicians installed a black one-button telephone to connect the Mark Hopkins to the Kremlin. Dour Russian security guards carrying Geiger counters paced through the rooms, looking for hidden deposits of radioactive cobalt which might have been placed to poison the premier. At the railroad yard where Khrushchev was scheduled to arrive, police were X-raying all the cars to be used by the official party, looking for explosives. Outside the Mark Hopkins, other police were posting signs and removing all the cars from the streets around the hotel.

The Hearst-owned *Examiner* made its special effort to welcome the premier. Calling him "The most dangerous man in history," it warned San Franciscans to be "coldly polite. There are sound historical reasons why feelings of hatred and hostility should exist. The memory of Hungary, Poland and Korea is still strong." Some business groups handed out black ribbons to be worn in protest, and Hungarian freedom fighters marched down Market Street carrying signs reading KHRUSHCHEV, YOU'RE WELCOME IN HELL.

When Khrushchev's train, escorted by highway patrol cars

on the road alongside and a helicopter overhead, arrived in the Southern Pacific yards, the Russian security men were nervous, peering through the train windows to see the hostile crowds. Only there weren't any.

Khrushchev, his wife, two daughters, son, son-in-law and the rest of the official party climbed into the line of waiting cars. Preceded by two police cars, Khrushchev's Cadillac, which he shared with San Francisco Mayor George Christopher, began the drive downtown to the Mark Hopkins. Khrushchev pointed to a building under construction. "In Russia we are more efficient," the premier told Christopher. "We have precast concrete."

Christopher smiled. "We want to be friends, but I can't concede that Russian methods of efficiency are better than ours."

"True," Khrushchev said. "You are first in efficiency now. But it won't be long until you are in third place."

"Who'll be in second?"

"China."

"China is a very old country," Christopher replied. "It's five thousand years old, and they haven't passed us yet. We're only two hundred."

"Ah," Khrushchev said, "we are only forty years old and look what we've done to you already."

Now they were passing the first crowds along the route. To Khrushchev's delight, they smiled and applauded. He rolled down the window of the Cadillac and waved at them, then, seeing a billboard from Christopher's reelection campaign, grinned and said something to his interpreter. The interpreter turned to Christopher. "He asks if you would like him to campaign for you?" Khrushchev slapped Christopher on the back.

Even the Russian security men were smiling when the premier's car arrived at the Mark Hopkins. Ten thousand people were gathered on top of Nob Hill, and they burst into applause when Khrushchev got out of the car. He beamed, raised his hands together like a boxer, waved and bowed as he went into the hotel.

That night Khrushchev had a brief meeting in the hotel with American labor union leaders. He described the can-can dancing he had seen in Hollywood, calling it "the culture of a surfeited and depraved people. The Soviet people would scorn such a spectacle." Then he did his own parody of the can-can.

While he was talking to the labor leaders, Nina Khrushchev was given an automobile tour of the city, driving to the Golden Gate Bridge, along Grant Avenue through Chinatown, to Fisherman's Wharf and back to the hotel. In the Mark Hopkins kitchen the hotel chef and a consulting Russian chef prepared a meal for the premier, while a dour Soviet security man poked a Geiger counter through the salad, looking for radioactive cobalt.

Early the next morning Khrushchev startled his bodyguards by taking a stroll from the hotel across the top of Nob Hill, looking at the Masonic Hall and at Grace Cathedral and the view of the Bay. "This is the most beautiful American city I've seen," he told an American escort. Then he strolled back under the Russian flag over the entrance of the hotel.

After breakfast, a parade of limousines took him down to the wharf, where he boarded a Coast Guard cutter for a tour of the Bay. "I'll tell you about our submarine strength," he told a startled coast guardsman as they circled the harbor, "but you'd say I was bragging and trying to intimidate the American Navy. Actually, we are now using our submarines to catch herring."

"How do you catch herring with a submarine?" a puzzled reporter asked.

"I don't know, I'm no fisherman," Khrushchev said, and roared with laughter.

After he was landed back at the wharf, Khrushchev startled everyone by asking to break his itinerary and visit Harry Bridges and his dockworkers at the Longshoremen's Hall. After a flurry of schedule changes and arguments among protocol officers, the change was made, and the fleet of cars drove to the hall.

Bridges and his pregnant wife met the premier at the door. The renegade union leader, who had been leading waterfront strikes since the 1930s, said, "As you can see, she is expecting a baby. In fact, it's due today. I hope he will grow up in peace and meet you someday." Khrushchev was handed a white longshoreman's cap, which he put on, and he spoke to the gathering of workers: "Ladies and gentlemen, may I address you as we address the workers in Russia? May I call you comrades?" They clapped and cheered.

When he finished at the Longshoremen's Hall, Khrushchev was driven down the Peninsula to tour an IBM factory. Meanwhile, Mrs. Khrushchev had been on a shopping spree at Sears Roebuck. After spending thirty minutes at the hosiery counter, she had bought blankets, stuffed animals and car seats with toy steering wheels as gifts for her grandchildren, and then she was driven to Trader Vic's for her first hamburger. Khrushchev himself, as he returned from the IBM plant, stopped at the Stonestown Shopping Center to see what a supermarket looked like. While the premier solemnly inspected frozen fish sticks, shook milk cartons and sniffed melons, reporters turned the aisles of the market into a madhouse, climbing on top of counters and knocking over piles of cans as they frantically tried to get pictures. Khrushchev seemed to enjoy every minute of it.

That night he ate dinner in the Garden Court of the Palace and afterward addressed a combined gathering of the Commonwealth Club and the World Affairs Council. The Rose Room and the Concert Room had been opened to make room for the audience of 2,100 and another 1,800 were listening over loudspeakers in the corridor.

It was a very different speech from that he had given before, without threats and bluster. "We do not want war, with its horrible consequences, he said, "ever again to be visited on mankind. . . . All prejudices and ill will must be discarded.

"It isn't only in oil and gold that you are rich in California. . . .You have everything. The people of San Francisco positively charmed us. I felt as though I was among real friends, who are thinking the same thoughts the people of the Soviet Union are thinking."

The next morning the black telephone to the Kremlin was disconnected and the premier left the Mark Hopkins, after giving the bellhops little Lenin medals and the maids little models of the Luna. An ecstatic Mark Hopkins public relations man swore to reporters he heard the premier say, "This is the finest hotel I've ever seen."

History notes that Premier Khrushchev flew that morning from San Francisco to Iowa, then to Pittsburgh, then to Washington for talks with President Eisenhower and finally back to the Soviet Union. It recalls that he said on boarding his plane, "Let me thank you from the bottom of my heart for your kind hospitality, for your bread and salt." Later, as we saw, when he could have destroyed the world, he didn't. Let historians say what they may about diplomatic maneuvers, nuclear sufficiency, threats and counterthreats. Give San Francisco credit because it greeted Khrushchev, when he came, not as an enemy, but as a guest.

23

Kennedy

THE decade of the sixties arrived literally with a crash. In the kitchen of the Sheraton-Palace, the busboys were just picking up huge platters of food and the waitresses silver coffeepots, when there was a clamor and shrieks from one end of the room. "I see him! I see him!" the waitresses began screaming, and coffee slopped to the floor and platters tumbled in the sudden rush to be near the man who was walking through the kitchen, smiling. His name was John Fitzgerald Kennedy, and in a week he would be elected president of the United States.

Kennedy, after shaking hands with the busboys, walked out to the dais and received the applause of the Democratic fund raisers of San Francisco with a wave and a smile. When their applause had died down, he said, "I'm deeply touched. Not as deeply touched as you have been, of course, but deeply touched. . . . About campaign contributions. I have said that contributions are not a qualification for embassies. Since then, my father hasn't contributed a cent to my campaign." Then, turning serious, he thanked the diners, each of whom had paid $100 to be there. "You," he told them, "are the people who have kept this campaign going."

After a dinner of spring chicken and string beans, Kennedy was in a car on the way to the Cow Palace, reading over his speech. The polls showed that the election was very nearly tied; that same day Vice President Nixon was appearing with President Eisenhower in New York. He needed something imaginative to catch the attention of the nation, and he thought he had it, in a proposal he meant to give this night.

Thirty thousand people had jammed inside the Cow Palace, chanting over and over, "We want Kennedy! We want Kennedy!" in a great roar. Then, in the apex of the spotlights, lit by hundreds of popping flashbulbs, Kennedy was there, waving, and they were standing on their seats, cheering him. When they had quieted down, his New England accent echoed over the loudspeakers through the Cow Palace: "This country needs progress and action. There must be a new machinery to win the struggle for peace and freedom. I therefore propose a peace corps of talented young men willing and able to serve their country for three years as an alternative to peacetime selective service. . . ."

Then he held out his hand. "So I come here today, and ask you to give me your hand, give me your voice, and let us move this country forward. . . ."

24

New New York

IN April, 1960, the streets of downtown San Francisco were ablaze with French tricolors; Charles de Gaulle was being driven through the financial district, standing stiffly in the back of an open limousine, nodding and waving to the cheering crowds and murmuring, *"Merci, merci."*

At the Mark Hopkins, George Smith made a final critical inspection of De Gaulle's bedroom, noting with approval the eight-food bed his carpenter had built for the six-foot-four French president.

That night, before returning to the Mark Hopkins, De Gaulle sipped California wine and addressed a huge audience in the Civic Auditorium, ending his speech with raised arms and a rousing tribute to his host city: *"Vive Chicago!"* he shouted. *"Vive les États-Unis!"*

"Long live San Francisco!" the interpreter translated. "Long live the United States!" De Gaulle beamed.

We can presume that De Gaulle was carried away by the wine and the enthusiasm, but consider what a Sausalito artist said when he returned home after an absence of several years and looked across the Bay at San Francisco: "It looks like a graveyard. And, as is the custom, the richer the dead, the bigger the gravestone."

When he had left, the city he saw across the Bay had been white and clung to the hills like a Mediterranean town. Now, from its white heart there rose an eerie forest of black glass towers, tall and cold.

Between 1966 and 1971, thirty-one skyscrapers rose from downtown San Francisco, built around the brown rock and glass tower of the world headquarters of the Bank of America, the tallest in the city.

The towers were the children of two Europeans, Ludwig Miës van der Rohe and Charles Édouard Jeanneret, who called himself Le Corbusier, neither of whom ever saw what they had done to San Francisco.

Le Corbusier, working in France in the 1930s, was determined to do for architecture what Picasso had done for painting: to throw all the old standards out the window. He proclaimed that all architecture from the Parthenon to the present was dead; buildings were henceforth to be "machines to live in," modeled not after cathedrals or temples but after automobiles and refrigerators, pure and functional. He produced a new urban plan for the city of Paris which drew gasps from the Parisians: He proposed leveling the entire city, from Notre Dame to the Eiffel Tower, and replacing it with a cluster of skyscrapers connected by freeways.

Few people permitted Le Corbusier to design buildings for them, but his ideas caught hold with the new generation of architects, who promptly looked for ways to annihilate the architectural past. Mies was the most accomplished of the new architects. His buildings, from the Seagram Building in New York to the Lake Shore Drive Apartments in Chicago, were triumphant examples of his own proclamation "Less is more," tall, severe, cold, perfectly proportioned steel and glass shafts, reflecting the passing clouds in their icy black windows.

San Francisco was largely oblivious to what was happening across the country. It was enjoying its own peculiar jumble of architecture. San Francisco's Victorians, resplendent with gingerbread trim, scrolled cornices, fluted columns and ornate bay windows, were almost absurdly silly-looking by themselves, like oversize cuckoo clocks, but bunched together in rows on the hillsides, they were magnificent, as colorful and picturesque as rows of toy soldiers. Downtown San Francisco was the same way; the architecture, from the lacquer and gold ornament of Chinatown to the Art Nouveau windows of Willis Polk's Hallidie Building to the WPA Egyptian shaft of Coit Tower, from the mansarded château roof of the Mark Hopkins to the palatial façade of the Fairmont, was so bizarre, so astonishing and so unexpected as to be utterly charming, mixed as it was with sudden and unexpected glimpses of the great bridges and the blue water of the Bay and the odd appearance of antique cable cars scuttling up the hills. It was unique, like nowhere else in the world, and that was why San Franciscans loved it.

Into this unruly paradise came the men who wanted San Francisco to be another New York, the administrative capital of the Pacific. They believed that great corporations had to have great buildings, and modern industries the most modern buildings possible; in the 1960s, that meant buildings styled after the icy towers of Miës van der Rohe. So it was, then, in the last years of the sixties, that great steel frames climbed skyward, shadows fell across the white buildings, and downtown San Francisco began to look like New York or Chicago or a graveyard, buried beneath the tall steel monuments to Alcoa, Levi Strauss and the Bank of America.

"If they don't like it," said Roger Lapham, Jr., the son of former Mayor Roger Lapham and a downtown real estate developer, "then let them go someplace else, but don't keep complaining about it, because that's what is going to happen, and nobody can stop it."

By 1968 there were so many skyscrapers downtown that they almost defeated their own purpose; what good was it for a corporation to have a massive steel and glass fudgesicle if it was surrounded by other corporations' black glass popsicles and cement vanilla bars?

The Transamerica Corporation, a conglomerate of insurance and real estate agencies that owned, among other things, rental cars and United Artists pictures, sought a unique way to advertise itself through the architecture of their new home office.

In January, 1969, TV and radio reporters and newspapermen were summoned to a meeting room at the Fairmont, where they were met by the chairman of the board of Transamerica, a public relations man, Mayor Joseph Alioto, William Pereira, the architect of Cape Canaveral, and a mysteriously draped object. After the opening speeches, Mayor Alioto and the board chairman joined to pull off the drapes. There was a gasp in the room. The mysterious object was a five-foot model pyramid.

Designing a 1,000-foot-high pyramid was considerably different from building one. Many San Franciscans, among them Mrs. Hans Klussmann, were willing to put up with black popsicles and fudge bars, but an inverted white ice-cream cone was a bit much. Committees were formed and lawsuits were filed to block construction of the pyramid.

The opponents of the pyramid failed to consider the ingenuity of Transamerica's public relations man, John Kresak. He knew that the building's opponents were waiting for the groundbreaking to make their strongest legal challenges. But if the building could be gotten under way without loud demonstrations and other harassment, he was sure it could be finished.

One day in December, 1969, during the lunch hour when there were few people about, an old pickup truck parked in front of City Hall. Out of the truck climbed a vice-president of Transamerica Corporation, who looked around to make sure he wasn't observed before he went inside to file a site permit. When he had filed the permit, he rushed to a telephone.

Kresak and the superintendent of the building's construction were waiting for the phone call in a restaurant across the street from the site. When it came, Kresak hurried to call selected newsmen and cameramen, who were waiting impatiently in nearby telephone booths. They hurried to the site, where they were met by Kresak and the superintendent.

The superintendent gave a signal, and out of a basement excavation hidden from the view of the street roared a truck and a tractor.

As Kresak smiled happily, the photographers surrounded the tractor and took its picture as it bit the first chunk out of the pavement. The Transamerica Pyramid was on its way to joining the San Francisco skyline.

The huge slab Holiday Inns that now sprang up in San Francisco, no less than five of them, were in line with Mies van der Rohe, although far less artfully done. It remained for the new Hyatt hotel chain to push modern architecture to a new frontier: that a building could be not only a machine to live in, but a circus as well, architecture as entertainment.

When the Hyatt Regency opened near the old Ferry Building in 1974, architectural critics searched for some way to describe it: One ventured that it looked as if it had caved in on one side; another said it looked like a giant typewriter. But it was the interior that was the glory of the Hyatt; it was hollow, containing a fifteen-story cavity decorated with enormous pieces of sculpture, cocktail pits, caged doves, an artificial stream, a fountain and elevators shaped like vitamin capsules that whizzed up to a revolving bar on the roof.

Allan Temko, the architecture critic of the *Chronicle*, after exploring the spaces and corners of the Hyatt Regency, finally realized what the Hyatt Regency, the ultimate 1970s hotel, looked like: "It is a convention machine, crammed with windowless meeting rooms . . . it is a cash register, in both shape and function."

If San Francisco was the victim of one cultural trend, it was the birthplace and baptismal font of another. In the summer of 1967, anger against President Lyndon Johnson and the steadily escalating war in Vietnam and a Swiss drug called lysergic acid diethylamide, or LSD, combined on the sidewalks of a run-down neighborhood around the intersection of Haight and Ashbury streets to create a new culture. Wearing flowers, beads and peace symbols, young people swarmed to San Francisco for "The Summer of Love," to listen to their own music by local bands called The Jefferson Airplane, Janis Joplin and the Grateful Dead, to attend great disorganized picnics, called be-ins, in Golden Gate Park and to sit for hours listening to the music of the Beatles on stereos in incense-filled rooms after licking LSD off small squares of paper.

The Gray Line tour buses which once drove through North Beach in search of beatniks now were rerouted to the Haight-Ashbury. They crawled slowly down the street, allowing the tourists to gape at the crowds of people, oddly dressed in fringed buckskin, long skirts and Indian headbands, who strolled the street or sat talking in doorways. On occasion, one of the youths would hold up a mirror and run alongside the bus.

The tourists on the buses paid little attention to one young man with long brown hair, flowered trousers, a denim jacket and lavender, heart-shaped glasses who was strolling along Haight Street. After a few blocks he turned into Golden Gate Park and walked up the side of what was known as Hippie Hill, where a man was playing the guitar for about twenty people seated on the hill.

The young man asked the guitar player if he could try the guitar. The guitar player nodded and handed it to him, and the young man began playing Beatle songs.

Suddenly one of the spectators realized something. She looked at the young man, looked away and looked again. "It's George Harrison!" she shouted. The shout was taken up throughout the park, and the Beatle was soon surrounded by admiring fans. He played for about ten minutes more and then walked back through the Haight, followed by the crowd. He had flown up for the day from Los Angeles, where he had been visiting Ravi Shankar, to see what was happening in San Francisco.

"What do you think of the Haight-Ashbury?" someone called.

"Wow, if it's all like this, it's too much," Harrison replied.

It was too much; it was over almost as soon as it started. The hippies traded their flowers for the surplus fatigue jackets of the antiwar movement or left town. Golden Gate Park was filled with vast antiwar demonstrations, and the Haight-Ashbury was soon overrun by heroin dealers.

Hollywood, in the meanwhile, playing with its new light and mobile film cameras, was discovering that San Francisco was a picturesque film location. For television they had created a San Francisco street in Universal City, near Los Angeles, to film the detective series *Ironside*. Now, with lightweight cameras, they used the real San Francisco to film another series, *Streets of San Francisco*. Dozens of movies were filmed in the city, ranging from the car-chase-filled *Bullitt* to Woody Allen's *Play It Again, Sam*, for which the locale was changed from New York to San Francisco.

The Japanese, unable to travel so far to take advantage of the city's charms, got their revenge by constructing San Francisco in miniature and then destroying it with a giant rubber octopus. Producer Irwin Allen borrowed the Bank of America's tower to roast an exceptional cast of actors in *The Towering Inferno*, and director Peter Bogdanovich ordered a car chase down a flight of stairs for Ryan O'Neal and Barbra Streisand in *What's Up, Doc?*, to the fury of city officials.

The Fairmont was used so often the doorman was required to join the Screen Actors Guild. Fairly typical was the filming of *Petulia*. The script required a noisy fund-raising benefit in the lobby for the opening scene. George C. Scott, Julie Christie and Richard Chamberlain were suitably dressed in evening clothes, and a little-known local band, which turned out to be Janis Joplin and Big Brother and the

Holding Company, was hired to provide the music, but there was a complication: A convention was occupying the Fairmont, and they were trying to raffle off an automobile. The automobile was parked in the lobby.

The film crew begged and pleaded with the conventioneers, but they refused to move the automobile. Finally, the script was rewritten to include the automobile, the actors were handed fake raffle tickets, and the band began to play, Scott, Christie and Chamberlain began to dance, and the cameras began to roll.

Sometimes, in the urgent 1960s, the pressure was almost unbearable. Nearly 140 reporters and photographers jammed around Judy Garland when she gave a press conference in the Top of the Mark in 1965.

"San Francisco is my favorite city," she declared.

"When are you going to marry Mr. Herron?" a reporter demanded. Mark Herron, looking uncomfortable, was standing beside her.

"You'd better ask Mr. Herron," Judy Garland said.

"Well, maybe in two or three weeks," Herron said. "Or maybe a year or so."

"What was your first picture?" a reporter asked.

"*Pigskin Parade*," she answered.

"And that was made in nineteen thirty. . . ."

"No about 1473, as I recall," she joked.

Near the end of the sparring, she was asked if she felt any animosity toward the press.

"No, I feel I'm a performer," she said, "and I'm paid for being a performer, and the public has to know that I'm around."

In the back of the room, a press agent whispered to the reporters, "You know, she got a much bigger turnout than Madame Chiang Kai-shek."

The 1960s were difficult for nearly everyone. Young Chinese in Chinatown were putting on Mao tunics and waving little red books of the sayings of Chairman Mao, and when a model of the proposed Chinatown Holiday Inn passed by in the Chinese New Year's Parade, they booed it loudly and threw firecrackers at it.

On Columbus Day ever since anyone could remember, Joe Cervetto, the owner of the building maintenance company, had proudly put on a wig, brocade costume and sword and had played the part of Columbus in a reenactment of his landing on a beach a few blocks from Fisherman's Wharf. On Columbus Day, 1970, when Cervetto, sword in hand, stepped from a rowboat onto the beach, he was met by American Indian activists in sunglasses and fatigue jackets, who pulled his wig off, tried to push him into the Bay and yelled at him to go back where he came from.

But the cruelest trick was played on the prophets of San Francisco as the capital of the Pacific. The census of 1960 showed that San Francisco had stopped growing and had actually begun to decline in population, as residents fled its congestion for the suburban tracts of Walnut Creek, San Mateo, Daly City and Hayward. San Francisco was surpassed in population now by even the new plastic and asphalt sprawl of Houston. Dozens of residents telephoned the newspapers to claim that the census had missed them, and volunteer teams were organized to make a recount, but it was useless: San Francisco was a small peninsula, with no room to expand; it could never compete in population with the sprawling desert cities of Houston and Los Angeles.

Nor was it the commerce center it once was. The once-bustling docks were now rotting away, unused. The ships passing through the Golden Gate were now passing by San Francisco to dock in Oakland, which had modern container ship facilities and direct truck and rail access to the east. San Francisco was forced to scrap its dream of a multi-skyscrapered world trade center; instead, the city cleaned out the old Ferry Building, hung a few old flags in a hallway and announced that it was San Francisco's World Trade Center.

San Francisco seemed doomed to become an enormous office, bustling during the daytime and deserted at night, while the surrounding neighborhoods decayed, were demolished, and the new neighborhoods decayed more. But help came from an unexpected place; from Lurline Roth, the owner of Filoli, the great estate south of the city, with its yew trees and chandeliers from the Palace of Versailles.

Society, too, had been changing. The Monday luncheons at the St. Francis, which once had determined who was where in society, ended in 1962. Headwaiter Ernest Gloor had died in 1959, and his successor, Barney, as one woman snapped, "made a number of serious mistakes," in whom he placed at what table. The Mural Room itself was demolished in 1970 to make room for the base of a 600-room tower, with which the St. Francis hoped to compete with the Fairmont. The murals were carefully removed and offered to museums, but they were too big, too expensive and out of style. They were finally stacked in a warehouse, where they still remain.

The membership of society was changing; the man who sold cigars had finally won a place in Burlingame next to the man who made cigars, only to find that his new neighbor was a man who imported cigars from Taiwan or synthesized them out of petroleum or lint. The old bankers and shippers and publishers were joined by electronics tycoons, aerospace barons and hamburger franchise kings. The newly rich built brand-new ranch-style mansions in Burlingame, up against the hedges of even-more exclusive Hillsborough, and slyly wrote their address as Hillsborough, unaware that the real Hillsboroughers slyly listed their address as Burlingame.

The whole way of being rich had changed. No longer did Peninsula families preside over great estates, rear enormous families and make a pilgrimage each summer to Del Monte; now they seemed to spend most of their time driving to San Francisco International Airport in San Mateo, catching a flight to a board meeting of one of their foundations in New York or to a newer and more sophisticated ski resort in Colorado or Switzerland than the one they had gone to the year before, which had already been overrun by social climbers.

This rapid new life-style made the great Peninsula estates costly white elephants, too expensive to hold onto. During the 1940s the Crocker family's elegant estate, New Place, was equipped with locker rooms and a caddy shop and turned into the Burlingame Country Club. George A. Pope's twenty-acre estate became a subdivision called Elmwood Gates, the Flood estate, Linden Towers, in Menlo Park, with its stately white-towered mansion, was turned into a housing tract called Lindenwood, and the Henry J. Crocker estate in Cloverdale was purchased and reopened as Slim Dunlop's Covered Wagon Dude Ranch.

William Bowers Bournes had sold Filoli to William P. Roth, the president of the Matson Navigation System, in 1937. After his death, Roth's widow, Lurline, lived in the enormous house in the center of the gardens of the huge estate. As the fifties moved into the sixties, Mrs. Roth watched the changes in San Francisco; she saw the once-gala sailing days of ocean liners from the port become fewer and fewer, until even the liner named after her, the Matson Line's *Lurline*, which had long made festive voyages between San Francisco and Honolulu, was sold to a Greek shipping line and sailed to the Mediterranean. A new *Lurline* was launched; but she was a cargo ship, and she docked only in Oakland.

Mrs. Roth began to think. Surely San Francisco was too special to die, too special to be another warren of office buildings. Surely there was a way to save whatever it was that made people think that San Francisco was different from any other place in the world.

She and her son found it down by Fisherman's Wharf. In 1847 James Lick had docked in San Francisco on the *Lady Adams*, carrying with him $30,000 and 600 pounds of chocolate made by a man in Lima, Peru, named Domingo Ghirardelli. The chocolate sold quickly, and two years later Ghirardelli himself sailed up from Peru to start a chocolate factory.

In 1893 Ghirardelli bought a block of land down by the waterfront containing an old brick mill that had once made woolen blankets and uniforms for the Union Army. He built more brick buildings for his expanding chocolate factory around a grassy courtyard for his employees and added a clock tower, copied from a French château, in 1915. Huge letters spelling "Ghirardelli" were erected over the factory and remained brightly lit, until they were turned off during the blackouts of 1942, and were kept off even after the war ended.

After the war the chocolate factory, needing more space, was moved to San Leandro, and the building was sold to the Golden Grain Macaroni Company. It seemed inevitable that the run-down brick buildings would soon be torn down and replaced with huge vanilla-ice-cream-bar apartment buildings.

But Mrs. Roth wanted the onrush of San Francisco to stop; she wanted to save something. She had memories of the huge "Ghirardelli" sign twinkling on shore, seen from the decks of the *Lurline* as she sailed in the Golden Gate.

So she and her son William, an attorney, bought the old

factory in 1962 and hired the local architects Wurster, Bernardi and Emmons and landscape architect Lawrence Halperin to do something interesting with the old buildings, putting up $5,000,000 for the remodeling.

The new Ghirardelli Square reopened on November 29, 1964, and the huge sign was lit up again for the first time since 1942. Had they seen it, Miës van der Rohe and Le Corbusier would have been appalled; there were no clean lines, no icy planes of black glass, no stark tower. Instead, there were sixty-five shops and restaurants, selling toys, books, music boxes, chocolate sundaes and dozens of other wares, jumbled about a courtyard where a fountain splashed and musicians played. The old brick buildings had been polished and decorated with flags and strings of lights and now bustled with the gay confusion of a street fair.

Ghirardelli Square and the old Del Monte Cannery down the street, which was remodeled to copy it, were soon crowded with tourists who rode the cable cars down from Union Square to visit them.

Critics wrote that Ghirardelli Square and the Cannery were too gaudy, too much for the tourists, but they forgot that all San Francisco was like that; San Franciscans, as every visitor from Rudyard Kipling on down noticed, loved to show off; they dressed gaudily, built extravagantly and filled the lobbies of their hotels with huge mirrors to admire themselves. New Yorkers hurried along the sidewalks of their city; San Franciscans perfected the art of strolling by practicing it since 1849. One reason the cable cars were able to survive so long was that San Franciscans were really never in a hurry to get anywhere, and they wanted to enjoy a look at their city on their way.

But being vain has its disadvantages; you sometimes come to think that if you do one thing well, you can do anything well. San Franciscans had thought they could be another New York, forgetting what they would have to give up to do it. Sometimes a Mrs. Klussmann or a Mrs. Roth had to remind them.

25

Chains

ONE afternoon in the fall of 1954 a slight gray-haired woman looked up from her carefully laid table in the Garden Court of the Palace and smiled faintly for a photographer.

"It's the trend of the times, isn't it?" she said to a reporter from *Time* magazine. "All the great hotels are going into chain operations."

She was Mrs. William Johnstone, the granddaughter of William Sharon and the owner of the Palace since 1939. She had been born in the hotel, and her family had owned it since the day it opened. Now she had just sold the Palace to Sheraton Hotels of America for $6,500,000.

The next week *Life* magazine showed a broad-faced man with piercing dark eyes and thinning black hair resting his hands on the balcony overlooking the Garden Court. *His* Garden Court. He was Ernest Henderson, president of Sheraton Hotels, and he had just captured the newest prize in a mad race with Conrad Hilton to control the most hotels in America. Hilton had bid $4,500,000 for the Palace and lost.

Old San Franciscans were outraged. The papers editorialized, columnists fumed, and veteran Palace lobby sitters refused (and still refuse) to add "Sheraton" to the name of their beloved hotel. They fought a valiant rear-guard battle against the giant corporation. When an item appeared on a luncheon menu, advertised as being served "at Sheraton Hotels everywhere," the *Chronicle* editorialized that San Franciscans would not be served "syndicated ragout of beef." The item was dropped from the menu. But the economic tide was irreversible. Today all four of San Francisco's great hotels are parts of chains.

Ellsworth P. Statler, the son of a German preacher, deserves the credit, or blame, for the first chain hotels, bringing together several St. Louis hotels under his name in 1908. His chain was swallowed up by Conrad Hilton in 1954.

Hilton, whose name had become synonymous with all that was good and bad about chain hotels, bought his first hotel, the Mobley, in Cisco, Texas, right after World War I. Exhausted after an unsuccessful business meeting, Hilton had tried to lie down in the lobby. The clerk told him that he couldn't sleep there unless he was a guest and that there were no rooms left. Left with the alternative of sleeping on the sidewalk, Hilton offered $50,000 and bought the hotel.

Hilton took a walk around his hotel and promptly ordered the staff to rip out half the front desk and to put beds in the dining room. This was the beginning of his secret of success, "utilization of every possible foot of space for the production of maximum income." This was the doctrine, combined with his motto, "Be Big, Think Big, Act Big, Dream Big," that prompted Hilton to buy America's most luxurious hotel, the Waldorf-Astoria and insert a new floor between the ceiling and the floor of the Grand Ballroom to make two ordinary ballrooms.

While Hilton had prowled Texas, looking for new hotels, his soon-to-be chief rival, Ernest Henderson, in his early twenties, his brother and a college roommate were pursuing their fortune in Boston. They had hit upon the idea of buying goods in inflation-torn Germany and reselling them at enormous profits in the United States. After trying binoculars and police dogs, they bought a lot of 40,000 men's suits at twenty cents each and shipped them to Boston, planning to sell them at sixty-eight cents a suit and make their fortune. Unfortunately, the suits, which were highly fashionable indoors, were made of a paper fiber which melted when exposed to humidity. After an eager rush, sales fell drastically, and it seemed the brothers were ruined. Just then a telephone call came from Chicago asking how many suits Henderson had left. Thirty-nine thousand, Henderson said. Fine, the man in Chicago said, I'll take the whole lot. The delighted Henderson later learned that the man was a buyer for a chain of Chicago mortuaries, faced with an overflow business owing to an influenza epidemic. The Sheraton Corporation was born.

The name came when Henderson, elated at the success of his first few hotels in the area, bought the Sheraton Hotel, named after the eighteenth-century English furniture designer, in Boston. He found that it would cost more to replace the enormous electric sign on the roof than it would to rename his other hotels, so they all became Sheratons.

"Making new and successful hotels out of old ones was even more exciting," Henderson once said, "than making 'almost' new Fords while we were still at college." His technique of remaking a hotel became legendary. He made his first hotel profitable by padlocking the cupboards so the employees couldn't eat any food; now "wrecking crews" of his Boston executives would descend on a new hotel, hunting for inefficiencies and new sources of profit under the name Operation Pay Dirt.

Teams of two executives would move into the bar, one inconspicuously watching from a corner booth, the other laying the money for drinks on the counter and leaving. The first man would watch to see if the money went into the cash register or the bartender's pocket.

Teams of twenty salesmen, under Henderson's name, "The Sheraton Sales Blitz," would ransack every corner of the city to sign up conventions, weddings and banquets. Every practice of the hotel was questioned. "Those who accept explanations at full face value may be burying their heads in the sands of delusion," Henderson snapped. Food costs, paint, light blubs, room rates, everything was divided into twenty-two categories by the Sheraton statistical department and plotted onto Operation Pay Dirt Charts. Suspicious of anything that seemed frivolous or unnecessary, Henderson would frequently refer to Athens and Sparta, hinting darkly that "the former was evidently allergic to the disciplines and austerity practiced by the Spartans, yet Athens eventually succumbed during the Peloponnesian War."

Henderson's Spartans, Pay Dirt Charts in hand, arrived in San Francisco fresh from conquering the Sheraton-Dallas, the Sheraton-Astor, the Penn-Sheraton, the Sheraton-Cadillac, the Sheraton-Blackstone and twenty-six lesser Sheratons. Walking into San Francisco's proud Palace, they immediately began frowning.

"It is no longer possible to maintain all the costly traditions that sentiment once dictated," Henderson announced. "Our predecessors, the Sharon family, had been more intent on maintaining the traditions of the past than the vitality of the profit and loss statement." Henderson pointed at the menu of the Garden Court. "Harsh economic facts relentlessly require recognition." The Garden Court and its cook, Lucien Heyraud, were "a relic of a bygone gastronomic age." He ordered oysters Kirkpatrick banished and replaced them with lamb chops and string beans. This, he recounted later, "At least partially restored some needed luster to the hotel's once meager monthly earnings reports."

Then there was the matter of redecorating the hotel to bring it into line with Sheraton standards. In 1954 Henderson had invited eight interior decorators to the Sheraton-Plaza in Boston, handed each $3,000 and a room key and asked them to create "The Hotel Room of Tomorrow." When the eight had finished sawing, painting and arranging, Henderson invited in 1,000 guests, offered them free cocktails and asked them to pick which room they liked best. The winner was a room designed by Mary Kennedy. Henderson promptly hired her to design rooms for the entire Sheraton chain, so that every room from Boston to Chicago to Philadelphia to New York to Dallas to San Francisco would have that Sheraton touch. When she was finished, a Sheraton guest could go to sleep in Baltimore and wake up in San Francisco without knowing the difference; this was the modern hotel at its most modern.

The staff of the Palace were not overjoyed at these innovations by Henderson and his "wrecking crew." The Sheraton president was carefully placed in the same bed where Harding had died, in the hope that it might be contagious. It wasn't.

But there is a law of the economic sea that no matter how big a fish is, there is a bigger and meaner fish somewhere that wants to eat it. In 1968 a team of cost accountants even meaner and pickier than Henderson's set upon the hapless Sheraton accountants, throwing down their briefcases and identifying themselves as employees of the bizarre worldwide conglomerate known as International Telephone and Telegraph, or ITT.

ITT was the creation of an economic buccaneer named Sosthenes Behn. In 1920 Behn, who was then buying and

selling sugar in the Caribbean, acquired the Puerto Rican
Telephone Company. Seeing a chance to rival Bell Telephone overseas, he was soon running telephone companies
from Spain to Argentina.

His particular genius lay in getting in on every side of a
business opportunity. In the early years of World War II, he
held a large interest in the Focke-Wulf aircraft factory in
Nazi Germany, whose bombers were being directed to Allied
convoys by German spies in Argentina using Behn's cable between Buenos Aires and Berlin, to be shot down by the British ships with the aid of electronic equipment manufactured
by Behn's English subsidiary.

Behn died in 1957 and the ITT empire was taken over by
Harold Geneen, an owlish master accountant who set about
trying to make it even bigger. He bought Avis rent-a-car,
bakeries, farms, lamp factories, insurance companies, motels
and business colleges, and, when he saw that Conrad Hilton's
hotels were making $140,000,000 a year, started looking for
a hotel chain. Geneen buried Henderson under an avalanche
of cost analyses and balance sheets, and Sheraton Hotels
were his. Every soap wrapper and cocktail napkin in the
Sheraton-Palace now blazed with the slogan "A world-wide
service of ITT."

But the law of the greedy fish still held. There was only so
much profit ITT could squeeze out of Sheraton, and only so
much Sheraton could squeeze out of the Palace; the accountants must have gritted their teeth every time they saw the
golden chandeliers and gilt and marble trim of the Garden
Court. So it was that in 1973, a new team of accountants, this
time from Japan, briefcases in hand, began poking through
the books of the Sheraton-Palace. Suddenly the Palace belonged to a Japanese corporation called Kyo-Ya, which translates roughly as "Fun House." Kyo-Ya, needless to say, had
long since been overwhelmed by the accountants of Kokusai
Kogyo of Japan, an Oriental ITT whose name translates as
"International Enterprises" and which runs taxi companies,
sightseeing buses, travel bureaus, auto agencies and, if the
travel business gets slow, makes military equipment. They re-
tained the Sheraton name and hired Sheraton Hotels to run
the Palace as it had before, as they did when they bought
Sheraton's hotel in Los Angeles, the Sheraton-West.

The St. Francis, built by the Crocker family, was still family-owned until the middle of World War II, directed by the hand of Jennie Crocker Whitman Henderson and her husband. Though the family owned it, it seemed to San Franciscans that it was the sole property of Dan London, its manager.

Dan London was the last of the great managers in San Francisco, the last of a breed that had included Baron Rieder at the Palace and James Wood of the St. Francis at the time of the earthquake. More than managers, they had the glamor of foreign correspondents or international spies and a style taken more from *Grand Hotel* than from the Cornell Hotel School. London's job was to represent the St. Francis, both in San Francisco and around the world. Tall, immaculately dressed and trimly mustached, London was almost a fixture in the lobbies of Claridge's in London, the Ritz in Paris and the Waldorf-Astoria in New York. It was he who lured Mac-Arthur to the St. Francis, he who walked with President Eisenhower to his room during the 1956 Republican convention, he who, when Admiral Nimitz returned to San Francisco after the end of the war, met the admiral on the high seas, swinging aboard the flagship of the Pacific Fleet in a bosun's chair. When he was in town, he put on a nautical cap, crowded visiting dignitaries on board his yacht and took them cruising on the Bay.

In August, 1944, the family had sold the hotel to Ben Swig, who had sold it to Edmund DeGolia, eighty-nine years old, who was a permanent patient of Notre Dame Hospital.

In 1954, the same year the Palace became a Sheraton, the St. Francis became the twenty-third piece of the Western Hotel chain, joining the Multnomah in Portland, the Oasis in Palm Springs, the Benjamin Franklin in Seattle and the Mayfair in Los Angeles. Western expanded into Western International, adding the prestigious new Century Plaza in Los Angeles and the Space Needle in Seattle. Then, in March, 1970, Western International was acquired by United Airlines, which was anxious to go into other pastures.

Dan London retired in 1965. His ship models remained in the office, but his place was taken by a quiet professional manager named William Quinn, who wore a corporate emblem on his lapel, the tiny nutcracker crushing the globe that symbolized Western International Hotels.

Atop Nob Hill, Ben Swig was infected by chain fever. He had elevated himself still further to board chairman and moved into Mrs. Flood's old penthouse on top of the hotel, letting his son Richard manage the hotel, but now it seemed time to expand still further. He purchased the old Roosevelt Hotel in the French Quarter of New Orleans, decorated it with the flamboyant *F*, and renamed it the Fairmont Roosevelt. In short order, for Ben Swig never dallied with anything, brand-new Fairmonts were being built in Dallas, Atlanta and Tulsa.

The Mark Hopkins, from the day it opened in 1926, was the private kingdom of George Smith. He was successful enough also to own the Fairmont from 1929 to 1941, when the Linnards were in financial trouble, but by 1960, he was having difficulty; the ultramodern 1950s Dorothy Draper decor looked sadly dated in 1960, and without the resources of a chain to back him, Smith couldn't afford a major refurbishing. Besides, he was seventy-one.

In 1962, eager to rest and travel, George Smith sold the Mark Hopkins for $10,000,000. The buyer was Louis Lurie, the "Wizard of Montgomery Street"; the Mark became his two hundred and sixty-seventh piece of real estate.

Lurie was seventy-two when he bought the Mark. A one-time Chicago newsboy, he came to San Francisco when he was twenty-six, in 1914, and took a $50-a-month room at the Palace. He lived in the Palace for thirteen years; during that time he turned his modest savings into a small fortune by playing the exploding city real estate market. He bought and sold office buildings, vacant lots, theaters and hotels as if they were pieces on a giant game board. Habitually dressed in black or dark gray suits, with a homburg set at a jaunty angle on his head, he became a familiar sight downtown as he negotiated deals on everything from the backing of Broadway plays (he was a large backer of *South Pacific* and *Teahouse of the August Moon*) to the hot dog concession at the 1939 Treasure Island fair.

When Lurie discovered something he liked, he clung to it fiercely; he enjoyed riding the elevator of the office building he owned at 333 Montgomery alone; if anyone else tried to get in the elevator, he ordered them out. He liked eating lunch at Jack's so much that he ate there every day for thirty-four years, always at the same table, a fact which not only endeared him to the management of the restaurant but which earned him a place in Ripley's "Believe It Or Not."

Besides real estate, the theater was his great love. When the Geary and Curran theaters, San Francisco's last legitimate theaters, encountered stormy financial waters and were on the verge of closing, Lurie bought them both and kept their stages lit. He delighted in surrounding himself by theater people, especially at his lunches at Jack's; it was almost a game for regular diners to look over to Lurie's table to see who his guest was that day: Noel Coward or Gertrude Lawrence or Maurice Chevalier.

Chevalier had a special spot in Lurie's heart. They were born six days apart and each year celebrated their birthdays together, with Chevalier, the younger, calling Lurie Pappa and Lurie calling Chevalier Sonny.

So George Smith moved out of his twelve-room suite on the eighteenth floor of the Mark, just below the Top of the Mark, and Lurie moved in. Not wishing to be jarred by totally new surroundings, he had the walnut-paneled entrance hall, dining room and living room of his home exactly reproduced and installed in the Mark. Then the movers carried in his armchairs, his ebony grand piano, his four-inch guppy in its bowl and the stone buddhas, antique Japanese screens and jade his dead wife had collected. In the bedroom they set one clock on either side of the bed so he wouldn't have to roll over to see what time it was, set up a rack for the *Wall Street Journal*, a humidor full of cigars, and installed the tape-recording machines that recorded every call.

The "Wizard of Montgomery Street," needless to say, didn't want to be bothered about bed counts and linen washing; he was too busy toying with the exhilarating chess board of real estate. He turned over the operation of his hotel to a singing cowboy from Tioga Springs, Texas.

Gene Autry was certainly better known for galloping across the screen on his horse Champion or for singing, in a heart-rending twang, "That Silver-Haired Daddy of Mine," which won him a place in the Country Music Hall of Fame in Nashville, than he was for running hotels, but he was a shrewd businessman. He had invested his movie earnings to build a minor empire of radio stations, television stations, the California Angels baseball team and the Gene Autry Hotel

Company. Now his men flew up from Los Angeles to see what they could do with the Mark Hopkins.

They couldn't do much; Gene Autry was more interested in profits than he was in repairing an aging hotel. They re-upholstered the sofas, moved the furniture around, re-named the restaurants and hung a plaque featuring two stallions and the legend "Where Good Friends Get Together" over the front entrance, but the Mark looked tacky compared to the Fairmont across the street, where the wealthy now went, and too expensive for the tourists, who were now being lured to the new Hilton and Holiday Inns. In 1967 Autry asked to pull out and leave this bit of range to somebody else, and Lurie agreed.

Loew's Hotels was the next choice. An offshoot of the theater chain, Loew's sent its managers through the Mark, where they once again reupholstered the sofas, rearranged the furniture and renamed the restaurants. Now the hotel looked like the lobby of one of Loew's theaters. This worked no better than Gene Autry's attempts had; Lurie soon threw them out of the hotel, holding a press conference to declare, "They're no good. I don't trust them."

George Smith was spared the spectacle of his hotel being used as a mannequin by succeeding waves of interior designers. He died unexpectedly of a heart attack on September 24, 1965.

This time Lurie gave the lease to the Bishop Corporation of Honolulu, which had hotels scattered from Guam to Bangkok, but none in the continental United States. During the following year, 1973, Bishop was swallowed up by Intercontinental Hotels, and the Mark Hopkins became a stepsister of the Warsaw Intercontinental, the Zagreb Intercontinental, the Saipan Intercontinental, the Managua Intercontinental and fifty-six other Intercontinental Hotels from Rawalpindi to San Salvador.

Louis Lurie never got to see his hotel join the Interconti-nental chain. He died on his eighty-fourth birthday, September 6, 1972.

Intercontinental, unlike the managers before them, was not paltry in spending money on its new child. It spent $2,000,000 to undo the damage Dorothy Draper had done with $100,000. It painted over the garish colors, converted the Lochinvar Room back to a quiet grill and scraped the paint off the skylight to let the first sunlight in twenty years into the old courtyard. The courtyard was faced with weathered brick, filled with hanging flowers and wicker furniture and opened as a garden bar. Every room, from the Top of the Mark to the lobby, was redone in the Intercontinental image.

In the meanwhile, the laws of big and bigger fish were still operating. Intercontinental was swallowed by Pan American Airways, which was busily diversifying.

Unfortunately, the Pan American executives were so busily diversifying that they neglected their original business, flying airplanes. As a result, the economic slump of 1974 caught them with hangars full of brand-new, enormously expensive Boeing 747 jumbo jets without enough passengers to fill them. The company was soon over its head in debt.

In Arthur Haley's popular novel *Hotel*, the imaginary St. Charles Hotel in New Orleans was saved from oblivion by a mysterious guest who purchased the hotel, to the delight of millions of readers and movie viewers. In a strange twist, the Mark Hopkins staff were startled to learn in February, 1975, that one of their regular guests had bought not only half of all the Intercontinental Hotels, but had put in $300,000,000 to rescue Pan American. The regular guest was Mohammed Reza Pahlevi, the shah of Iran.

26

San Francisco, 1976

UNDER the surface of Market Street, a white rapid transit train glided eerily out of the tube that lay on the bottom of San Francisco Bay and came to a stop beside a brightly lit brick platform. The doors slid open, and a crowd of people began walking along the platform to the escalators and stairs that led up to the streets of the financial district.

Soon people were emerging from the modern brick stairwell in front of the Sheraton-Palace Hotel. In the lobby of the hotel, fifty Japanese tourists, in black and gray business suits, and their wives sat very quietly beside a pile of suitcases, flight bags and camera cases, while their leader negotiated with the desk clerk. One of the tourists stood alone far down the hall, near the entrance to the kitchen, curiously inspecting the brass plaque that designated the Garden Court as a historical landmark. The Sheraton Corporation had fought the placing of the plaque, since it would prevent it from demolishing or remodeling the Garden Court. When it lost, it hid the plaque down the hallway so few people would see it.

A few blocks away, in a massive old office building on Market Street, Joseph Belardi, the head of the Hotel, Culinary Workers and Bartenders Union Executive Board frowned and leafed through pages of wage scales. A picture of Franklin D. Roosevelt hung on the wall in front of him.

He had been one of the pickets outside Harvey Toy's Manx Hotel in the 1937 strike. Now he was one of the most powerful men in San Francisco. He picked up the telephone, knowing that his call would be answered personally by the manager of any of the hotels.

Below the old office building, one of Andrew Hallidie's cable cars was being revolved on the turntable to begin another journey over Nob Hill to Fisherman's Wharf and the shops of the Cannery and Ghirardelli Square. A hundred tourists waited patiently in line, cameras in hand, to board the cable car. When as many as could fit had been seated on the old slat benches, the grip clanged the bell, pulled back on his lever, and the car began rattling up Powell Street toward Union Square.

The cable car clattered past the windowless brick and concrete department stores that loomed over Union Square and passed the front doors of the St. Francis Hotel.

In a cluttered modern office of the sales department on the third floor of the hotel, a young man in a well-cut black suit and black mustache leaned back at his desk and cradled a telephone by his ear, gently but firmly explaining to the president of a large business association that he could have the Presidential Suite at a reduced price, but he could not, under any circumstances, have a free bar in his room. While the other man talked, the salesman thought painfully about the recent convention of the Science Fiction and Fantasy Association; the delegates had arrived in top hats, opera capes and spacesuits, with bizarrely curled mustaches and shaved heads, carrying canes and live snakes, and had brought six-packs of beer and hamburgers into the hotel and held a picnic in the lobby.

In Dan London's old apartment upstairs, which was now an elegant suite where President Georges Pompidou of France had stayed, a maid dusted the small bust of Napoleon on the bookcase and then began dusting the books: Sinclair Lewis' *Babbitt*, *Northwest Passage*, the *Memoirs of Cassanova* and several biographies of Richard Nixon. The maid looked curiously at the last; they had only recently been put in the bookcase by the management, and the biographies of Herbert Hoover removed.

At the back of the hotel, glass elevators shot upward at 1,000 feet a minute to the Penthouse Bar and Victor's restaurant at the summit of the new thirty-two-story tower. Guests stepping from the elevators and walking into Victor's passed a large portrait of Victor Hirtzler, arms crossed, hat jauntily tilted on his head, looking like the toppler of kings and presidents.

Down below, in a small office behind the Dutch Kitchen,

Wolfgang Fellinger, the executive chef of the hotel, studied the banquet schedule for the day; his staff of fifty-four would be serving 25,000 meals that day. A master chef trained in Germany, he had cooked at the Ritz in Paris, the Kensington Palace Hotel in London and the Grand Hotel in Stockholm; he had served the queen of England, Premier Khrushchev, King Ibn Saud and Field Marshal Montgomery. Coming to the United States, he had discovered American tasts in food by cooking for Muhammed Ali at Chicago's Continental Plaza; Ali had ordered seven sirloin steaks and a glass of milk.

The lobby was jammed from one side to the other with 1,800 men talking noisily to each other, their name tags announcing that they were members of the Food Processing Machinery and National Canners Association. In the center of the sea of canners, the thirty delegates to the convention of the International Federation of Doll Clubs were trying vainly to get out of the lobby.

The cable car took on more passengers, hanging from the railings on the outside, and began the perilous climb up Nob Hill. Its bell ringing furiously, it rattled alongside the dark stones Mark Hopkins had laid as the foundation of his mansion that now supported the Mark Hopkins Hotel.

The gold and white lobby of the Mark was tranquil; a few guests sat in the deep leather armchairs. In the closet of a corner office, three dull green teletypes tapped out cryptic messages from a computer in Cedar Rapids, Michigan, which mysteriously ran the affairs of Pan American Airways and Intercontinental Hotels from Zagreb to San Francisco.

Upstairs, one maid polished the baby grand piano in the wood-paneled Presidential Suite, while another wiped the handles and faucets of the sink and shower, which were plated with gold.

Over their heads, a few graying men sat in a corner in the Top of the Mark, oblivious to the young people seated around them. They sipped their drinks and stared silently at the sweeping vista of the Golden Gate, remembering a night in 1943 and a laughing young man who had been with them that night, who was now dead somewhere under the Philippine Sea.

Across the street in the Fairmont, a group of plumbers were trying to decide why the tropical rainstorm in the Tonga Room had dribbled the night before. The doors of the

Venetian Room were closed, because Marlene Dietrich's pianist was practicing for her appearance that night.

Upstairs in the Penthouse, Ben Swig sat in his office, reading the reports of some of the charities he supported, in front of a wall covered with signed photographs of presidents, prime ministers and popes shaking hands with Ben Swig.

In the valet shop, Henry Kalfain's son was pressing the robes of the oil minister of an Arab country. Henry Kalfain himself, eighty-eight years old, wearing a black nautical cap, sat in the dim living room of his small house in the West Portal district, looking at an old framed photograph of a ball at the Fairmont he had helped serve sixty-five years earlier. He smiled at the stiff, unnatural expressions of the men in their strange clothes.

On the crest of Telegraph Hill, Mrs. Hans Klussmann sat in the living room of the huge red-shingle house she designed herself, talking on the telephone at a small desk. The room was decorated with porcelain and brass models of cable cars. Out the window she could see the black-glass towers of the financial district and, directly in front of her, the white Transamerica Pyramid. To the right of the towers she could see the yellow and white shaft of the Fairmont Tower, its elevator sliding up and down the outside like the mercury of a thermometer.

A group of teenage girls, dressed in long formal gowns for a wedding, stood waiting in the lobby, looking critically at their reflections in the great Florentine mirrors. A sports car was parked in the far corner of the lobby, attended by a young lady seated behind a table who was trying to sell tickets to raffle it off. Still looking over their shoulders and watching themselves, the girls moved down the corridor toward one of the ballrooms.

Behind them an employee moved from ashtray to ashtray, stirred the sand and then, with a cast-iron stamp, impressed the sand with an elegant script F.

Outside, the bell of the cable car clanged again, and then, people hanging from the outside, it plunged down the other side of Nob Hill on its way to Fisherman's Wharf.

Sources

Much has been written about San Francisco before the earthquake, and it can be read most easily in the new California History Room of the San Francisco Public Library. The Bancroft Library of the University of California in Berkeley has a larger collection, but being designed for specialists, it is surrounded by walls of security and paperwork and is difficult to use unless you know exactly what you want. The library of the California Historical Society, housed in an old mansion in the Pacific Heights area of San Francisco, has a quaint Victorian reading room and cartons stuffed with memorabilia, from old menus to handwritten proclamations by Emperor Norton. Unfortunately, they are organized in a curious system known only to the librarian, and he is unwilling to talk unless the reader has paid him a dollar user's fee and given his word that he won't steal the furniture or rip pages out of the books.

Much less has been written about San Francisco since 1906. The few books are in the California History Room of the library, along with an abundance of pamphlets and clippings. I chose to use the accounts in the *Chronicle* and *Examiner* on microfilm in the newspaper room for most of my research.

1. San Francisco, 1876

Rudyard Kipling's observations come from *The Western Gate—A San Francisco Reader,* ed. by Joseph Henry Jackson (New York: Farrar, Straus & Young, 1952). The "eastern reporter" is Samuel Williams, writing in *Scribner's* magazine in July, 1875. The "Englishman" is William Laird MacGregor, *San Francisco in 1876,* for private circulation only (Edinburgh: Thomas Laurie, 1876). The "local reporter" is B. E. Lloud, in *Lights and Shades of San Francisco* (San Francisco: Bancroft, 1876).

2. Gamblers

A new book by David Lavender, *Nothing Seemed Impossible* (Palo Alto: American West, 1975), will tell you more about William Ralston than you probably want to know. I used *Ralston's Ring,* by George Lyman (New York: Scribner's, 1937) for his life, and *Lights and Shades of San Francisco (ibid.)* for a description of the closing of the Bank of California. The story of the first hotels comes from *A Room for the Night: Hotels of the Old West,* by Richard A. Van Orman (Bloomington: Indiana University Press, 1966). The description of the building of the Palace is from *Bonanza Inn,* by Oscar Lewis and Carroll Hall (New York: Knopf, 1939), the definitive history of the Palace, by Lewis, surely the best historian of Old San Francisco. The story of James Fair comes from *The Silver Kings,* also by Oscar Lewis (New York: Knopf, 1947).

3. Heroes and Poets

Bonanza Inn was the principal source. Julia Cooley Altirocchi added observations about Patti's visit in her dizzy *The Spectacular San Franciscans* (New York: Dutton, 1949). The "foreign observer" is again William Laird MacGregor. The story of the first child born in the Palace is from a letter at the California Historical Society. The Joaquin Miller story is from *The Fantastic City,* by Amelia Ransome Neville (Boston: Houghton Mifflin, 1932).

4. Oysters and Champagne

The menus appeared in William Laird MacGregor's book, and he is again "the English observer." The Palace dining room is described in *Bonanza Inn;* other restaurants are described in Oscar Lewis' *Bay Window Bohemia* (New York: Doubleday, 1956) and *A Cook's Tour of San Francisco,* by Doris Muscatine (New York: Scribner's, 1969). The Campi story is from Robert O'Brien's "Riptides" column of May 1, 1946.

5.   *High Society*

Again, *Bonanza Inn* is the main source. Others were *Champagne Days in San Francisco,* by Evelyn Wells (New York: Doubleday, 1947) and William Chambliss' own appalling book, *Chambliss' Diary,* or *Society as It Really Is* (San Francisco: Chambliss & Co., 1894).

6.   *The Gray Lady and the Gambler*

Bonanza Inn described what happened at the Palace. Lucky Baldwin's hotel was described in clippings books at the public library, and the Zeb Kendall story came from an article about San Francisco hotels by Lucius Beebe in the April, 1961, issue of *Holiday.*

7.   *Teddy*

Theodore Roosevelt's adventures in San Francisco were described in the San Francisco *Chronicle,* May 14–20, 1903.

8.   *Cracks in the Rainbow*

Of the dozen books about the earthquake, the best two are probably *The Earth Shook, the Sky Burned,* by William Bronson (New York: Doubleday, 1959), and *The San Francisco Earthquake,* by Gordon Thomas and Max Morgan Wills (New York: Stein and Day, 1971). The Cook, Hertz, Bennet and Hopper quotes are from Thomas; the Farish quote and telegrams are from Bronson. Caruso's actions are hotly disputed, his own version being the least reliable account of all; I chose Thomas' version. The young St. Francis page's story is from the archives of that hotel. Jack London's story appeared in *Collier's Weekly,* May 5, 1906. Gertrude Atherton recalled the "Sheet of gold" in *My San Francisco* (New York: Bobbs-Merrill, 1946). The insurance investigators' report is called "Report of the Committee of Five to the Thirty-Five Companies on the San Francisco Conflagration, December 31, 1906." Will Irwin's eulogy, "The City That Was," written for the New York *Sun,* was reprinted as a book (New York: B. W. Huebsch, 1906). The accounts of Tetrazzini's concert are from *The Fantastic City (op. cit.)* and *Tales of San Francisco,* by Samuel Dickson (Palo Alto: Stanford University Press, 1957).

9. The Long Waltz

The description of the new Palace is from a special section of *The Western Hotel Reporter,* December, 1909. The Fairmont is described from its own brochures of the time. The resorts are described from their advertisements in a local magazine, the *News-Letter,* and from *Bay Window Bohemia (op. cit.).* The diversions of the time are taken from old social programs at the California Historical Society, the *News-Letter,* and a guidebook of the time, *San Francisco as It Was, as It Is and How to See It,* by Helen Throop Purdy (San Francisco: Paul Elder & Co., 1912). I found the young Isoroku Yamamoto's name on an old guest list in the *News-Letter* of December 3, 1910, and confirmed his presence in the area from a biography. The opening program of the 1915 Exposition is from the February 20, 1915, *News-Letter.* The visits of Ford, Edison, Sunday, Bryan, Roosevelt and Paderewski are from the *Examiner;* the description of the German war films is from the *News-Letter.*

10. War

The Mardi Gras of 1917 was described in the society pages of the *Examiner.* The story of the Burlingame Cavalry Troop and of Bert Hall were in the *News-Letter.* The war stories are from the *Examiner.* The Von Papen story was told me by Henry Kalfain himself and confirmed by accounts in the papers of the time.

11. Wilson

The background comes from *When the Cheering Stopped: The Last Years of Woodrow Wilson,* by Gene Smith (New York: William Morrow, 1966). The story of his visit and texts of his speeches are from the *Chronicle.*

12. "Your President Is Dead"

Lardner, Cobb and Runyan's accounts of the convention were syndicated in the *Examiner.* The background and the story of Colonel Forbes' junket came from *The Shadow of Blooming Grove: Warren G. Harding in His Times,* by Francis Russell (New York: McGraw-Hill, 1968). The descriptions of his death came from the *Chronicle* and Russell *(ibid.).*

13. The Jazz Hotel

Almira Bailey's remarks are from *Vignettes of San Francisco* (San Francisco: San Francisco *Journal,* 1921). The rise of jazz was recorded in the *News-Letter* and the *Chronicle.* The "Golden Bear Growl" is from an old St. Francis menu at the California Historical Society. The descriptions of the St. Francis and its staff come from the hotel's brochures and its newsletter, *Annals of the Hotel St. Francis,* which appeared from January, 1916, to December, 1918. Victor's story comes from the *Annals,* from his *Hotel St. Francis Cookbook* (Chicago: Hotel Monthly Press, 1919), and from Robert O'Brien's "Riptides" column of September 8, 1950. Leroy Linnard's radio station was reported in the *Chronicle* of March 21, 1922, and his airline in the same paper of March 26–28 of the same year. The Prohibition stories came from the *Chronicle* and *Examiner* from January, 1920, to December, 1933.

14. The Orgy

James Agee on Arbuckle came from *Agee on Film* (New York: McDowell, Obolensky, 1958). The story of the scandal comes from the *Chronicle* and *Examiner* from September, 1921, to April, 1922. Arbuckle's last years are from his obituary in the New York *Times* on June 30, 1933. The animated cow episode is from *Crazy Sundays; F. Scott Fitzgerald in Hollywood,* by Aaron Latham (New York: Viking, 1971).

15. New Lights on the Hill

The background of George Smith came from his obituary in the September 25, 1965, *Chronicle.* The story of the old Mark Hopkins mansion was in "The Mark from Top to Bottom," by Ferol Egan, in *San Francisco* magazine's March, 1966, issue. The description of the hotel came from *San Francisco Business,* which featured the hotel in its December, 1926, issue.

16. The Strike

President Hoover's visit was reported in the *Examiner* of November 9, 1932. The description of the death of Sperry and Bordoise and the general strike are from *Treasure Island: San Francisco's Exposition Years,* by Richard Reinhardt (San Francisco: Scrimshaw Press, 1973). The hotel strike was covered in the *Chronicle* from May, 1937, to July, 1937, in the *Catering Industry Employee* of the same months, in negotiating documents, and from the recollection of Joseph Belardi. The Shaw visit was reported in the *Chronicle* of March 16, 1936.

17. Treasure Island

The adventures of Gertrude Stein and Alice B. Toklas are from the *Alice B. Toklas Cookbook* (New York: Harper and Row, 1954). The story of the parties and life on the peninsula are from *The Spectacular San Franciscans (op. cit.).* Description of the fair is from Reinhardt *(op. cit.);* of the visitors, from the *Chronicle.* The Kurusu-Yamamoto exchange is from William Manchester's *The Glory and the Dream* (Boston: Little, Brown, 1973).

18.   "Is the Ocean Ours or Theirs?"

The news bulletin is from Manchester *(op. cit.)*. The events following Pearl Harbor were reported in the *Examiner* and *Chronicle.* The Dos Passos quote is from the March, 1944, issue of *Harper's.* The Top of the Mark story is from "The Mark from Top to Bottom" *(op. cit.)*. The Oppenheimer story is from Manchester and *The Oppenheimer Case: Security on Trial,* by Philip M. Stern (New York: Harper and Row, 1969). The description of the Russians at the St. Francis is from the *Saturday Evening Post* of January 10, 1953.

19.   MacArthur

The background on General MacArthur came from Manchester *(op. cit.)*; the report of his visit from the *Examiner.*

20.   Zen and Château Lafite Rothschild

The Jane Russell and Joseph McCarthy stories are from the *Chronicle.* The Eisenhower story was told me by Henry Kalfain. The opera of the 1950s is from *The Spectacular San Franciscans (op. cit.)*; and the social pages of the *Chronicle.* The story of the new bohemians came from *San Francisco: An Informal Guide,* by Ben Adams (New York: Hill and Wang, 1961). Lucius Beebe described his adventure in "A Spendthrift Tour of San Francisco" in the *Holiday* magazine of September, 1958, and told the story of Lucien in the August issue of the same magazine. He also recorded the battle to save the cable cars in *Cable Car Carnival* (Oakland: Grahame Hardy, 1951), which I supplemented from the files of the San Francisco Public Library and with brief talks with Mary Ball, who witnessed the race between the cable car and the bus and now runs the lost and found of the Municipal Railway, and Mrs. Klussmann herself.

21. Ben Swig's Tower

Ben Swig's career was adoringly followed in *Ben Swig, the Measure of a Man*, by Walter Blum (San Francisco: Lawton & Alfred Kennedy, 1968). Dorothy Draper's atrocities were vividly illustrated in the Mark's own brochures and press releases. The battle over the tower was reported in both the *Chronicle* and the *Examiner* in December, 1950. The opening of the Jack Tar Hotel was heralded in the August, 1961, issue of *Popular Mechanics*.

22. Khrushchev

The story of Nikita Khrushchev's visit is taken from the reporting of the *Examiner*.

23. Kennedy

John Kennedy's visit was also taken from descriptions in the *Examiner*.

24. New New York

The De Gaulle story is from the April 27, 1960, *Chronicle*. The graveyard quote, the Lapham quote, and the construction statistics are from Bruce Brugmann and Greggar Sletteland's important book, *The Ultimate Highrise* (San Francisco: San Francisco Bay Guardian Books, 1971). The groundbreaking of the pyramid was described by Kresak himself in a public relations publication article which was reprinted in *Ultimate Highrise*. Allan Temko's review was in the *Chronicle* on September 13, 1974. The George Harrison story was in the *Chronicle* during the celebrated summer of 1967. The Judy Garland press conference was in the *Examiner* of August 26, 1965. The story of Ghirardelli Square comes from the literature of the builders.

25. *Chains*

Mrs. Johnstone's picture and remarks appeared in *Time* on October 25, 1954. Hilton's life is recorded in his own book, *Be My Guest,* which was once found in the desk drawer of every Hilton hotel room, but which has since been relegated to the dark closets of the housekeeping departments. Henderson wrote a rival book, *The World of "Mr. Sheraton,"* which proved him a better humorist if not a better hotelier than Hilton. The story of ITT is told in *The Sovereign State of ITT,* by Anthony Sampson (New York: Stein & Day, 1973). Kyo-Ya's takeover was reported in the *Chronicle* on April 15, 1973. The biography of Louis Lurie came from his obituary in the *Chronicle* on September 7, 1972, and Herb Caen's remembrances in his column that same day.

Index

254